ARROW'S EDGE MC

PRAISE FOR FREYA BARKER

Freya Barker writes a mean romance, I tell you! A REAL romance, with real characters and real conflict.

~Author M. Lynne Cunning

I've said it before and I'll say it again and again, Freya Barker is one of the BEST storytellers out there.

~Turning Pages At MidnightBook Blog

God, Freya Barker gets me every time I read one of her books. She's a master at creating a beautiful story that you lose yourself in the moment you start reading.

~Britt Red Hatter Book Blog

Freya Barker has woven a delicate balance of honest emotions and well-formed characters into a tale that is as unique as it is gripping.

~Ginger Scott, bestselling young and new adult author and Goodreads Choice Awards finalist

Such a truly beautiful story! The writing is gorgeous, the scenery is beautiful...

~Author Tia Louise

From Dust by Freya Barker is one of those special books. One of those whose plotline and characters remain with you for days after you finished it.

~Jeri's Book Attic

No amount of words could describe how this story made me feel, I think this is one I will remember forever, absolutely freaking awesome is not even close to how I felt about it.

~Lilian's Book Blog

Still Air was insightful, eye-opening, and I paused numerous times to think about my relationships with my own children. Anytime a book can evoke a myriad of emotions while teaching life lessons you'll continue to carry with you, it's a 5-star read.

~ Bestselling Author CP Smith

In my opinion, there is nothing better than a Freya Barker book. With her final installment in her Portland, ME series, Still Air, she does not disappoint. From start to finish I was completely captivated by Pam, Dino, and the entire Portland family.

~ Author RB Hilliard

The one thing you can always be sure of with Freya's writing is that it will pull on ALL of your emotions; it's expressive, meaningful, sarcastic, so very true to life, real, hard-hitting and heartbreaking at times and, as is the case with this series especially, the story is at points raw, painful and occasionally fugly BUT it is also sweet, hopeful, uplifting, humorous and heart-warming.

~ Book Loving Pixies

ALSO BY FREYA BARKER

ON CALL SERIES (Operation Alpha):
BURNING FOR AUTUMN
COVERING OLLIE
TRACKING TAHLULA
ABSOLVING BLUE
REVEALING ANNIE
ROCK POINT SERIES:
KEEPING 6
CABIN 12
HWY 550
10-CODE
NORTHERN LIGHTS COLLECTION:
A CHANGE IN TIDE
A CHANGE OF VIEW
A CHANGE OF PACE
SNAPSHOT SERIES:
SHUTTER SPEED
FREEZE FRAME
IDEAL IMAGE
PORTLAND, ME, NOVELS:
FROM DUST
CRUEL WATER
THROUGH FIRE
STILL AIR
LULLAY: A CHRISTMAS NOVELLA
CEDAR TREE SERIES:
SLIM TO NONE
HUNDRED TO ONE
AGAINST ME
CLEAN LINES
UPPER HAND
LIKE ARROWS
HEAD START
STANDALONE BOOKS:
WHEN HOPE ENDS
VICTIM OF CIRCUMSTANCE

EDGE
OF
TOMORROW

ARROW'S EDGE MC

FREYA BARKER

ISBN: 9781988733555

Cover Design:
Freya Barker

Cover Image:
Jean Maureen Woodfin (JW Photography and Covers)

Cover Models:
Darrin James Dedmon & Baby John

Editing:
Karen Hrdlicka

Proofing:
Joanne Thompson

Formatting:
CP Smith

ACKNOWLEDGMENTS

I have to thank the awesome Barks & Bites, my reader group. These ladies keep me motivated on days when I'd rather head back to bed and pull the blankets over my head. They're also very welcoming so if you enjoy my books and would like to join, you can do it here:
https://www.facebook.com/groups/FreyasBarksandBites/

At my back (and often at the drop of a hat) are Karen Hrdlicka and Joanne Thompson, my fabulous editing/proofreading team; Deb Blake, Pam Buchanan & Petra Gleason, my beta readers for Edge Of Tomorrow; and CP Smith for her fabulous formatting.

Also putting up with me (and I'm not always easy!!) my agent, Stephanie Phillips of SBR Media; my promo queen Debra Presley & my advertising guru Drue Hoffman of Buoni Amici Press, my publicists; Krystal Weiss, my awesome personal assistant; and finally every amazing blogger, who promote and recommend my books.
But, as always, the biggest thanks goes to you, my readers. You give each new story I put out there a warm, enthusiastic welcome, and never fail to warm my cold heart with your kind words!

Love you all.

EDGE
OF
TOMORROW

1

LISA

"Don't forget your lunch!"

Ezrah—who bailed out of the car the moment the wheels stopped turning—grinds to a halt halfway to the front door of the school and comes running back. I lean over to hand him his lunch bag through the passenger window.

"Best not be getting another call from the principal's office today, boy," I warn him.

All I get is a grunt in response. Dear Lord, but that child tests my patience.

Ever since we found a home in Durango two years ago, my grandson has gone from a timid, beaten down little boy to this mouthy child with an attitude that won't fit through the door. He never fails to find an argument, it doesn't matter who's across from him. Yesterday he went head-to-head with his teacher during history class. Argued with her when she claimed slavery was abolished in the US since 1865. Ezrah disagreed. Loudly.

My grandson was not wrong, given that up until two years ago we lived in service to a family of white supremacists, but calling his teacher bat-shit crazy wasn't the right way to convey the message. I ended up having to pick him up from the principal's office, and back at home had Trunk sit him down for a good talk.

Ezrah looks up to Trunk, our resident child psychologist and a black man. My poor grandchildren haven't really known any father figures—anyone to take guidance from—until we came here. Of course, in an MC testosterone runs rampant, and although all good, decent men, they're not known for their tact. My grandson emulates what he sees.

I watch him run to the door and slip inside.

"Nana, is Ezrah in trouble?"

I turn around in my seat and look at my baby, my Kiara.

"Not if he behaves. Now, let's get you off to school."

Kiara just started first grade this past August, but not at the same school as Ezrah. I did that on purpose. The boy is so protective of his sister, she wouldn't get a chance to forge friendships of her own, which is important. She's surrounded by boys at home, she needs some space to develop her own person.

I park at her school, not ready to let her walk in by herself. She's my baby; I practically raised her from birth, after their momma disappeared.

I was sixteen when my daughter Sunny was born, and head over heels for her father, a twenty-year-old neighborhood punk named James Weston. She'd been an easy child and our life in the tight, one-bedroom apartment, on the wrong side of town, had felt like a dream come true. Until James was killed in a drive-by shooting that riddled our small apartment with bullets when Sunny was only three months old.

Life wasn't so idyllic after that, but I managed— even without a high school diploma—to keep us afloat. Despite my determination to give my daughter a better life than mine, she fell in with the wrong crowd. She got pregnant at nineteen, had Ezrah at twenty, and by the time she disappeared at just twenty-four, she had two kids and no clue who their fathers were. She was found dead of an overdose two months later.

I'd been only forty at the time and left with a four-year-old and an infant to raise.

"Have a good day in school, baby," I tell Kiara, when she turns at the door and tries to fit her small arms around my waist.

"Bye, Nana."

She lifts her face for a kiss and I pull the door open for her, scooting her inside before returning to my car. It's starting to rain again.

Normally, I do groceries with the aid of one of the club's prospects to help me haul them, but with this impending thunderstorm I don't want to go out more than is necessary. I'm only two blocks from the grocery store, so I decide to get them now before the weather gets worse.

By the time I pile my second grocery cart high, I can see conditions haven't improved outside. The skies are dark and I can see the wind has picked up. Once I cash out, one of the baggers is kind enough to wheel the second cart to my car, despite the steady rain coming down. I slip him a few dollars for his help before loading up my little Toyota to the brim with bags.

I'm a drowned rat when I get behind the wheel, sitting in a puddle. The hair I get up an hour early every morning to subdue into smooth waves springs out in rebellious little curls I'll have to live with the rest of the day. Curls now, untamed frizz when it dries. Lovely.

A burst of lightning followed almost immediately by a loud crack of thunder rattles me when I turn up Junction Creek Road. The rain is now coming down in sheets and my windshield wipers work hard to give me at least a glimpse at the road ahead. At some point, halfway up the mountain, a river of rainwater is coming down the road and—afraid my little car will start hydroplaning—I quickly pull off onto the shoulder. Better to wait it out.

I've sat here for a few minutes when my phone starts ringing in my purse. It's the garage.

"Hi."

"Where the hell are you?" Brick barks and instantly my hackles go up.

"Good morning to you too."

Brick joined the Arrow's Edge MC around the same time I started working for them. He runs the garage up at the compound. A rugged, rough around the edges, but at times kind man who seems to have infinite patience for the boys, but none for me. Sometimes I think he's doing some kind of penance, looking out for me, because he certainly doesn't seem happy about it.

Not that I ever asked for anything, he just seems to feel the need to jump in and rescue me. I can't lie; there've been times I would've been up shit creek without a paddle if not for him stepping in. Like when Ezrah busted open his head and I ended up in the hospital with him without insurance. Brick walked in, handed over his credit card, and told me to put a sock in it when I objected.

I think he sees me as some kind of charity case.

"You left two hours ago, it normally takes you half an hour tops to run the kids to school, and the weather is shit. For all I know you're in a goddamn ditch somewhere," he grumbles.

I roll my eyes but realize he can't see that.

"I pulled off to the side to wait out the storm. The road is a bit of a mess."

"Where?"

"Halfway up Junction. I think the rain is getting a little lighter, I'll try again in a few minutes."

"I'm on my way."

"I'm fine," I snap, but the next thing I know the line is dead.

See? It's like he doesn't even hear me. I'm not some wilting flower. I've seen and been subjected to more shit in my life than many ever will, but still he acts like I can't take care of myself.

5

The fact I've developed a thing for the man over the past two years doesn't exactly help.

He still pisses me off.

BRICK

DAMN STUBBORN WOMAN.

She nips at my hand every goddamn time I reach one out.

So pigheadedly independent.

"Shilah, need you to come with me."

The young prospect, or cub as they're called in this club, wipes his hands on a rag and jogs after me to the truck.

"Where are we going?"

"Picking up Lisa, she's stuck on the mountain in this weather. You're gonna drive her car home."

I crank the heat in the cab of the truck and drive out of the gates.

"There."

Shilah points at Lisa's piece of shit car, barely visible through the windshield. I drive past, hit up the first driveway I come across, and turn back up the mountain. I pull up beside her car and tell Shilah to get out.

"Get her in here. Pull her the hell out if you need to," I grumble, even though I know he'd never do that.

I watch as he opens her driver's side door and gestures at the truck. I can't see her reaction, but I can guess. The moment she gets out, her angry dark eyes meet mine, but she climbs into the truck. I try not to notice the way her clothes look—drenched and plastered to her body—as she buckles in, her generous mouth pressed into a tight line.

"Your hair looks nice."

Don't ask me what makes me say that. The only excuse I have is I'm trying hard not to check out the hard nipples visible, even through the sweater she's wearing, so I focused on her hair. I think this is the first time I've seen it natural and I like it.

"Save it. The hair's a mess and you know it," she snaps, keeping her head averted as she looks out the side window.

I figure it's better just to keep my mouth shut, until I let Shilah pull her car out in front of me and see the back of her car packed with grocery bags.

"Groceries? Why would you go—"

She holds a hand to my face, effectively silencing me.

"Just don't, Brick." Her voice sounds tired, weary, and instead of tearing a strip off her for going to the store without help, I shut my mouth and put the truck in gear.

Back at the compound, Shilah is already unloading the groceries as I pull up right outside the clubhouse so she can get out without getting wet. The moment she unclips the seat belt I reach over and touch her arm.

"I'll go pick up the kids this afternoon."

She turns to me, a little smile on her lips but she keeps her eyes down.

"Thanks, Brick, but I'm sure the storm will have blown over by then."

"For crap's sake, woman, would you let someone lend a hand from time to time? You're plum worn-out 'cuz you're too stubborn to accept any help."

So much for my good intentions.

"I'm fine. I do fine by myself."

"I ain't debating that, and if it was just me I wouldn't argue at all—I know you can barely stand to be around me—but plenty of other folks have offered and you turn us all down. Don't know if you noticed, but being family is a huge part of being part of an MC. We have each other's backs."

"Good for you," she spits, getting out of the truck before turning to face me. "I'm not part of any MC, I'm just the cook."

With that she throws the door shut and stomps into the clubhouse. I curse under my breath and put the truck in gear, pulling it up to the garage.

That afternoon I watch her climb into her wreck of a car and head back down the mountain to pick her kids up from school.

She probably already has something going for dinner, which she cooks for anywhere from six to nine kids and between six and a dozen adults. It all depends what is going on, and who is pulling up a chair at any given meal. Club events, holidays, cookouts, there are even more mouths to feed. On top of that she cleans, does laundry, and has her own place behind the clubhouse to maintain. Sure, she gets help from the kids, but sometimes I wonder if that's not more of a headache than it's worth.

Seven days a week, and as far as I know, she's barely

had a single day off since she came here. From what little I know, she's been looking after others her entire life. That's gotta change. I'm going to have to have a word with Ouray.

With Shilah finishing up the brake job we were working on, I head inside to catch Ouray before Lisa gets back.

I find him in his office.

"Got a minute?"

He drops his pen and leans back in his chair.

"Sure. Sit."

I take a seat across from him but then don't know where to start.

"It's about Lisa." Ouray folds his arms over his chest and waits me out. Typical Ouray. "She's tired. She needs a break."

"Did she tell you that?"

"No, and that's the problem. I can see it in her, Chief, she's worn but she'd never ask anything for herself."

He leans forward, his forearms on the desk, hands folded.

"What would you like me to do? Think I haven't offered her time off? Most she was ever willing to take was a weekend and she ended up back in the kitchen by Sunday afternoon. I can hardly force her to take time."

Trunk walks in, stops, and looks from Ouray to me and back.

"Am I interrupting?"

"No," Ouray says, just as I tell Trunk, "Yes."

The asshole grins wide and pulls up a chair. Last

thing I need is our resident psychologist to sit in on a conversation I'm already regretting.

"Brick here is worried about Lisa."

Trunk turns to me, his eyebrow raised.

"Shee-it. About fucking time, brother."

"Jesus," I grumble, standing up. "The woman could use some time off, that's all. You idiots wanna make more outta that, do it on your own damn time."

I turn for the door and almost run into the subject of conversation, and she's not happy.

"Lisa…" But she's already moving down the hall.

I want to go after her but Trunk grabs my arm.

"Brother, word to the wise," he shares. "Glad as fuck to see you're pulling your head outta your ass, but that woman is an uphill battle. Think Mount Everest."

I pull out of his hold.

"Thanks, fucking Ann Landers, but I'm just worried she's gonna keel over on the job one day. Then where'd we be?"

I walk out of there, but not fast enough to miss Ouray's comment.

"Goddamn it, we're heading for another round of drama around here."

Jesus, these guys are worse than a fucking quilting bee.

I find Lisa busy in the kitchen. Ezrah and Kiara are sitting at the table having a snack.

"I'm busy, Brick," she says, her back to me. I lean my hip against the counter beside her.

"You're not Superwoman, Lisa."

"I know that," she hisses, glaring at me, but her eyes are shiny.

Fuck, is she gonna cry?

Deciding whether to grab the tissues, or run for the nearest exit, my phone rings. The perfect distraction; I don't even bother checking before I answer.

"Yeah."

There's a heavy silence, and then a painfully familiar voice.

"Dad?"

2

LISA

"NEED A HAND?"

Lissie, Yuma's wife and a rare friend to me, walks into the kitchen where I'm struggling to pull the roast out of the industrial-sized oven.

I'm a strong woman, always have been, but lately it's like my energy saps at double the rate. My arms feel weak and I don't trust myself to lift the large Dutch oven onto the stainless steel counter.

"Yeah. Take a towel and grab the other side of this? Damn thing's so heavy."

Together we manage to hoist it up on the counter. Lissie lifts the lid and peeks inside.

"Oh my God, that smells so good."

"You hanging around for dinner? I've got plenty."

Her husband, Yuma, is in a club meeting and their adopted son, Jesse, wanted to hang with the boys. As a result the whole family dropped in, including four-month-old baby, Lettie, named after Momma, who ruled the roost here before she passed away last year.

"You sure? Jesse would love to. He says he misses your cooking."

I knew Jesse as Thomas who, along with his big brother, Michael, was one of the boys who were being groomed by the Hinckle family to be part of the new American Nationalist League's militia.

When I took the job with the Hinckle family as their cook and housekeeper six years ago, I had no idea what I'd been getting myself into. I had just found out Sunny was dead, leaving me with then four-year-old Ezrah, and Kiara had been an infant. I was desperate to find something that would keep a roof over our heads and food on our table, and didn't look as closely as I should have at my new employers. By the time I realized what I'd stepped into was nothing more than modern-day slavery, it was too late.

Margaret, one of the Hinckle daughters, made it very clear to me she wouldn't think twice slicing my *nappy mongrel* kids' necks if I stepped out of line. I had no doubt she would.

I'd become very good at staying silent and as invisible as I could make myself. I'd been mostly successful.

These days I still sometimes have to pinch myself to make sure I'm not dreaming. When the FBI raided the compound, outside Moab two years ago, I had a hard time believing it was truly over, but then this club adopted me and my kids, showing me a level of kindness I'd never experienced before. I'm forever in their debt, which is why every day I can take care of them is a gift.

"Positive," I assure Lissie.

I stick my head into the clubhouse and call Ravi and Michael, two of the club's charges, to start setting out plates and cutlery, and set the table for the kids. With the larger dinner crowd tonight, buffet style will be easier. I spot Nosh, who is sitting at a table by the bar with Lettie in her carrier on the floor beside him, but he's staring at the beer bottle in front of him.

"Your father-in-law looks lost," I tell Lissie.

"I know. We thought naming Lettie for her grandmother would make him happy, but it just seems to make him miss her more."

"Grief is unpredictable. Especially for those who try to push it out of the way, it's bound to hit you upside the head when you least expect it. He'll find his way through."

"Hope so, anyway," she says, clearly changing the subject as she rubs her hands on her jeans. "What's next?"

I point at the large pot of potatoes I already drained. "Those need mashing, while I slice the beef."

The bean casserole and salad are already done, and by the time I catch sight of Brick passing the kitchen—a sign the meeting is over—the food is ready to go out on the table.

For two days I've tried to forget about the few

words I heard Brick mumble to whomever had called him before he moved out of earshot. *"Kelsey,"* he'd said before adding, *"sweetheart."* His voice had been rough with emotion. I'm not sure what to think but I can't deny it stung.

Ridiculous, since I keep snapping at the man when he comes too close, but the way he hasn't even acknowledged my presence since then doesn't feel good. Guess it serves me right.

"Kiara," I call out to my girl, who apparently got bored with the boys and is now on her knees beside Lettie's car seat. "Come sit down for dinner."

I load up a plate for Nosh while Lissie takes care of the younger kids. Then she and I get our own before giving the all-clear to the menfolk. If we were to wait until after, there wouldn't be any food left. Well, maybe salad.

Trunk, the only other black adult and my grandson's idol, flips two fingers at me before he ducks out the door. Heading home to Jamie and their kids, I'm sure.

Five of the guys live here. Nosh, Tse, and Brick have rooms in the clubhouse, and Wapi and Shilah have their quarters in the younger kids' dorm out back. The other guys live elsewhere, but some have stuck around for dinner.

The kids and I have our own place, what used to be Momma and Nosh's cottage, set back from the clubhouse. The old man gave that house to us last year after his wife died. Said it needed new life and it came with the job. For the first time ever, my grandchildren have their own rooms.

Another reason why, even if I were to work out the rest of my days here, it would still not come close to repaying these people for what they've done for my family. So whenever Brick offers help, I feel that scale tipping again.

I dart a glance at Nosh's table, where Brick has taken his plate and joined the old man. His head is bent over his dinner.

"Let me clear these off," Lissie stands up and starts collecting empty plates.

"Sit your butt down, I've got it." I get to my feet and push her back down in her seat.

It doesn't take me long to clear the table, but when I carry the now empty Dutch oven into the kitchen, I suddenly feel the world spinning.

The last thing I remember is a loud crash.

BRICK

I'M UP AND out of my seat, running for the kitchen.

Lissie is ahead of me, already bending down in the narrow space where Lisa is lying on the floor.

"Get out of my way."

I unceremoniously grab Lissie under her arms and swing her behind me.

Lisa's eyes are closed, her skin an almost gray quality that scares the crap out of me, but she seems to be breathing. I look for her pulse, which may be a little slow. When I turn I see Lissie lifting her feet on her lap so they're elevated.

"She okay?" Ouray asks from the doorway.

"She's on the fucking floor of the kitchen, so I'd say no," I snap, angry at him, angry at Lisa, but mostly angry at myself, because I fucking knew she wasn't well.

"Language," she whispers, blinking those dark brown eyes open. She looks a little disoriented and tries to sit up. "What…"

"Stay put."

"Ambulance is on the way," I hear Yuma call out.

"I'm fine. Just a little dizzy is all."

"Right. Dizzy." Sarcasm drips from my voice but I can't help it. "You hit the floor, woman. Passed out cold. You're gonna stay down until the ambulance gets here so they can check you out."

She glares at me but doesn't argue. I have a sneaky suspicion she may be more shaken than she lets on. Good, maybe now she'll start taking care of herself.

"Nana?"

I twist my head to see Kiara slip through the large bodies of Ouray and Tse blocking the doorway.

"Come here, Princess," I call her, watching as her bottom lip begins to tremble. She shuffles closer and leans her whole body into my side. "Your nana's fine, see? She fell and now she's waiting for the ambulance to come check her out."

Lisa reaches for her granddaughter's hand.

"No crying, child. I'm fine. You listen to Mr. Brick. Nana's just tired is all."

"Here," Lissie gets up and holds out her hand to the

girl. "I think Lettie needs a clean diaper and a bottle. Wanna help me with that?"

She takes Kiara out of the kitchen, shooing the guys back from the doorway as she goes.

"Dear Lord, that's embarrassing," Lisa mutters. "I should get up."

"Do me that one favor and stay where you are," I plead. "Humor me."

She studies my face and tries to read my eyes, but I make sure not to let anything show.

It's been tough these last few days since that surprise phone call ripped those old wounds right open. I thought I was gonna have a coronary when I heard her say, "Dad."

My daughter, Kelsey. The last time I saw her was about eight years ago when she told me, in no uncertain terms, she didn't want anything to do with me. Fuck, that hurt, but I understood. She'd been just a little girl when I left.

I did ten years in prison for aggravated auto theft. In simple terms, I'd run a chop shop for my old club. It had taken Kelsey's mother five years before she filed for divorce and I didn't blame her one bit. In fact, I'd told her not to wait enough times. Sadly she waited too long.

She'd just been getting her life in order, away from the club, when she was diagnosed with liver cancer. By the time I found out, she was already dead. My then seventeen-year-old daughter had been looking after her ailing mother for two years on her own, and there was nothing I could do, I had another two years to go before I'd be eligible for parole.

Needless to say, my daughter blamed me and I can't fault her for that. She told me the only thing she wanted from me was to be left in peace. It was the least I could do for her, but I did remind her if ever she needed anything to call me.

Two days ago she did, after eight years of silence.

She was in trouble, I could hear it in her voice, but she wouldn't tell me over the phone. She asked where I was and said she'd talk to me when she got here. Then she hung up. I've tried calling her back a few times but she's not answering.

"Hey, Lisa. What happened?"

Sumo, one of the Durango Fire Department's EMTs, walks into the kitchen, followed closely by his partner, Blue.

I scoot out of their way, but stick close by, listening with half an ear when they start firing off questions and help her into a sitting position. It's not until I hear Blue say she'd like to take Lisa in to get her checked out that I focus on the conversation.

"I'll be fine."

"Still," Sumo tries, "it wouldn't hurt to get yourself checked out."

"Can't I stop in at the doctor's tomorrow?" She lowers her voice and I have to strain to hear her next words. "The kids are already upset. I can do it after I drop them off at school."

Sumo turns to look at Blue, who shrugs, but before they can answer I put in my two cents.

"I'll make sure she goes." I know she's about to

protest so I throw her a glare. Her mouth snaps shut, but I can tell she's not happy with me. Tough, I can live with that. "We'll drop off the kids at school and go straight from there."

"Sounds good to me. I don't think you have a concussion, but it still wouldn't be a bad idea to have someone around tonight," Blue carefully suggests, her eyes drifting to me.

"She won't be alone."

Despite Lisa's protests, I walk her and the kids to her cottage, the boys at the clubhouse taking care of cleaning the kitchen.

"You don't need to stay here. If there's a problem we're close enough to the clubhouse," she says, blocking the doorway after letting the kids inside.

"What if you pass out again?"

"Then the kids can come get you."

I let my head fall back on my shoulders and take a deep breath in. It's still not enough to take the sting out of my words.

"And put the responsibility to look after you on their narrow shoulders? Not gonna happen."

I know I hit dead center when she sucks in a breath and pales even further. Without a word, she turns and walks into the house, leaving the door open. I follow inside.

Instead of feeling good about my small victory, I'm sick to my stomach at the pain I glimpsed in her eyes.

3

LISA

I WAKE UP at the sound of Kiara chattering away in the kitchen, and the low rumble responding immediately reminds of the man who slept on my couch.

We didn't talk much when we got here. I was busy getting Kiara ready for bed and assuring her Nana was just fine, and after that sat down with Ezrah to make sure he had his homework done. After he went down, I basically pulled out an extra pillow and blanket, handed it to Brick, and locked myself in my bedroom.

At first I didn't think I'd get to sleep last night, but I was out like a light in no time. Only problem is, even after a solid night's rest, I still feel tired.

I swing my legs out of bed and stumble to the bathroom. Normally I'd first get coffee going, but there's no way I'm walking into the kitchen with my hair looking the way I know it will. My reflection confirms that was a good call, and I once again consider going for a haircut. I've thought about it, going short so it's easier to manage, but so far I've chickened out every time.

Ezrah is up as well when I finally emerge from the bathroom, but Brick is nowhere to be seen.

"Where's Mr. Brick?" I ask, walking to the coffee machine to see the pot is already full. Bless his heart.

"Shower," Ezrah explains. "Said he'd be back to pick us up."

I note the dishes in the sink.

"Had breakfast already?"

"Yup, Mr. Brick said I could have Lucky Charms," Kiara chirps, knowing damn well those are saved for the weekends.

I give her an admonishing look because I'm sure she never mentioned that to the man.

"Book bag ready, boy?" I direct at Ezrah.

"Uh-uh." He eyes me suspiciously. "Why is he pickin' us up? You still sick?"

In the past I might've tried brushing him off with some excuse, but the boy is ten going on twenty-five with everything he's seen in his young life.

"Mostly just tired. I'm gonna see the doctor, make sure that's all there's to it."

He stares at me a few seconds longer before turning back to whatever TV show they're watching, while I get some toast and coffee down.

Five minutes before we normally leave, a knock

sounds at the door and Kiara runs to open it. Brick's eyes are on me as he steps inside.

"Y'all ready?"

"Don't forget your lunches, and get in the truck already," I tell the kids. "I'm just gonna grab my things."

They're already in the back of the truck's crew cab when I pull the front door shut behind me. Brick is waiting for me on the passenger side and opens the door. I avoid his eyes, and climb in after mumbling, "Thank you."

As usual, Kiara is chattering from the back seat, giving me a headache.

"Child, save some of that for your friends at school, all right? You're not gonna have any stories left."

"Sure I will. I have lots more stories. Like when—"

"Princess, give it a rest, yeah?" Brick rumbles, softening his words with a wink in the rearview mirror.

My grandbaby, the little traitor, smiles and answers obediently, "Okay."

What's missing this morning is Ezrah's attitude. He always has something to say to his sister, most of it not particularly complimentary, but he's been suspiciously quiet this morning.

I twist in my seat to look at Ezrah, who appears to be turned to the window, but he's looking at me from the corner of his eye. His face is tight. My boy is worried about me.

It doesn't surprise me. Kiara was too young to have any memories of her mother, but Ezrah was hurt when she disappeared. Poor kid started asking when Mama would be home, then moved to asking if she'd come back, and finally I had to tell him she was dead when I got word. Eventually he stopped talking about her altogether.

I'm the only constant the kids have had in their lives. Last night must've freaked him out.

I throw him a smile before straightening in my seat, just as Brick pulls up to Ezrah's school. He's already half out of the truck when I call him back.

"Bag, lunch…and a thank-you for Mr. Brick," I snap.

Ezrah mumbles something that may have been gratitude and I'm about to call him out on it when Brick glances over and ever so slightly shakes his head.

As usual I walk Kiara to the door, kissing her head when she hugs my middle, and opening the door for her. Brick has an inscrutable expression on his face when I climb back in the truck. I suddenly feel uneasy.

"What?"

He shakes his head.

"Nothin'." He pulls away from the curb. "Where's your doctor at?"

"Clinic by the hospital." It's quiet in the car, but I can't shake that look in his gray eyes. "What was that look for?" I finally ask.

His gaze is focused on the road ahead, but I keep my eyes on him. He knows I'm not letting up.

"You. You've got this tough exterior—bristly—but every now and then, when you think no one's lookin', you're showing your soft side."

I turn my head to look out the side window, but I can't keep myself from mumbling, "Pot meet kettle."

His deep chuckle fills the cab of the truck and I don't bother hiding my smile. It's quiet after and I keep my eyes out the side window, although I can feel him looking over from time to time. He unsettles me, makes me feel off-balance. Conflicted is probably a better description.

Brick's been nothing but nice to me, although he sometimes has a bossy way about him. Heck, everyone at the clubhouse has been nice and it's taken me a long time to get used to it. But Brick appears to have taken a personal interest I don't quite know what to do with.

There's a reason I've been trying to avoid spending too much time in his presence. I'm attracted to him. Something that's not easy for me to admit, even to myself. White men paying me any attention in the past have always been after one thing, and one thing only.

"Thanks. You can just pull up front," I tell him when he turns into the clinic's parking lot. "I can grab an Uber back."

"Right," is all he says in response before I jump out of the truck and rush inside.

"Was this the first time you passed out?"

Dr. Weinberg sits down behind his desk, the ECG strip in front of him.

Ouray gave me his name last year, after an incident when Ezrah had needed stitches. Brick had come to my rescue then as well. I'm not sure what the club's arrangement with the doctor is, but I know he's the one the boys see and I've been here a few times for my babies. I've just never been here for myself.

After a preliminary examination, I had to stop at the lab for some blood work and an ECG before I was called into his office.

"Yes, I've been light-headed before, but the first time I fainted."

He nods and looks down at the strip.

"Never had any cardiac complaints?"

"No."

"And how long have you been feeling tired and light-headed?"

I snort, because the truth is, I've felt like that for a good long time.

"A while now."

"Hmm. Ever noticed an irregular heartbeat? Felt out of breath?"

My hand automatically comes up to my chest. The memory of my mother dying of a heart attack, at the ridiculously young age of thirty-nine, suddenly surges to the forefront. A hard time in my life I've relegated to the far recesses of my mind.

"Not really."

"What about family, any history of cardiac issues?"

I walk out of his office twenty minutes later with an appointment with a cardiologist at Mercy for the day after tomorrow. I sit down on a bench just outside the clinic doors, taking a moment to gather myself. Dr. Weinberg assured me it was just one of several things he wanted to check out, but that given my mother's history, and the fact I showed an irregular heartbeat, he felt a visit with a cardiologist should be first.

My God, I'm scared. Not for myself, but my poor babies.

BRICK

I SEE HER come out of the clinic and take a seat on the bench.

Then I watch her drop her head in her hands and her shoulders jerk.

I'm out of the truck in a flash.

"Hey…" I crouch in front of her and try to lift her face, surprised to see her cheeks wet. Only other time I ever saw her cry was when Nosh gave her the key to the cottage. "Sugar, what's wrong?"

She tries to hide her face, but I'm not letting her shake me off.

"What did he say?" I try again, but she doesn't seem willing, or even able, to talk.

Someone comes walking out of the clinic and looks our way. I do my best to shield Lisa with my body. She's a very private woman and doesn't need gawkers watch her break down.

"Come on, let's get you out of here."

She lets me pull her to her feet and keep my arm around her as we make our way to my truck. I help her in, pull open the glove compartment where I stuff fast food napkins, and tuck a wad of them in her hand before closing the door.

FREYA BARKER

"Lisa, talk to me."

Her face looks ravaged when she turns to me and I instinctively grab for her hand.

"I'm scared."

"What happened in there?"

She shakes her head but talks anyway.

"I was fourteen when Mama died of a massive heart attack. She never even knew she was sick. She was thirty-nine."

"I'm sorry."

It's a useless thing to say but I say it anyway, for lack of anything better. It takes a second for the possible relevance of what she's telling me to register. Damn.

"I know I'm overreacting, it's probably nothing, but I'm the only thing my babies have and it scares me."

"Babe, right now you're scaring me. What'd the doc say?"

"He's not sure, but my blood pressure's too high, my heartbeat is irregular. He set me up an appointment with a cardiologist for further testing the day after tomorrow. Said it could be other things: infection, anemia, the change…" She gives me a side-glance but quickly diverts her attention back outside. "Never been sick a day in my life. What am I gonna do if—"

"One step at a time. Sugar, look at me," I urge her and she finally complies. Her tears have dried but the fear is still there. "Don't borrow trouble. We'll deal with whatever comes, but it's no use worryin' until we have ta."

"We?"

This time it's me who breaks eye contact. Two fucking years I've been keeping my distance, biding my time, but fuck if time couldn't be running out right in front of me. I look back at her and brush the back of my fingers over her silky soft cheek before cupping her face.

"Fucking right, *we*. Whatever happens, you ain't alone. Not anymore."

She grabs my wrist and leans her face into my palm. "Brick…"

"Not just me. The club's your family, Lisa. There ain't a single brother who'd hesitate even a second to take your back."

She closes her eyes, giving me a chance to take in her face. She's a classic beauty: high cheekbones, full mouth, glowing, rich brown skin. Right now her hair is tied at the nape of her neck, but I love the way it flowed free around her face the other day.

"I'm forty-six, Brick."

"Not news, Lisa."

Her brown eyes turn to me. "I've outlived my mama by seven years already."

I'm not sure if it's the defeat in her eyes or the two years of hanging onto my restraint, but I lean in and take her mouth. Fuck, I've exerted an iron will for a long goddamn time, but one taste of those luscious lips and it's clear there's no going back.

It's far from a one-sided kiss as her hand touches my face and her mouth welcomes me, but I force myself to release her.

"Don't borrow trouble," I repeat.

She pulls her hand back, dropping it on her lap as she sits back in the seat and her eyes drift out the window.

"You're right, and this didn't happen," she says, refusing to look at me. "Let's get home. I've got stuff to do."

"Oh, it fuckin' happened, but I'll take you home."

"Language," she snaps, which makes me grin. There she is.

"Fine, I'll mind my language if you promise to take it easy."

I don't get an answer but I didn't really expect one. She's a proud woman.

The twenty-minute, silent drive back to the compound allows me to think about the phone conversation I just had while waiting for Lisa in the parking lot.

After Kelsey's call, I talked to one of the brothers, Paco, who's smart with computers. I gave him her name and number and he'd promised to see what he could find. So far he got a DMV listing with an old address in Denver—she apparently hadn't lived there for close to a year according to her landlord—and the registration for a 2017 Nissan Rogue.

The thought she'd been so close to me all this time didn't sit well.

He hadn't been able to do much with the phone number, which looks to be linked to a pay-as-you-go account. He suggested maybe talking to Luna, the wife of our president, Ouray, and also an FBI agent.

If I don't hear from her today, I might just do that.

When I pull into the compound, I drive straight to

Lisa's cottage.

"You could've dropped me off at the clubhouse, I want to make a start on dinner before I pick the kids up this afternoon."

I stop outside her front door, put the truck in park, and turn toward her.

"I'm picking up the kids, and I'm sure the guys can manage dinner. Why don't you take some time?"

Her eyes narrow on me.

"You're the one who told me not to worry until I had to."

"Yeah, but that doesn't mean you should pretend like nothin' happened," I fire back. "For once, would you look after yourself? Have a bath, read a book, watch TV, whatever, just…" I take a deep breath before adding in a gentler voice, "Just look after yourself. Please?"

She's silent for a moment, her eyes scanning my face. Then she nods.

"Okay."

I grab her hand and kiss the back of it.

"Thank you."

4

LISA

I WAKE UP on the couch, a little disoriented, but it only takes me a second to figure out why I'm here and not in the kitchen at the clubhouse.

Sleeping had been a welcome escape from the wide range of emotions I was overwhelmed with earlier. Heck, still am to a point.

Mama's unexpected death and the suppressed memory of standing over her grave, feeling so utterly lost without her, had hit me like a freight train in the doctor's office. It was so easy to imagine my babies standing over my grave, lost and rudderless. My fear had been instant and I let panic take over. The thought of my grandchildren going through something like that when they've already been through so much in their short lives was more than I could handle.

You think you finally have a grasp on life, only to discover what a joke that is. My carefully honed, tough exterior disintegrated on the spot. I was having an honest to God anxiety attack on that damn bench.

Then Brick was there. His mere presence having more of an impact than I should let it. It wasn't the first time he stepped up right when I needed it, but it was the first time he made me believe maybe I'm not alone.

Of course that kiss helped. Oh boy, it sure did. It pulled me in and left my mind blissfully empty. That is, until he broke away and reality hit me like a ton of bricks.

I get up off the couch to get a glass of water from the kitchen when a knock sounds at the door.

"Hey."

Lissie is standing on my doorstep with the baby's car seat in hand.

"Come in. What brings you here?"

I step aside and let her through. She sets Lettie down on the couch and turns to face me.

"I see," I tell her, noting the expression on her face. "Brick." Damn that man.

"Don't blame him. I came by to check on you and bumped into him. All he told me was he took you to the doctor this morning and to check in with you."

Damn, another tick up on the man's trust factor, letting me decide if I want to share.

"I was grabbing something to drink, you want anything?" I ask, delaying the inevitable.

Lissie was a detective with the Durango PD when

I met her and I'm sure she'll dig until I give her the goods. She's a stay-at-home mom now, with a new baby girl and an eight-year old adopted son, I'm sure those interrogation skills will come in handy.

"Tea or water, either is fine."

I lean over the couch to give sleeping Lettie a kiss on her downy head before I head to the kitchen. Tea sounds good. It's getting chilly.

While I put on the kettle, Lissie pulls out a chair at the small kitchen table, and I can feel her eyes following my every move.

"So the doctor?" she prompts me.

"Said I should take it easy until we know what's going on."

I'm being evasive I know, but I immediately feel guilty keeping her in the dark when I turn around and see her face. She's become a good friend, even better since Lettie's birth. She trusted me with her insecurities around motherhood, her tears when she was hit with baby blues. Lissie deserves my trust in return.

"He is sending me to a cardiologist," I reveal, sitting down across from her.

I relay the visit, and then tell her about Mama. It's something we have in common, losing our mothers at a much too young age. Lissie can relate all too well and when the water starts boiling we're both already crying.

Good Lord, I haven't cried this much in years. I thought my tears had plumb dried up since my Sunny passed away, but maybe I'd just gotten really good at blocking them.

"So…Brick?"

It's on my tongue to blow Lissie off, but with a sip of my tea and the shared tears still drying on my face, I decide to share some more.

"He's nice."

Lissie rolls her eyes. "Tell me something I don't know."

"I mean, the man is *nice*. I never could figure why he was always there to lend a hand. Thought maybe…heck, I don't know what I thought, but as it turns out it could be he thinks I'm nice too."

Lissie snorts and bites her lip, obviously trying not to laugh at me.

"Ya think? Not that it was news to me anyway, but when you went down last night, he all but threw me aside to get to you. That man always seems to have his eyes on you, keeping track of your kids, and treating them like they are his own. Only person who never picked up on that was you. The rest of the club already knows."

I know she's right; it's just embarrassing I'm the last to clue in. I'm not usually this dense.

"He kissed me," I confess and watch as Lissie cracks a wide smile.

"Yay, Brick. About bloody time. And?"

Now it's my time to snort. "What are we, fifteen?"

"Come on, give me something."

"It was nice."

That is an understatement of epic proportions, given the fact I can't remember the last time I was kissed like that.

"Nice? Again? You're gonna need some new adjectives."

"All right. Given I was having a breakdown when he kissed me, and it took me a minute to remember my own dang name after, I'd say it was good."

"So now what?" she asks with barely veiled enthusiasm.

"What do you mean, now what? Now nothing. I've gotta take care of my health so I'm around to raise my babies right, and look after this club that's done so much for me. I ain't got time for fantasies."

Lissie snickers as she gets up to grab a fussy Lettie, who's apparently hungry.

"This is gonna be so much fun to watch," she mumbles.

When the subject of conversation comes walking in ten minutes later—no knock from him—I'm on the couch burping the baby while Lissie is using the bathroom. He walks straight over, and bends down to kiss Lettie's head. For a second I thought he was going to kiss me and am annoyed at myself for being disappointed.

"I'm heading out to pick up the kids. Need anything from town?" he asks instead. "We're ordering pizza for dinner, but maybe you need somethin' else?"

"I should be fine. I'm a little low on milk but it's enough for breakfast. I can always grab some at the clubhouse."

I get to my feet, Lettie almost asleep on my shoulder, and gently place her in the baby carrier. When I turn around, Brick is only inches away. He curves a hand around my neck and my breath stills in my throat. I see the kiss coming and there's no mistaking who it's intended for. Forgetting everything I told Lissie this afternoon about not having time for fantasies, I automatically lift my face.

This time his tongue slides along my bottom lip, teasing me into opening for him, which I do without thought. His deep groan when he invades my mouth reverberates through my body, waking up parts long gone dormant.

"Oops. Sorry."

I abruptly pull away from the kiss, catching Lissie grinning behind her hand.

"I'm just gonna grab Lettie and get out of your hair."

"Not on my account," Brick announces. "I gotta go get the rugrats anyway." But before he leaves, he pulls on a curl by my ear. "I'll take the kids to the clubhouse. Bring 'em over with pizza when it gets here."

I nod my response, not even registering what I'm agreeing to.

Lissie chuckles when the door shuts behind him.

"Now nothing, huh? That didn't look like nothing. It looked like a whole lotta something to me. Hot."

She grins big, fanning herself excessively.

"Dear Lord, help me," I mutter, shaking my head.

"Don't think you'll need the Lord's help with this, honey. Brick looks like he's got it covered."

BRICK

"THIS IS GOD-awful," I mumble under my breath, trying to swallow down the bite.

Wapi chuckles beside me.

We had pizza last night, but tonight Tse offered to make lasagna for the guys. Wisely, Ouray had opted to eat dinner at home, so it ended up just being the four boys, Paco, and the four brothers living here at the table, being subjected to the brother's version of what should be an Italian classic.

It's like chewing glue. I wince when I think of the small tray I dropped off with the kids at Lisa's for their dinner. I hope she has something else to feed the kids because this isn't fit for pig slop.

"Tastes better if you wash it down with beer," Wapi suggests.

The only saving grace is the garlic bread, which was store-bought, and the salad that came from a bag. It's no surprise for once the boys are taking second helpings of the salad.

"Tse, man," I call out to where he's sitting in Lisa's chair at the head of the table. "Appreciate the effort and I love you like a brother—hell, I'd take a bullet for you—but please don't ever ask me to eat your cookin' again."

Loud hooting and hollering goes up around the table. Tse, who's one of the most easy-going guys I know, shrugs and smiles as he demonstratively stuffs another forkful in his mouth. But even he can't eat the stuff without making a face.

"Seemed easy enough on the YouTube video," he says, tossing back the remainder of his beer before he looks around the table. "Which one of you fuckers are gonna try tomorrow?"

"Language!"

All heads turn to Lisa, who just walked in the door. I'm about to ask her what the hell she thinks she's doing here, but I'm silenced with a single hand gesture. She keeps walking to the kitchen door and peeks inside before her sharp gaze goes around the table.

"Them boys need a proper meal, so I'll be back in that kitchen tomorrow. But, come hell or high water, you boys better make sure that mess in there is cleaned up and my kitchen is spotless."

With that she marches right back out. As I get up to go after her, Nosh chuckles, shaking his head.

"A sharp tongue and a big heart, that one," he signs. *"Just like Momma."*

I didn't know Momma well, but from what I've been told about her that's a big compliment to Lisa. I wish she'd heard it.

She's already halfway back to the cottage when I catch up with her.

"Hey, hold up. What was that all about?"

She stops and turns around so I can catch up. Then to my surprise she starts laughing, and fuck if that isn't the best sound I've ever heard.

"I'm bored," she says when she can speak again. "Spent two days in that house and I came this close…" she holds her thumb and forefinger together, "… to braidin' my hair in cornrows I haven't worn since nineteen ninety-six." She turns and starts walking again so I keep up with her. "Besides, I can't sit by while these boys are fed…whatever the hell that was. Who wrecked my kitchen?"

I chuckle at her rant.

"That'd be Tse. He watched a YouTube video." I burst out laughing at her slack mouth and bulging eyes.

She shakes her head. "That man better clean up that mess he made."

She pushes open the door and seems to expect me to walk in after her. I step inside and close the door behind me, when Kiara comes running up.

"Mr. Brick! Wanna see my book?"

"Inside voice, child," I hear Lisa call from the kitchen as her granddaughter grabs my hand, pulling me into the living room.

"Look."

She points at a book on the couch I instantly recognize. It was one of Kelsey's most treasured ones, *Goodbye Moon*. I'm suddenly hit with a wave of nostalgia as I remember reading to her in bed those nights I was home.

I briefly talked to Luna this afternoon when she dropped by to pick up Ahiga, and she said she'd see what she could find out for me. She also pointed out there was little law enforcement would be able to do in this situation. Kelsey is an adult, I really haven't been part of her life for the past eighteen years, and just my interpretation of her phone call wouldn't be enough to open a case, but she promised to do what she could.

"Brick?"

"Yeah."

"I'm making grilled cheese, do you want one or did you actually eat that stuff?"

"Hell to the no. One bite was enough. Not gonna say no to grilled cheese."

Ezrah is sitting at the kitchen table and looks up from what looks like schoolbooks to lift his chin at me. Ten going on twenty-five, complete with attitude. He imitates the brothers at the club, but he's way too young to pull it off. I keep my chuckle to myself

"Come sit," Kiara says, patting the couch beside her.

"All right, Princess."

I sit down and she immediately crawls on my lap, book in hand.

"Will you read to me?"

Fuck.

She snuggles in against my chest when I open the book, but I've barely read a page when my cell rings in my pocket. I lift Kiara off my lap and hand her the book. Pulling my phone out, I note it's the clubhouse phone.

"Yeah?"

"Got a visitor. You coming here or want—"

"On my way." I don't let Paco finish.

Then I walk into the kitchen where Lisa is flipping grilled cheese sandwiches on a large griddle.

"Hate to bail, Sugar, but I've gotta run up to the clubhouse. Something's come up."

Her eyes are worried when she turns to me.

"Everything okay?"

"It's fine. Sorry about the sandwich. I'll check in later, yeah?"

I give her a quick kiss on the cheek, when I notice Ezrah watching our interaction closely. I won't hold back forever, but I'm not going to lay one on her when I'm about to run out the door.

"Later, Ezrah. Princess." I ruffle her hair when I pass the couch. "We'll have to finish that story some other time, all right?"

As soon as I have the door closed, I start jogging over to the clubhouse. Paco is behind the bar when I walk in and cocks his thumb down the hall at the back.

"Ouray's office."

My heart is pounding in my chest, anticipation high, and I stop outside the office to take a few deep breaths before pushing open the door.

Luna and Ouray are the only ones in the office.

"What's going on?"

"Brother, have a seat."

I glare at Ouray and stay standing.

"Just tell me."

It's Luna who starts talking.

5

BRICK

"YESTERDAY STATE POLICE came across a breached guardrail on Highway 550, about ten miles south of Silverton."

My knees go weak and I reach behind me to find a chair, sitting down hard. Ouray shoves a glass in my hand and I don't even look to see what it is, I just throw it back.

"They found a silver Nissan SUV halfway down the gulley. Took them 'til last night to get to the wreck. I'm so sorry, Brick, they think it was your daughter behind the wheel. She didn't survive the crash."

She's still talking but I don't hear anything anymore, all I see is that little girl curling up beside me in her bed as I read her a nighttime story. Years lost, so many years lost.

A pained roar rips from my chest and before I can stop myself, the glass is flying through the room, crashing against the wall.

"Brother…" I feel Ouray's hand clamp down on my shoulder. "Brace. There's more."

I force my gaze to Luna, whose face is carefully shielded—professional—but she can't hide the sheen in her eyes.

"Brick, when we talked earlier you didn't mention a baby…"

It takes a second to register.

"Baby?" My voice sounds hoarse, emotions clogging my throat.

"They found a baby in the car with her. Did you know she…?"

"Hers?"

She nods. "They went through her purse, found a birth certificate for Finn Ernest Paver, date of birth July 27th."

There's no way to stop the sob wrenched from my chest. Ouray's fingers dig into my shoulder, and I welcome that pain over the other.

She gave him my name.

"He's alive, Brick," Luna says softly. "The baby was protected in his seat. He has some superficial injuries and was dehydrated and hypothermic, but he's alive."

"I need to…" I start, but I don't know what I need to do. I'm reeling from the information and nearly breathless with this deep ache pressing on my chest.

"Here's what we're gonna do," Ouray says behind me. "We're taking you to see your daughter at Hood Mortuary. I'm gonna stand by you while you identify your daughter, and once that's done, we're going to go see your grandson at Mercy Hospital, brother."

A grandson. *Jesus*.

I barely notice the curious looks when Ouray escorts me through the clubhouse, his wife leading the way. I just concentrate on putting one foot in front of the other until Luna opens the door to Ouray's new Toyota 4Runner and I get in.

As Ouray drives us toward town, questions start surfacing and I twist in my seat to look at Luna.

"Was it an accident?"

"Unsure at this point. State Patrol called in the Colorado Bureau of Investigations' forensic team. The SUV was brought to the DPD lab here in Durango. Hopefully we'll hear more on that in the next day or so. I told the CBI investigator I spoke with about your phone call with her."

I try to remember the sound of Kelsey's voice, but I can't.

"The father? On the birth certificate?" I clarify.

"Blank. The CBI investigator will be connecting with their colleagues in Denver to see who she was connected to. He promised to keep me updated, and I'll let you know when I do."

When we pull into a parking spot at the mortuary, I'm suddenly not so sure I can do this. Ouray doesn't give me a chance to think, he gets out and opens the door on my side.

"Let's get this over with," he says gruffly.

Luna walked ahead to talk to a guy, who has his eyes on me, as Ouray and I approach.

"Brick, meet CBI agent, Terry Mullin. Terry, this is Brick Paver and that's my husband, Ouray," Luna introduces us.

The man's handshake is firm and his face somber.

"Brick?"

"Road name. My driver's license says Ernest."

The slight flick of his eyes at Luna tells me he's seen the baby's birth certificate.

"Right. Why don't we get this over with?"

Without waiting for an answer, he leads the way inside. I've been here before, but that was for Momma's funeral last year. This is very different. We follow him down a set of stairs and through large swinging doors into a hallway that reeks of chemicals and death. My stomach recoils and as if he could feel it too, Ouray's hand grabs onto my shoulder again.

This sterile place, all white tile and stainless steel, is not where I want to imagine my baby girl, but one look at the sheet-covered body and I know in my bones it's my Kelsey.

A woman in a white coat stands beside the gurney and reaches for the sheet.

"Are you ready, Mr. Paver?" the agent asks me, and I feel Ouray's fingers tighten.

I nod.

My eyes stay focused on the beautiful blonde hair

she inherited from her mother for a long time, until I finally force my gaze lower.

So pale. Her skin is almost translucent. I involuntarily take a step closer. Despite the marks where I suspect glass may have cut her, she looks peaceful. Beautiful, even now.

"That's Kelsey," I whisper.

"We'll give you a minute."

I hear feet shuffling out of the room, but when I feel Ouray's hand retreat, I quickly cover it with mine. I need someone to hold me up. He squeezes my shoulder in understanding.

As I stand here, looking at her, I wonder if she knows the depth of my regret. The span of my pain. I'm not a religious person, but I hope and pray with everything I am she is with her mother now.

My tears blur her face and I bend down and kiss her forehead. The first kiss I've given her in eighteen years and her skin is cold.

"Swear I'll look after your boy, baby girl. I'll do right by him, as God is my witness."

I WALK UP to the crib and meet the blue eyes of my grandson.

He's beautiful like his momma, but darker, like me. He looks up at me with curiosity as I take stock of the cuts on his little body.

"Hey, Little Man," I rumble, and his eyes blink a few

times, startled at the sound. "Can I touch him?" I ask the nurse who let me in.

She smiles at me. "Yes, you can. Like I said, he's feeling a lot better now that he's nice and toasty and has his belly full. If you'd like, you can take a seat and I'll hand him to you? It's time for his bottle."

She must be worried I'll keel over, which isn't beyond the realm of possibilities. I'm spinning.

Once I'm seated, she carries over the baby and I take him from her. So light. Hardly any weight to him yet. I settle him in the crook of my arm as she hands me the bottle. His eyes never leave my face, like he's trying to study me. Not even when I tease his lips with the nipple and he eagerly latches on.

"Brother…" Ouray sticks his head in the door. "I'm just gonna run Luna home and then I'll come back. Is there anything you need?"

"Lisa."

It's the first time I think of her since running out of her house, but her name is also the first thing that comes mind.

"Give me an hour to get things sorted back at the clubhouse and I'll bring Lisa with me."

I nod. Then I put my head back when the nurse files out behind Ouray, leaving me alone with my grandson.

Lisa

My head barely hits the pillow when I can hear knocking at my door.

My first thought is Brick has come back.

I haven't heard from him since he left earlier tonight, but when eleven o'clock came and went, I had to get some sleep. I have my appointment with the cardiologist in the morning, and if I am to head back to the clubhouse in the afternoon, I'll need my rest.

I slip on my robe and pad down the stairs. The figure on my step is not Brick, it's Ouray, and instantly red flags go up as I yank open the door.

"Sorry to catch you so late," he says.

"Is something wrong with Brick?"

"Yes and no. Can I come in for a second?"

Twenty minutes later we're on our way to the hospital, Wapi staying with my kids. My mind is still trying to process what Ouray told me. Brick has a daughter—had—and apparently I wasn't the only one in the dark. No one in the club had known. He has a grandson too, and not even Brick had known about the baby.

My heart breaks for him and when Ouray said he'd asked for me, I was dressed and ready to go in minutes. Not that I have any idea what to do for him.

"How old is the baby?"

"Almost three months."

"How badly was he hurt?" I'd like to know before I walk in the room. I can handle a lot of things, but I have a hard time seeing innocent children hurt. I'd need to mentally prepare for that.

"He just has a few scratches on his body from flying glass. Little guy was lucky. The CBI agent said they estimate the accident happened sometime in the twenty-four hours before they were found. The baby was dehydrated and cold."

I blink back the tears, thinking about what might have happened to that poor little thing if they hadn't found the car when they did.

"Did she suffer?"

I feel Ouray's eyes on me right before his hand covers mine.

"We won't know for sure until they do the autopsy, which is scheduled for tomorrow, but from what I understand it's likely she died quickly."

"I hope so," I whisper, wishing for Brick's sake they would be able to at least give him that.

I follow Ouray down the long halls when we get there, until he stops outside a room. I look in through the window and see Brick sitting in a chair, eyes closed, the baby cuddled against his shoulder.

"You go ahead, I'll be in the waiting room."

I toss Ouray a grateful smile before quietly pushing the door open.

Not quietly enough apparently, Brick's eyes pop open, red-rimmed and filled with a pain I recognize all too well. He reaches out a hand for me and I grab hold, letting him pull me right up to his side. He doesn't let go.

"Look at that beautiful little boy," I whisper, stroking the fingers of my other hand over the baby's back. "Do you know his name?"

"Finn," he answers, his voice cracking as he leans his head against my stomach.

My hand immediately goes to his hair, running my

fingers through the strands.

"That's a good name."

"She called a few days ago—Kelsey. First time in eight years I heard her voice." I keep stroking his head, willing him to keep talking. "She didn't say much, only that she was on her way to see me. I never even knew she had a child. It's fuckin' unreal."

"You're holding him. He's real."

He lifts his head and tilts it up at me.

"You're crying."

"My heart hurts for you," I tell him honestly, but I notice him startle.

He suddenly gets up.

"Sit." When I don't move right away, he says, "Please sit down, I'll grab another chair. Are you okay holding him?"

"My name Lisa?"

Like I would say no to holding a little one. I take a seat and hold out my arms, noting how carefully he handles the baby.

"I'm afraid to let go of him."

The baby doesn't seem to wake when I cradle him in one arm, and stroke Brick's face with my hand.

"I'll keep him safe."

He looks down on me, his eyes solemn.

"I know. That's why I asked for you." He straightens up and walks to the door before turning around. "Is Ouray around?"

"Waiting room."

"Good. I'm gonna need his help."

He opens the door when I call him back.

"Brick? What do you need help with?"

"Child Protective Services will be here in the morning."

"What for?"

"Making sure I'm fit to look after him, I guess."

I feel instantly protective.

"Of course you are," I assure him.

"I live in a room in the clubhouse of an MC, was always good enough for me, but it could be argued it's not a good place for a baby."

"Then tell them you live with me."

I'm not sure what prompts me to say it, and I certainly have no idea how it comes across, but now that it's out there I'm not taking it back. I tilt my chin up, bracing myself for him to laugh in my face.

He doesn't. Instead he lets go of the door and walks back over, crouching in front of me.

"Last thing I wanna do is take you for granted, but I was hoping you could help me with him. Been a long time since I dealt with a baby." He falls silent for a minute, his head tilting to one side as he scrutinizes my face. "Do you mean it?"

"Wouldn't'a said it otherwise."

He lowers his forehead to my knees and I hear him sigh.

"I shouldn't put this on you. You have enough on your plate."

My free hand goes back to his hair, the tips of my fingers stroking the hairline at the base of his skull.

"You didn't. I offered."

We sit like that for a few minutes when a nurse walks in, and Brick straightens before standing up.

"I just need to do vitals," she says, looking from Brick to me and back.

"This is Lisa, my woman."

I swallow hard.

The nurse throws me a friendly smile.

"Would you mind putting him in his crib? It's easier."

"Sure." I get up and carry the baby over, laying him down gently. Then I turn to Brick. "Go talk to Ouray and grab an extra chair."

"Will you stay with him?"

"Not moving an inch," I assure him.

With a curt nod and a last look at his grandson, he walks out the door.

6

BRICK

DIDN'T THINK THE first time I'd sleep with Lisa it would be in a couple of recliners in a hospital room beside my grandson's crib.

Half the night I alternated between watching her and my grandson sleep, before I finally dozed off. I wake up to crying, Finn's crying. I'm quickly by his bedside and lift him in my arms before he wakes Lisa up as well, but when I turn with him in my arms, I see she has her eyes open and is watching us.

"Go back to sleep, Sugar."

She smiles sweetly and closes her eyes again. We talked quite bit before she fell asleep at around two this morning, and I'm sure she's still tired. I fed the baby around three and eventually dozed off as well.

I'd sent Ouray home earlier, didn't see the need for him to hang around the hospital. He said to call him when we're ready to come home. He also promised to get in touch with his contact in Child Protective Services. He deals with the CPS fairly regularly in regard to the boys the club fosters.

I'm just changing Finn's diaper since it was soaked through—a skill I apparently retained over the years—when the door opens and a new nurse sticks her head in. I put my finger to my lips, indicating Lisa. She slips into the room and steps up beside me.

"Want me to get his bottle?" she whispers.

"Please."

Twenty minutes later Finn is dozing off in my arms, his bottle empty, when Lisa stirs.

"How is he?"

"His belly's full and he's asleep, so I'm guessing pretty good."

I watch as she stretches with her arms over her head. Another fantasy I'd envisioned much differently.

"What time is it?"

"Coming up on eight."

She suddenly shoots out of her chair.

"Where's the bathroom? I have to get cleaned up. My appointment with the cardiologist is at eight thirty."

Shit. I'd totally forgotten about that and immediately feel guilty.

Something must've shown on my face because she leans down, her face in mine.

"Don't. I know where your mind's goin' and I'll have

none of that."

Then she completely blows me away when she initiates a sweet kiss, drops one on Finn's downy head, and walks out of the room.

I use the opportunity to call Wapi and make sure the kids are taken care of and have lunches for school. Apparently the whole club is in the know already because according to Wapi, Lissie showed up early and is dropping them off at school, along with her Jesse.

Twenty minutes later she's back, with a brown paper bag and two coffees she puts on the nightstand. Then she walks over and plucks Finn off my lap, carrying him to his crib.

"Let's eat. I have about ten minutes until my appointment."

She hands me one of the coffees and pulls some kind of breakfast wrap from the bag, handing it to me.

"What about you?"

"I got a muffin. That's about all I can handle right now."

"Nervous?" I ask, already chewing.

"Little."

We eat in silence, except I think I may have groaned at my first sip of coffee. Sleeping in a recliner is not ideal.

"I should've checked on the kids, make sure—"

"Talked to Wapi. Lissie's got them."

She smiles at me. "Any other time I would've snapped at you for taking over, but I'm thanking you today."

Despite the persistent ache that returned in my chest after spending twenty minutes reliving yesterday's hell,

I manage a wink back.

"I should come with you," I change the subject, but Lisa shakes her head as she brushes crumbs off her lap and gets up.

"You need to be here with that precious boy. I'll come right back after and we'll make a list of things we'll need for him."

She stops in front of me and bends down. I hook my hand behind her neck and give her a hard close-mouthed kiss.

"Thanks, Sugar."

With Finn sleeping and Lisa at her appointment, I call Ouray.

"Have you heard anything?" he asks.

"Waiting for the doctor, no sign yet of CPS."

"Yeah, I just talked to Joyce, my contact there. She's finding out who the caseworker is and will try to get hold of them before they show up over there. She doesn't think there'll be a problem, they prefer to place kids with family when possible."

I have to say, it makes me feel a little better. I'm not ready to give up the one thing still connecting me with my daughter.

"I know it's still early, but anything on Kelsey?" Even just saying her name is difficult.

"Luna left to meet up with Terry Mullin. The autopsy is scheduled for nine thirty and they want to be present."

I squeeze my eyes shut to fight off the images of my baby girl lying on that cold slab.

"Okay."

"Brother, hate to do this to you, but we've got to start thinking about a funeral."

"Her mother was buried in Grand Junction but with Finn here in Durango, I'd like to think she'd want to be close to him."

"Probably a good call. I can put a call in to Hood, set something up for us to go in this week and get that sorted."

That isn't something I ever thought I'd be faced with—planning Kelsey's funeral—but I have to do right by her.

"That'd be good."

"I talked to the brothers, spread the word. We're all here for you."

Even after only two years with Arrow's Edge, I know in my bones he's telling the truth. The brotherhood is strong.

"Appreciated. I'll call you later."

I quickly hang up before emotions get the best of me, just as Finn starts fussing in his crib. Needing to feel the connection, I lift him out and settle him against my chest where he immediately calms down.

LISA

MY HEAD IS spinning with information when I walk out of radiology.

The cardiologist, Dr. Husse, sent me there for an echocardiogram. Something about assessing the function of my heart. I've also been outfitted with a Holter monitor to track heart rhythm over the next couple of days, and the wireless pack is clipped onto my waistband. She warned me there might be more tests. I don't really care as long as they figure out the problem. I'd rather know what I'm dealing with.

I've been gone for a couple of hours when I return to the room, and Brick is not alone. I hesitate in the entrance but Brick sees me and waves me over.

"Perfect timing," he mumbles in my ear. To the two women on the other side of Finn's crib he says, "This is Lisa Rawlings."

Both women introduce themselves. One is the hospital social worker and the other is a CPS caseworker.

They have a lot of questions, a lot of forms for Brick to fill out. At some point, I can sense he's spent all his 'polite' for the day when the CPS lady points out it's unusual for someone at fifty—which is apparently Brick's age—to be raising an infant. I can feel him gearing up and quickly put my hand on his arm.

"Plenty of men becoming parents again at a later age," I tell the woman. "Or women for that matter. I'm forty-six and am raisin' my two young grandchildren. It's not like either of us is new at this parenting thing."

"And how old are the other two children in the house?"

"Ten and six. Boy and girl."

She has a few more questions, mainly about the house and space for the baby, and I calmly explain we haven't really had a chance to work out all the logistics, given the circumstances. It seems to satisfy them for now, and the caseworker hands Brick an information sheet and a phone number to call once we're settled in so she can do a home visit.

He's still bristling when they're gone.

"He's my own goddamn flesh and blood and they're gonna decide what's best for him? Fuck that."

"You could adopt him," I suggest. "You're the boy's only surviving relative. Set those wheels in motion. Get a lawyer."

He bends down and drops his head in his hands.

"My fuckin' head's gonna explode."

I understand how he feels. I remember being so overwhelmed when Sunny was found dead I didn't know where to start.

"One thing at a time," I tell him gently, placing a hand on his back. "Let's get this baby home first."

"I believe I can help with that," the nurse says, walking in with a diaper bag and some paperwork. "The bag is his. EMTs brought it in with him, and I have his discharge right here."

"Shit."

Brick turns around in the front seat of Ouray's SUV to look at me.

"Forgot to ask how your appointment was this morning."

I notice Ouray's head come up and his eyes catch mine in the rearview mirror. I haven't told him yet, but in my defense, the past day or two have been chaotic to say the least.

"They did some tests and put a Holter monitor on me. I've got another appointment on Monday. Hope we'll know more then."

"Wanna fill me in?" Ouray asks.

"Doc Weinberg said I had high blood pressure and arrhythmia, and sent me to a cardiologist, who's tryin' to find out what the problem is."

I'm trying to sound casual. There's enough going on, no one needs something else to worry about.

"Her mother died of a heart attack at thirty-nine," Brick fills in for me.

So much for downplaying it.

"That's it. I don't want you near the clubhouse," Ouray snaps.

"Actually, Dr. Husse—that's the cardiologist—told me I should go about my regular day with this thing on."

He glares at me in the mirror but I lift my chin defiantly. I don't want to become a burden, especially now. Brick is the one who'll need the support.

"Fine, but you'll have help. And while I'm at it, we need to talk about the garage. Shilah seems to be hanging in, but I'm putting Tse in there for the time being." When it looks like Brick is going to protest, Ouray holds his hand up. "No argument, brother. I'm not takin' anything away from you, I'm just making sure things can keep running the way they should and taking some pressure off you in the meantime. Your hands are gonna be full. We're family, lots of people ready to jump in if need be.

For both of ya."

Finn starts fussing in his car seat, and I use the excuse to lean over him and hide the emotion on my face.

"Clubhouse or cottage?" Ouray asks, when we turn up the drive to the compound.

"Cottage," Brick answers, but then turns to me for confirmation.

"Agreed."

The clubhouse can wait another day. We need some time to process.

"Cottage it is." He drives past the boys' bunkhouse and pulls up in front of my place. "Some of the women have been busy this morning, pulling together a few things you might need for the little one."

Brick, who was about to get out of the truck just manages to nod, so I do the talking. I put a hand on Ouray's shoulder.

"Tell the girls thank you."

He pats my hand. "Sure thing."

Bags line the small hallway walking into the house. In the living room a foldable playpen/travel bed is set up.

"Jesus," Brick mumbles, as he carries the borrowed baby seat over to the couch, setting it down before he rubs his hands over his face.

"They even brought formula and bottles," I tell him, peeking in the bags. The others hold baby clothes, a monitor, changing pad, baby shampoo, and diapers.

"Where the hell are we gonna leave all that?"

He sits down heavily beside his grandson, a proprietary hand covering the baby's belly.

"Was thinking about that; my bedroom's big enough for a crib and it's quiet up there. I have plenty of room in the walk-in closet for stuff and it won't take much to clear out a couple'a drawers in my dresser, so we can use that to change him. Or," I add, wanting to give him another option. "I can clear out Kiara's room, have her move into my room and you and the baby can have hers."

"No way. Not putting that girl out of her room. Not gonna happen."

I walk over and sit on the coffee table in front of him, putting my hands on his knees.

"Go have a shower—think about it—I've got your boy. I'm gonna get this stuff sorted and tucked away, and get his bottle ready. Small steps. Besides, if whatever we decide to do doesn't pan out, we can always change it until we find somethin' that works."

"Christ, what a mess," he mumbles, shaking his head as he looks at my hands.

"Yeah, but we'll work our way through."

His head comes up, eyes shimmering silver with unshed tears. His pain raw.

"First time I saw her in eight years and she was cold as ice. Couldn't even tell her I love her."

Not knowing what else to do, I climb on his lap and wrap myself around him as best I can.

"She knew, baby. She knew. Or she wouldn't'a come looking for you."

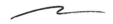

"WHAT'S ALL THIS, Nana?"

"Hush, child," I tell Kiara when she walks in the door. "The baby's sleeping. You can go peek but don't wake him up."

"Who is that?" Ezrah, who walks in right behind her, asks.

"That's Mr. Brick's grandbaby. His name is Finn. Finn's mama died in a car crash, so he'll be stayin' with us for now."

His face is worried when he turns to me.

"She died? She Mr. Brick's daughter?"

"Yeah."

"That why Wapi stayed wit' us last night?" I nod in response. "Mr. Brick sad?"

"Yeah, honey. He's sleepin' upstairs—he was up most the night—so keep it down a bit, all right?"

Ezrah walks over to the crib where his sister is already hanging over the side.

"He's little."

"I know. You guys hungry? Want a snack before you do your homework?"

Both of them nod, more subdued than they'd normally be. I get them set up at the table with a snack, a drink, and homework. It reminds me, I have to call Lissie. I'm pretty sure it was her who filled my fridge.

It's not until I'm on the couch feeding Finn, with Kiara tucked to my side; Brick comes down the stairs. My little girl jumps up from the couch and runs to him, wrapping her arms around his legs.

"I'm sorry, Mr. Brick. Are you sad?" She tilts her

head back and Brick picks her up.

"Yeah, Princess. I am." He walks over to the couch with Kiara perched on his hip, doing the chin lift thing with Ezrah, who is watching the older man closely. "Thanks for lettin' me sleep," he says with a forced little smile for me as he sits down, my little girl on his lap. Then he turns his attention to the baby. "How is he?"

"He's a good baby."

"I was helping Nana change his diaper and he pulled my braid," Kiara pipes up, startling the little boy.

"Inside voice," I remind her.

"Oops. But it didn't hurt," she finishes telling Brick in a stage whisper. This time his smile seems more genuine.

I remember that too, the guilt every time you felt something other than grief.

"Here, why don't you two look after this peanut and I'll finish up dinner?"

Bits of conversation filter through while I throw together a salad and get Ezrah to set the table. But I stop to listen when I hear Kiara ask something.

"Are you gonna stay here too?"

"Would that be okay with you? If I stayed on the couch for a bit?"

"Sure," my honest-as-the-day-is-long granddaughter replies. "But Nana's got a real big bed. If you ask her nice, I'm sure she'd let you sleep there."

My gaze flits to Ezrah, who is also suddenly all ears.

"Thanks, Princess. I'll start on the couch, but if I don't like it, I'll be sure to ask your nana real nice."

He twists his head and his gray eyes pin me to the spot.

Oh, Lordy.

1

Brick

I'M STILL AWAKE, the TV on but muted, when I hear Finn upstairs.

It's my second night on the couch and there hasn't been a lot of sleeping. Tonight was especially tough, since I had to arrange my daughter's funeral today.

This morning, Luna stopped by to let me know the autopsy report had shown nothing more than injuries from the impact of the crash. Kelsey hadn't been under the influence of any illegal substances or alcohol that might have impaired her.

Ouray picked me up this afternoon to talk to the funeral director. I'd missed Lisa by my side but I wouldn't have trusted anyone else to look after Finn, so she stayed home. I was grateful for Ouray, who took matters in hand, making suggestions and guiding me through it. We decided to hold off the service for five days to give law enforcement some more time to dig into her life. Ouray pointed out she may have friends, a boyfriend; colleagues who might want to pay their respects.

That's what kept me awake tonight, thinking about the kind of life she led, and the fact I remember the little girl but never got to know the adult she became.

From upstairs, I hear Finn again and I get off the couch, hurrying up the stairs in hopes I'll get there before he utilizes those fine lungs he turns out to have. I tiptoe into Lisa's bedroom just as she sits up and startles when she sees me.

"I'll get him. Go back to sleep."

"Sure?"

"Yeah. I've got him."

She lies back down and I walk over to his little bed. His eyes are open and his face is already scrunching up. I quickly reach in, pop his soother in his mouth, and lift him out. Then I grab a diaper, baby wipes, and tiptoe out of the room.

Downstairs I heat up some water for his bottle before quickly changing his diaper on the couch.

"That feel better? Yeah, I thought so."

I lift him up and settle him against my shoulder, my hand covering his little butt. I grab one of the bottles Lisa prepped before she went to bed and plop it in the hot water. I'd suggested microwaving it the first night home, but Lisa shot me down. She says it's safer just to set it in hot water; it heats more evenly that way. Since I can't even remember if I ever got a bottle ready when Kelsey was a baby, I'm gonna take Lisa's word for it.

Finn gets restless and his little head is bobbing up and down, his fist shoved in his mouth.

"Patience, buddy. It's coming."

It takes him no time at all to finish the bottle, once I sit down with him on the couch. His eyes start fluttering closed when he gets three-quarters through and the nipple slips from his mouth. The love I already feel for this little human is as overwhelming as the loss of his mother is.

It's easy to drift off with his warm body snuggled against me, but I'm afraid if I fall asleep I might drop him, so I force myself to my feet and head back upstairs to put him to bed.

I glance at the bed, where Lisa's form is motionless under the covers, her breaths deep and even. The moment I put Finn down in his bed, his face scrunches up and I quickly pop in his pacifier. He sucks a few times and settles right back down. When I turn to head back downstairs, I hear the rustle of covers and Lisa's soft voice.

"Everything okay?"

"He's good."

"Are you sleeping?" she asks, when I make my way to the door.

I stop and turn. Lisa is sitting up in bed, and by the light coming in from the hallway I recognize the concern on her face.

Rather than answer I grunt and watch as she flips back the covers.

"Get in, Brick. You heard Kiara, plenty of room."

Fuck. Tempting, but I don't know if it's wise. I shove a hand in my hair.

"You need to get some rest," she urges, and before I have a chance to make up my mind, my feet are already moving.

The moment I lie down beside her, she rolls toward me, putting her head on my shoulder and a hand on my chest. My arm automatically curls around her. Her soft body pressed against me, she sighs, and only moments later her breathing evens out with sleep.

I lie looking up at the ceiling, not wanting to miss a second of her heat warming my body and her scent teasing my nose; a dream realized in the middle of my nightmare. Then I close my eyes and allow myself to drift off.

At some point I feel her kiss me and whisper, "Rest, I've got this," against my lips.

The next time I wake up, I hear Kiara's excited chatter from downstairs. I glance over at the alarm clock on the other side of the bed and notice it's already quarter to eight.

Suddenly full of energy, I swing my legs out of bed, peek in the small bed to see Finn is missing, and dart into the bathroom for a two-minute shower. I quickly get dressed in the walk-in closet, where Lisa had me store some of my clothes, and head downstairs. There I find the kids dressed and ready for school and Finn strapped into his car seat.

"Morning."

"Told you Nana's bed was big enough," Kiara chirps, clamping her arms around my hips in an awkward hug.

I look down and stroke her head as she looks up at me with a big grin on her face.

"So you did, Princess. So you did."

My gaze drifts to Ezrah, who is standing by the front door, his eyes narrowed. I'm about to say something to him when Lisa comes walking from the kitchen, the kids' lunch bags in her hands.

"I was gonna let you sleep. Figured I'd bring Finn along to drop off the kids, and take him with me to my appointment."

Right. She's getting her tests back and getting the monitor removed. I notice his diaper bag sitting on the floor beside him.

I've been holed up in her house since we brought the baby home, but maybe today is a good day to face life again.

"Coming with you," I announce, as Lisa shrugs into her coat. "Just let me grab a coffee to go."

"I'll do it," she says, already heading to the kitchen. "You get the kids in the car."

I'm about to tell her we'll take the truck when I realize Ouray installed the base for the baby seat in the Toyota when we got home. We'll have to get one for my truck as well.

The kids are buckled in the back, a bit of a tight fit with the car seat in there as well, but they manage, and I'm folded behind the wheel. Lisa walks out with a travel mug and a brown paper bag, and stops a few steps from the car, eyeing me sharply before she gets into the passenger side.

"My car," she grumbles, shoving the mug in the drink holder and keeping the bag on her lap.

"Need to get you something safer," I let her know, ignoring her complaint.

My only response to that is a grunt.

I'm sure she has an opinion, but won't fight me in front of the kids; she'll save it for after we drop them off. Fine by me, I'll be ready with my perfectly reasonable point.

When Lisa walks Kiara to the door of the school, I wolf down the ham and cheese sandwich she somehow managed to throw together in two seconds, and check Finn behind me. He's sleeping. I'd forgotten how much babies sleep.

"The snow will be here soon," I start talking the moment she gets back in the car. "Tires have barely any tread left on 'em and you're due for a new timing belt. This piece of scrap has over two-hundred thousand miles on it and there are so many fucking things that could—"

"Language!" she snaps, her eyes shooting fire at me when I glance over.

"Go wrong," I finish, turning onto the street.

"Not telling me anything new, Brick, but both kids have grown out of their winter gear, and Ezrah's likely gonna need braces soon, so the car will have to wait for next year."

"What if I—"

"Don't."

"Hear me out. I'm tryin' to be practical here." I stop for the red light and turn to face her. Her lips are pressed in a tight line. "You go up and down that mountain every day, you drive around your kids and now Finn in this car. On top of that, you're letting me and my grandson live in your house. I haven't had my head on straight these past couple'a days, but it's clear this mornin' because you also let me sleep in your goddam bed while you looked after everyone. And you do all that while you're struggling with your health." The light turns and my eyes are back to the road. "Let me get you something reliable. Let me do something back for all the good you're givin' me."

LISA

I FORCE MYSELF to hear him out as he asked, determined to hang on to my independence. Unfortunately, what he says is fair, which means there's a war waging between my pride and my common sense.

"All right."

He pulls into an empty spot outside Mercy, turns off the engine, and turns to me expectantly.

"Was waiting for an argument," he finally says. "Does that mean you'll let me—"

"No argument, but nothing fancy or new."

"Sugar, I'm not hurtin'."

"Be that as it may, secondhand is good enough for me."

I can tell he may have something to say about that, but I don't give him a chance and open my door.

Finn starts fussing when he lifts him out of the car.

"I brought a warm bottle. Figured he might be getting hungry," I tell Brick. "It's tucked in the diaper bag."

"I'll feed him in the waiting room."

The baby's almost done with his bottle when a nurse comes to fetch me. As much as this man's presence would be a support, I want to do this on my own. With everything he's gone through these past days, I don't want him blindsided with any bad news I might hear.

"Be right back," I promise Brick, who nods his understanding.

I'm taken into a small treatment room, where I hand over the wireless monitor and take my top off as instructed. The nurse has me lie down and hooks up wires to the electrodes still stuck to my body.

"Another ECG?"

"Yes, Dr. Husse wants to see how you're doing today. The results for the monitor will take a week or more to process."

It doesn't take long before she announces I'm done and removes the electrodes.

"I'll leave you to get dressed, I'll just be a few minutes," she says, taking the strip of paper and walking out.

It ends up being more like ten when she returns and asks me to follow her to Dr. Husse's office.

"Ah, Ms. Rawlings, have a seat. First the good news, your ultrasound shows no blockages or irregularities in your heart." I blow out a sigh of relief. "But I see your heart is still irregular, so until the results of the monitor come back, I'm going to prescribe some medication. Low doses to start, so we can see if that'll help regulate your heart."

"And if it doesn't?" I ask right away.

"Why don't we worry about that when the time comes?"

Typical doctor speak, but what she doesn't know is I do better with the full picture.

"Actually, it's easier for me to know it all. I have two young kids I'm responsible for and preparation is everything."

She observes me closely before answering.

"If we can get the beta-blockers to work, great, but we'll need to continue monitoring closely. If not, and once the monitor results show the type of arrhythmia you have, there are various further options possible. Anywhere from different or more medications, to more invasive procedures, like an implantable device that helps regulate the heartbeat."

"Like a pacemaker?"

"For instance."

I swallow at that. I always thought that was something for old people, but in the end I'll do whatever it takes to see my babies grow up.

"Should I be doing something? Eating better? Or are there things I shouldn't be doing?"

She smiles reassuringly.

"I can send you to a nutritionist to talk about foods to avoid, but I can tell you right off the bat that alcohol and caffeine aren't your friend. Try to exercise; it helps strengthen your heart muscle, even just a walk around the block after dinner. Other than that, keep as active as you can, continue with your regular life, and avoid stress."

I almost laugh out loud at that. Those last two are mutually exclusive, but the rest I can handle. I'm relieved to know if pills don't work, there are other things that can be done.

When I join Brick in the waiting room, he's walking around, bouncing the baby on his shoulder.

"He all right?"

"Fussy. Maybe gas."

"Here, give him to me."

I take Finn, put him upside down on my forearm, his legs on either side of my elbow and my hand cupping his jaw. Then I rub little circles over the middle of his back while I fill Brick in on what the doctor said.

"She says plenty'a people lead a full and active life."

"That's good," he mumbles, pulling me toward him with a hand in my neck, "Real good," and kisses me soundly in the middle of the waiting room.

What a sight we must make; a white, gray-bearded biker, who picked today to wear his do-rag, and a black middle-aged spinster with a little baby in her arms. Surprisingly, both the elderly women sitting in the waiting room, and the young nurse behind the reception desk are smiling.

We tuck Finn, who fell asleep on my arm, into his seat and head back home. Yes, with Brick behind the wheel. But when we're about to drive by the clubhouse he suddenly pulls up in front.

"Do you mind?" he asks.

"Not at all, I was planning to head over here to start prepping for dinner anyway. Are you sure?"

Brick had been keeping his distance, and other than Ouray, no one had a chance to meet the baby yet. I hadn't pushed him, not even when I went back to work the past two days.

He takes a long look at the door and I'm guessing he's bracing himself for condolences.

"No," he says, but gets out of the car anyway.

I grab the diaper bag from the back seat while he lifts the baby carrier out, and I follow him inside.

Tse and Paco are at the bar, eating.

"Finally we get to see the rugrat," Tse calls out, before shoving the last of a sandwich in his mouth. Then he gets off the stool and walks over to where Brick sets the baby on a table. "Hope he don't look like his gramps," he jokes, clapping a hand on his brother's shoulder as he leans in to take a peek. "Damn, kid's lucky, no resemblance. He's cute."

"Fuck off," Brick grumbles, but his mouth is twitching.

"Good to see you, brother." Paco, who's come up on Brick's other side grabs his neck, giving it a squeeze. "Sorry 'bout your girl, but she sure left you somethin' beautiful."

"That she did," he replies gruffly.

I have to blink to keep the tears at bay and drop the bag on the table.

"I'll be in the kitchen," I announce, but before I can

get away Brick grabs my hand, pulling me close. He bends down, planting a hard kiss on my mouth before letting me go.

The statement is clear, and I blush when I walk away, listening to the guys giving Brick a hard time. I'm about to duck into the kitchen when I see Kaga, Ouray's right-hand man, and the chief himself come walking from the hallway in the back.

One last glance at Brick, surrounded by his brothers, looking down at the newest Arrow's Edge member, then I quickly duck into the kitchen, before waterworks take over.

The place looks like a damn tornado went through and I stick my head out the door to holler, "Tse! You been in my kitchen again?"

ARROW'S EDGE MC

8

BRICK

"YO, HAND ME that ratchet extender?"

Shilah saunters over and drops the tool in my hand.

"Figured it out yet?" he asks, peering into the engine compartment of the Lexus I'm working on.

"Not yet." The owner brought it in with a rattle and for the life of me, I can't fucking find where the noise is coming from. "Did you get the winter tires on the Jeep?"

"Yup, done."

"Okay, why don't you grab lunch, tell Tse to get his ass in here. He can get started on that brake job."

"You taking lunch?"

"I'll be there in a bit."

He saunters off again, dragging his boots. He's a good kid, becoming a good mechanic, but he annoys the shit out me.

"Lift your fucking feet!" I yell after him.

I woke up in Lisa's bed again this morning. She told me that's where I'd be sleeping and she wouldn't take no for an answer. Her soft body was draped over me like a warm blanket and I woke up with a goddamn woody.

She'd slipped her hand under my T-shirt and was moving it toward the waistband of the sports shorts I wore to bed. God, I wanted to feel her hand around my cock, but then I heard the baby move and I shot out of bed like I'd been bitten.

I almost went where I've wanted to go for too fucking long, and the guilt was instant. Finn, Jesus, right there in the room. My grandson, whose mother is on a cold slab in the morgue, waiting for me to put her in the goddamn ground.

Can't remember the last time I threw on clothes and barreled out of a woman's house like that. I went straight to the garage where I could get lost in work. I had Shilah grab me a coffee from the clubhouse, but skipped breakfast.

When Tse walks in, I hand him the ratchet.

"You try and find that dang rattle. I give up. I'm gonna grab some lunch and take Finn from Lisa. Be back tomorrow morning."

Paco, Ouray, Shilah, and Nosh are sitting at the big table, eating. Lisa's nowhere to be seen, but Finn's carrier is in the middle of the table, the baby the center of attention. I feel a pang of regret for walking out this morning, without paying him any mind, especially when his little legs start kicking the moment his blue eyes find me.

"Hey, buddy. Keeping the uncles entertained?" I mutter at him, as I unclip him from his car seat.

"You need a stroller," Paco suggests.

"Or one of those harnesses you can carry the baby in," Shilah contributes.

"Since you two are such experts," I tell the two bachelors, "why don't you go shoppin' for me?"

Lifting Finn from his seat, I leave Ouray snickering at the two dimwits, and go in search of Lisa.

She looks up when I walk into the kitchen, but quickly turns back to what she was doing.

"I was just warming his bottle."

"Lisa, look at me."

She swings around, chin high and proud, and her eyes full of challenge.

"What?"

"What happened this morning…" I hesitate too long and she turns her back again. This time I don't ask her to look at me, but close the distance between us. "It's my head. My body wants—fuck, Sugar, my heart wants— but when I take what you offered this morning, I want to have my head in the game." I can feel the tension coming off her. "I want to do more than take comfort in your body, I want to worship it."

She braces her hands on the edge of the counter and hangs her head down. I shift Finn in my arms and bend to press my lips to the back of her neck.

"I'm embarrassed," she mumbles barely audible.

"Don't be. I shouldn't'a run out. Should'a stayed and explained."

Finn finally decides he's waited long enough and starts crying.

"Give him," she says, turning around and immediately taking the baby from me. "Too much talk, right, Little Man? Let's get you in a clean diaper first."

She tries to walk past me with the baby, but I block her way.

"Am I forgiven?"

Her beautiful brown eyes meet mine and I watch as her face softens.

"Wasn't ever mad at you, was mad at me. Still am. Let the mood take over when the time wasn't right."

"Time's gonna be right soon, Sugar. Can't wait for a taste of that mood of yours."

She shakes her head but her mouth is smiling.

"You can get yourself a sandwich, my favorite guy needs his bottle," she sasses, heading out the door with my grandson.

When I walk out of the kitchen, a few minutes later, most of the guys are gone. Lisa is sitting at the table with Luna, who is feeding Finn his bottle. She looks up when I approach.

"This baby is way too cute to be related to you," she teases with a smile.

I take a seat across from her and start on my lunch.

"Not working?" I ask between bites, but when she winces I add, "Or are you?"

I already know the answer before she responds and

put my sandwich down; suddenly it lost its appeal.

"We've had some…interdepartmental snags to work out," she starts cautiously. "State Police, the Silverton's Sheriff's Office, Denver Police, and the CBI all had bits of information around your daughter's death. As a result, we've only this morning received a more complete picture we could've had days ago."

"Which is?" I snap, fully focused.

Luna takes a deep breath in before speaking.

"Evidence indicates that Kelsey's SUV was forced off the road. The lab found traces of navy-colored paint on the bumper, as well as on the driver's side door and front fender. State Police accident investigators confirmed through tire tracks there was another vehicle involved in the crash. The day of the crash, a witness showed up at the Silverton's Sheriff's Office to report they'd almost been run off the road by a large, dark-colored pickup truck trying to swing around a silver SUV, which seemed to be swerving to stay on the road."

"Fuck!"

I slam my fist on the table and kick my chair back. The baby promptly bursts out crying, and Lisa quickly takes him from Luna's lap and starts bouncing him on her shoulder. The guilt is immediate. Especially when Ouray comes stalking out of his office and takes a hard look at me before pulling out a chair next to his wife.

"He's fine," Lisa says softly, recognizing the regret on my face.

"I'm sorry," Luna says. "There's more. Sit down."

I rub my hands over my face, force myself to calm

down, and take a seat.

"The last piece is what got the FBI officially involved as of this morning; Denver PD received a missing person's report early last week. A woman by the name of Sophia Vieira came in with the claim a friend and her infant son had not been heard of since before the weekend."

The hair on the back of my neck stands on end, and I hear Lisa inhale sharply.

"The cop who took the statement didn't take the claim seriously. Not until the CBI showed up at the station after speaking to Sophia Vieira, who wasn't only a friend of Kelsey's but a colleague as well. Turns out she had reason to worry."

"Sonofabitch," I mutter, narrowly reminding myself to keep it down so I don't scare Finn again, but my hands clench in fists on the table.

My eyes find Lisa, who mouths, *"Take a breath."*

I follow her suggestion and take a few deep ones, forcing my hands to relax.

"I'm sorry, Brick," Luna says gently. "I realize this must be upsetting."

I bark out a strangled laugh.

Upsetting is an understatement. Someone killed my baby girl, could've killed my grandson.

I'm downright murderous.

LISA

IT'S VISIBLE, THE moment when Brick's grief turns from pain to rage.

I don't blame him. I didn't know his daughter, but I already love her little boy. If the person who ran them off the road were standing in front of me, I'd tear the son of a bitch apart with my bare hands. Instead, I gently bounce her baby to sleep on my shoulder.

"So now what?" Brick wants to know.

"Kelsey worked for Safe Loads, a security contractor specializing in the safe escort of military transports. She was the executive assistant and her friend works in the accounting department. Because of the sensitive nature of that type of business, the FBI is taking over the investigation."

"Are you saying it's because of her work Kelsey's dead?"

Luna is clearly uncomfortable with Brick's question and reluctant to answer.

"This is the part I fucking hate," she admits. "It's not our office in charge of the investigation but the Denver office, which…" she seems to struggle to find a word before finally settling on, "…limits what I'm able to share. What I *can* tell you is it's a possibility her death is linked to her job."

"So that's a yes," Brick stubbornly persists, pacing back and forth.

"Brother…" Ouray interjects, but Luna takes over.

"That's a 'possibly' and that's all I can give you for now. We're dealing with a military contractor, I'm sure you can see why that would be like rattling a powder keg. We've gotta tread carefully or otherwise this investigation could get shut down and we'll never know what happened."

"I need answers," Brick bites off. "She called *me*, Luna. *Me*. Last thing she said eight years ago was to leave her the hell be. I did, yet she called me asking for help, and now she's dead."

"Trust my wife, brother," Ouray reasons. "You know she won't rest until she finds you answers."

Brick nods and drops his head. Figuring it's time to cut through the thick tension, I change the subject.

"Do you have contact information for Kelsey's friend?" I ask Luna, carefully putting a sleeping Finn back in his seat. "Maybe we can give her a call. She may want to be here for Kelsey's funeral."

"Yeah, sure. I can text you her information when I get back to the office."

I sidle up to Brick and put a hand on his back.

"Maybe she can help fill in some of the blanks 'bout the woman Kelsey grew into," I suggest carefully, even though Brick's head stays down.

"She's welcome to stay here," Ouray volunteers before tagging his wife by the hand. "Need a few minutes before you go, Sprite."

The two of them walk off to his office and I step in front of Brick, facing him. He slowly lifts his head, eyes glassy, and I put my hands on his cheeks.

"Coming out of my skin," he mumbles.

"I know."

"I wanna hurt someone."

"I know that too."

I remember the blind rage that makes you want

somebody, anybody, to pay for the life you've lost. Instead you're left with all these emotions, no clear direction, and it tears you up inside.

"Guess you would," he agrees, folding me in his arms and burying his face in my hair. "Be lost without you, Lisa," I hear him whisper.

"Just hang on to me, honey. I'll walk you through."

Not sure how long we stand like that but I don't let go until he straightens up.

"What do I do?"

I try for a smile. "You put one foot in front of the other until it comes natural again."

"Hey, where is everybody?"

Trunk comes walking into the clubhouse and I give Brick a little nudge.

"I'm just about to get goin' in the kitchen. I'll leave you guys to it."

I go up on my toes to reach Brick's cheek for a kiss and make my way to the kitchen. I'll let those two figure it out.

After getting dinner started, it's about time to pick up the kids from school. When I walk through the clubhouse, there's no sign of Brick, Trunk, or the baby, but Ouray sits at the bar, talking to Nosh.

"He's with the baby in Trunk's office," Ouray volunteers.

"Good." I nod. "Gonna go grab the kids, in case he comes looking," I announce. "There's formula in the fridge if the little one is hungry."

Ouray lifts his chin in acknowledgement.

As usual, Kiara is full of beans, excited because she got a star from the teacher for her artwork. Ezrah is quiet, observant, and I make a mental note to take some time alone with the boy—figure out what he's got going on in his head—but he surprises me when he speaks up.

"Mr. Brick gonna be there tonight?"

I glance in the rearview mirror. The boy is looking right back at me.

"Course he is. Where else would he be?"

"Wasn't there this mornin'."

Yes, very observant. I didn't raise a fool.

"He wanted to get an early start at the garage. First day back."

It's stretching the truth, but I'm not about to tell my ten-year-old grandson his nana took liberties she shouldn't have.

I knew it the moment he shot out of bed. I hadn't really been thinking, just gave in to the moment, still half asleep.

"He livin' with us for good now?"

"I want Mr. Brick and Finn to stay forever!" Kiara announces.

Not a surprise since my baby gives her heart easily and freely. She's blissfully unaware. Her brother is far more cautious. Has more reason to be, given what he's seen in his young life. I know he likes the man, but he's also very protective of his sister and his nana.

It's not the definitive answer either of my children

is waiting for, but it's the best I can do for the moment.

"Mr. Brick and that sweet baby are welcome to stay as long as they want."

9

Brick

I DON'T KNOW why I'm nervous, but my palms are sweaty as I stand in the window, watching my truck approach.

I would've picked the woman up myself, but Lisa suggested it might be an emotional first meeting and thought it might be easier for both of us to meet at her place. She's at the clubhouse and is keeping the kids there until after dinner to give me the space.

Wapi, who drove my truck to the airport, jumps out and hustles to the passenger side door to help Sophia out. She's young, thirties I would guess, pretty, short brown hair, and legs that appear to have drawn the attention of young Wapi. I'll have to tell him paws off.

My young brother gets back in the truck and heads

for the clubhouse, leaving the girl standing out front.

I startle her when I pull the door open and her eyes take me in. I'm trying to imagine what she sees looking at me. An aging, gray, scruffy biker is likely not what she expected. Although, I did ditch my do-rag.

"Sophia?"

She nods, starts walking toward me, and doesn't stop until she's hugging me. I have no option but to put my arms around her and pat her back.

"I'm sorry," she mumbles, wiping at her face as she takes a step back. "It's just, you're exactly like she described."

Talk about a punch in the gut. Guess the surprise is on me, I didn't expect Kelsey had told anyone about my existence, let alone describe me.

"Come in," I mumble, inviting her to lead the way. "Would you like a coffee? Something else?"

"Coffee would be great." I walk ahead into the kitchen and hear her following me. "What a lovely place."

"It's Lisa's," I tell her. "You'll meet her later."

While I get busy making a pot of coffee, I try to come up with a way to get the conversation started. It feels strange; I know so little of my daughter I'm embarrassed to ask.

But I shouldn't have worried; Sophia apparently doesn't have that problem.

"I'm so sorry for your loss, Mr. Paver."

"Thank you, and you for yours."

I pour the water in the machine before I collect myself enough to turn around. Sophia is dabbing a tissue at her eyes.

I'm about to open my mouth when the baby announces himself over the baby monitor.

"Oh my God, is that Finn?"

She's already off her stool, but I'm not ready to invite her upstairs into Lisa's bedroom.

"I'll go fetch him, it's almost time for his bottle."

I rush upstairs and find Finn with his eyes wide open, his arms waving, and little legs kicking. Every time he does that just by looking at me, he cements himself a little farther in my heart.

Making quick work of his diaper, I carry him down the stairs where Sophia is waiting. She has her hands pressed against her mouth.

"Why don't you hold him while I get his bottle ready?"

She reaches out immediately and I hand him over.

"Hey, Finny. Hey, my boy. Look at you." I listen to her coo at him while I get going on his bottle. "He looks so healthy. I've been so worried."

"He was lucky." I turn to look at her. She's taken a seat at the table and is holding the baby up in front of her face. He's grabbing at her hair and she doesn't seem to mind. "You're good with him."

She glances at me, a sad little smile on her face.

"I was around a lot." She settles him on her lap, now giving her attention to me. "I was with Kelsey when he was born," she continues softly.

"Where was the father in all this?"

I can't seem to help the harsh tone, but I've been

thinking about this a lot and the more I think, the angrier I get. There must've been someone in her life. What I know of my daughter, the way she stood up to me, I'm convinced she would've told whoever the father is.

"Out of the picture."

"Who is it?"

Her eyes never waver and I take what she tells me as the truth.

"She never told me that, only that it was complicated and a mistake."

Finn starts fussing, probably hungry, and I turn to see if his formula is warm enough.

"You wanna feed him?"

"Please."

I walk over and hand her the bottle, and the way she settles the baby in the crook of her arm and entices him to take the nipple proves it's not the first time she's done this.

"What do you take in your coffee?"

"A little cream if you have it."

I fix us both a cup and sit at the table across from her, observing Finn, his eyes on her face and his hands on the bottle, looking comfortable. I'm trying to imagine Kelsey in Sophia's place, holding her child.

Suddenly a thought occurs to me.

"Do you have pictures of her? Kelsey?"

A big smile spreads over her face.

"I do. Lots. Well, lots since this little peanut was born but a few from before too. I'll grab my phone when he's done with his bottle."

After Finn falls asleep, we put him in his car seat on the table so we can watch him, and we spend the rest of the afternoon looking at Sophia's pictures and sharing memories of my daughter. I'm surprised how much time has passed by the time Lisa and the kids walk in.

"Mr. Brick, guess what?"

Of course Kiara walks through the door already chattering, and I can barely get up from the table when her little body slams against my legs.

"Child, mind your manners," Lisa says, walking in behind Ezrah, who is eyeing Sophia with caution.

Lisa herself seems a little apprehensive, so I hoist Kiara on my hip and approach her, bending down for a quick kiss hello before I introduce her and the kids to the younger woman.

"Guess what?"

Kiara, still perched on my hip, puts her hand on my face to get my attention.

"What?"

"Nana says I can wear my pretty dress tomorrow."

"That's perfect, Princess."

I kiss her head and put her back on her own feet.

"You haven't eaten?" Lisa comments as she walks into the kitchen, darting a glance my way, but Sophia answers.

"I'm afraid that's my fault; I started showing pictures of Kels and every single one came with a story."

Lisa smiles warmly at the woman.

"Oh, I love pictures," Kiara pipes up. "Can I see?"

"Sure," Sophia smiles at her.

"I wouldn't mind seeing them either," Lisa declares, "but let me get you something to eat first."

"You guys look at pictures. I'll fix us something." Lisa looks at me as if she sees water burning. "What? You don't think I can whip up some grilled cheese sandwiches?"

Her mouth twitches. "Good to know."

"I'd actually love a grilled cheese," Sophia announces.

"I'll eat one."

That comes from Ezrah, who's been quiet so far, and earns him a sharp look from his nana.

"You just had dinner," she points out.

"So? I got room."

In the end, I'm in the kitchen, making a stack of sandwiches, while everyone else is clustered around the table—Finn still sleeping in his seat on top—looking at pictures of my daughter.

It almost feels like she's here with us.

LISA

THE SERVICE HELD in the funeral home chapel was simple.

Brick had requested the casket be closed, but a large craft board with a collection of pictures stood on an easel beside it.

At some point between last night—after Brick walked Sophia over to the clubhouse—and the service, she had put this together with some of the brothers. It meant the world to Brick, who hugged her tightly.

The entire club had come out. Every single member. Brick insisted the kids and I sit by him in the front row, Finn on his lap. Right before the service started, I peeked over my shoulder and was surprised to see a bunch of other familiar faces mixed in with the Arrow's Edge club. The chapel was almost full to capacity.

The funeral director welcomes those gathered, and then invites anyone who wants to say a few words up to the front.

Ouray is first. He talks about the brotherhood and the value Brick has added over the past years. He mentions regret they never had a chance to know his daughter, but vows her son, Finn, will always have a home with the club.

I can tell his words mean the world to Brick, who holds on to my hand like a lifeline.

Then Sophia surprises me by walking to the front and sharing a few anecdotes of Kelsey, giving everyone a glimpse of the woman she was. She shares what a loving mother she was to her baby son, and the best of friends to her. Finally she turns to Brick and I can feel him stiffen beside me.

"Kelsey lived with regrets, especially since she became pregnant. She spoke of you often, wishing for a time when she could share her son with her father. She'd be so happy to see what I'm looking at. At peace to know Finn will be loved."

I want to bet there's not a dry eye in the chapel, but the only person I'm concerned with is Brick. Sophia walks up and I quickly take the baby from him as he stands to hug her.

After a few closing words by the funeral director, we follow the hearse to the cemetery. There is nothing official planned for after, but Ouray mentioned last night Lissie organized a lunch at The Brewer's, a pub and grill owned by the club, following the cemetery.

It's early November and the temperatures have dropped over the last days, so I make sure the kids are bundled up before we make the trek to the open grave. There we form a circle around the casket.

I've learned Brick isn't a particularly religious person, and to be honest, neither am I anymore. Still, there are beautiful words of redemption, which never fail to move me, I'd mentioned to Ouray I wanted to share. Not just for Kelsey, but for her father as well.

A few snowflakes start coming down when Ouray gives me a nod.

It's been many years since I've last sung, but the words are engrained in my soul. I fill my lungs, tighten my hold on Brick's hand, and close my eyes.

"Ah-mazing Grace, how sweet…"

By the time I start the second verse many voices have joined me.

With the first snow of the year softly falling around us, we put Brick's daughter to rest.

"WHY ARE WE going to the airport?"

Kiara is tucked in the back seat between the car seat

and Ezrah.

"Sophia has to catch her flight home," I answer, twisting my head so I can see her.

"She isn't coming for lunch?"

"No, baby, but she says she's coming back to visit soon."

Wapi, who is driving Sophia, turns into the airport parking lot ahead of us, and pulls up at the curb. Brick parks his truck behind them and we all get out to say our goodbyes.

"Send me pictures?" Sophia asks, tears in her eyes.

"You bet, and you come back soon, you hear?" I tell her.

She nods and turns to Brick.

"Thank you so much for including me."

He pulls her close for a hug. "Stay in touch," he says gruffly. "You're always welcome here."

"Thank you."

She heads toward Wapi, who is waiting on the sidewalk with her things, and we watch her give him a hug as well before disappearing into the terminal.

The Brewer's door is marked 'closed for private function,' but it's still packed when we walk in. Lunch is a regular rowdy club affair, but cut short for us when Finn starts crying and can't be comforted.

"You should take him home," Lissie suggests. "Too much going on around him, too much noise, too many impressions, he needs some quiet time."

The kids haven't quite finished their lunches but Lissie offers to take them to her place after. Her son,

Jesse, fits right between Ezrah and Kiara in age, and the three get along well.

"Can we go please, Nana?" my baby asks, and when I look over at her brother he nods enthusiastically as well.

The kids have been quiet and well-behaved this morning and probably have some energy to burn off.

"Oh, all right. But you behave," I caution them.

Poor Finn is still wailing when Brick clips his car seat on the base.

"You sure there's nothin' wrong?" he asks, concern on his face.

"I'm sure Lissie's right. We're just not used to him crying a lot. I'll get in the back with him, keep an eye out."

The sudden quiet and the truck's motion quickly lull him. By the time we pull into the drive to the compound he's fast asleep.

"What the fuck?" I hear Brick say, as he suddenly stops the truck in the middle of the driveway.

Up ahead the gate is swung open, chain and padlock hanging useless.

He pulls out his phone.

"Ouray, who left the compound last?"

ARROW'S EDGE MC

10

BRICK

"YOU HAVE *GOT* to be shitting me?"

Ouray is stomping around the clubhouse like a caged bear.

"You know this, Ouray," his wife tries to calm him down.

The chief is pissed because Luna had called the Durango PD on their way up to the compound. They were refusing him entry to his office and the bedrooms in the rear. All were apparently tossed and the wait is for the forensics team to get here.

Despite his good relationship with local law enforcement, he still doesn't like them up in his business. Frankly, neither do I.

We've all been relegated to the main room. Lisa and

myself were told to wait here until the cops go through her cottage and the boys' bunkhouse to see if anything is disturbed there.

"It's my own goddamn stuff. Not like my fingerprints won't be all over the place already."

"Suck it up," the five foot nothing FBI agent spits at her husband, not in the least intimidated by the sheer bulk he holds over her, or the fierce scowl on his face. "We're in the middle of investigating the death of the daughter of one of our own, who happened to be on her way here. You're a smart man, Ouray, I know you don't believe in coincidences either. Sit down, have a fucking beer, and chill your tits."

I can't help the snort, Lisa barely claps her hand over her mouth to stifle her snicker, but the rest of the guys have no such compunctions and bust out laughing.

It looks like Ouray is struggling to contain his own smile, hooking his wife behind the neck and giving her a hard kiss.

"Chill my tits, Sprite?"

I can't believe we just came from my daughter's funeral to find someone broke into the compound while we were gone, and yet here we are, the whole clubhouse laughing.

It feels good, and oddly enough there is no guilt.

As heartbreaking as the funeral was, it also brought me some peace. Part of that was the words Ouray and Sophia shared during the service, they went a long way toward healing the guilt that's been eating at me. But what felt like absolution was Lisa's rich, soulful voice singing about grace and salvation, while her hand clung to mine.

I had no idea she could sing like that. I don't think anyone else did either. Another layer of appeal added to the countless other qualities Lisa checks off. Some of those are no more than a promise so far, but I have every intention to sample.

"I'm glad the kids aren't here," Lisa mutters beside me.

"Agreed."

I put an arm around her shoulders and kiss the side of her head.

"Do you think they were in the cottage?"

"Actually," Luna says, walking up. "Ramirez called me a bit ago. He's at your house and it does look like they were in there. Not too bad," she quickly adds at Lisa's sharp hiss. "From what I understand the search was more methodical than destructive. Besides, it sounds like they may have been interrupted. They never made it up to the bedrooms."

"Someone tipped them off," I suggest. "Kept an eye on us?"

"Did you notice anything?"

I try to remember if I'd seen anything out of the ordinary, but I can't remember. I wasn't exactly looking for anything.

"Did you?" I ask Lisa, but she shakes her head, I turn to Luna. "What the fuck could they be looking for?"

She takes a sip of the coffee Lisa put on earlier and looks at me.

"Be a hell of a lot easier if we knew. Kelsey was on her way here—that's a fact—she was in some kind of trouble, and someone was upset enough to run her off the road. It's possible she had something they want back. Maybe information they don't want out there."

"You think it's connected to Safe Load?"

"Can't rule anything out at this point, Brick."

Tony Ramirez walks into the clubhouse and his eyes find me. He just nudges his head and walks right back out.

"Sugar, I'll be right back," I let Lisa know. "You good with Finn?"

She snorts and rolls her eyes.

"Like you need to ask. He's good here. I'm gonna start on dinner soon anyway."

I plant a quick kiss on her mouth and follow Ramirez outside. He's waiting by the drive up to the cottage.

"Would you be able to tell if anything was out of place in the cottage?"

He starts walking toward Lisa's place and I fall in step beside him.

"Surface stuff, yes."

"Good." We walk around a forensics van parked in front of the cottage. "They're finishing up, but I want to make sure we didn't miss anything."

The wardrobe closet is open, kids shoes and coats piled on the floor. Somebody tossed the couch pillows, and the drawers from the TV stand are pulled open. Yet the TV is still there, as well as the tablet underneath, even the remote seems to have been left alone. A lot of the surfaces are covered with a thin film of fingerprint powder, but it shouldn't take much to put this back together.

The kitchen is a different story. The fridge and freezer doors are open and most of the contents are tossed on the floor. Drawers dumped out, some cupboards opened, boxes of cereal, crackers, even a bag of flour emptied on the floor of the small pantry.

"Fuck, what a mess."

"Detective Ramirez?" One of the techs comes walking in. "I think you should come outside."

Tony starts moving right away and I'm close behind him, but I freeze in my tracks when I see the CPS caseworker standing in the hallway, looking around the place with her mouth hanging open.

"Can I help you?" Ramirez asks her, but her gaze lands on me, and stays there.

"Mr. Paver," she starts, and I can tell from the tone of her voice I'm not going to like where this is going. "I'm afraid I'll have to ask you where the child is?"

"Why?" My tone is less than friendly, given the day I've had. "What are you doing here?"

"We received a phone call from a concerned citizen."

I'm desperately hanging on to the end of my rope as I take a menacing step closer. She takes a small step back.

"A 'concerned' citizen?" I ask, my voice dripping sarcasm, when Tony intervenes and pulls me back.

"Do you have a warrant?"

That gets the woman's attention.

"I'm…well…this is just a welfare-check," she

stutters at Tony. "We don't usually need a warrant for that."

"You do when you walk into a house uninvited."

She takes a few steps back before lifting her chin. "I'll still need to do a welfare-check on the child."

"It's fine," I tell Ramirez. "I'll take her to the clubhouse."

She turns and walks out in front of us.

"So who was the caller?" I ask, catching up with her.

"I'm afraid that information is confidential."

She firmly presses her lips together to indicate she doesn't plan to say another word.

Ouray is outside, having a smoke when we round the corner, takes one look at the caseworker, and then shifts his gaze to me.

"Trouble?"

"CPS," I tell him

"Trouble," Ouray accurately concludes, opening the door for the woman.

LISA

I'M IN THE kitchen fishing Finn's bottle from the warm water when I notice it's gotten really quiet in the clubhouse.

Nosh volunteered to watch the baby, who seemed happy enough to blow bubbles and tug on the old man's beard. I didn't even think twice leaving the baby in his care. I've seen him with Lettie, who absolutely adores her grandpa.

I walk in at the moment a woman—who takes me a second to recognize—plucks the baby from Nosh's hands, the sudden move making him cry.

"Excuse me," I call out, marching up to her.

I'm about to grab Finn from her when a firm arm circles my waist and stops me.

"Child Protective Services," Brick whispers in my ear.

"I don't care if she's the First Lady," I snap, pulling from his hold. In the same move, I divest the woman of the baby and immediately turn my back.

Finn, bless his little heart, immediately stops crying and I tuck him in the crook of my arm, offering him the bottle before turning back. Nosh, the old coot, barks out a phlegmy chuckle.

"Sugar…" Brick tries to soothe me, but I'm paying him no mind; my eyes are shooting fire at the woman.

"Who do you think you are? You can't just walk in here and grab that baby," I snipe.

"Actually, I'm here to check on the child's well-being."

Her arrogance rubs me exactly the wrong way.

"As you can see he's perfectly fine unless manhandled by strangers."

The woman—I can't for the life of me remember her name, nor do I much care—raises an eyebrow and looks around the clubhouse where every head is turned our way.

"I'm afraid this is an unsuitable environment for the child, surrounded by hoodlums."

My blood is boiling but before I let loose, I turn around and hand Finn and bottle to Brick, before facing her again, my hands free.

"Unsuitable environment? You mean this family?" I wave my arm to include everyone in the room. "This man?" I step aside and point at Brick. "We just buried his only child this morning; Finn's mother. While this entire family was by his side doing that, some coward broke into the clubhouse, into our home, and you stand here and dare call this an unsuitable environment? Do you even know what these people stand for?"

"Lisa." Trunk walks up, the corner of his mouth twitching as he throws an arm around my shoulders. I suspect to keep me from wailing on the sanctimonious bitch, which I'm this close to doing. "I'm Dr. Rae," he says sticking out his free hand. "I'm the club's child psychologist."

"Jane Lunsden," she mumbles, taken aback as I'm sure was Trunk's intent.

"Ms. Lunsden. I'm not sure what brought you out here, today of all days, but I'm sure you'll agree with me—given the circumstances—perhaps another day would be more appropriate for a visit."

I love it when a brother flaunts his smarts instead of his temper. I'm instantly flooded with shame, because not only did I lose mine, but also my behavior wasn't exactly smart either. I'm supposed to be helping Brick's case, not hindering it.

"But…we received a complaint, we're mandated to investigate," she sputters.

"I understand," Trunk placates, "however, as you can see Finn is well taken care of, has loving grandparents and a clubhouse full of adults looking out for him. In addition, there is plenty of law enforcement here willing to vouch for it."

Her gaze darts around the room before landing on Brick, feeding the baby. I know exactly what she's looking at, the large, gruff-looking man, holding that tiny person like he has the world in his arms.

"Very well, but I'll be by next week to check in on him," she says, her eyes challenging me.

I swallow a few choice words, thinking it might not be a good idea to tell her what I think when she's about to march out of here. The moment Trunk closes the door behind her, though; I swing around on Brick.

"Tomorrow you find a lawyer and put an end to this nonsense."

"Yes, ma'am."

He sounds serious enough but I notice his mouth is twitching. I'm not about to wait for that smile to break through or I may be forced to hurt him. I'm still so angry she dared show up today, of all days.

I turn back to the kitchen, determined to give my itching hands something useful to do, when Nosh grabs my arm as I walk by the table.

"Momma'd be proud of you," he croaks in his rarely used, monotone voice.

I manage a smile for him before I dart into my sanctuary to hide the sudden wave of a different emotion. It's been some day.

Any residual anger I'm taking out on the poor vegetables. The way I'm chopping, it's a miracle I haven't hacked off a finger with my chef's knife.

I can sense him before I hear his boots on the tile floor. Arms slip around me from behind as Brick rests his chin on my shoulder.

"You okay?"

"Yeah. Where's the baby?"

"Back with Nosh."

"Good."

I close my eyes and lean back into him for a moment, enjoying the feel of his body surrounding me. Maybe soon.

"Thank you, Sugar," he rumbles in my ear. "Beautiful thing to see your momma bear coming out. Got a clubhouse full of men ready to lay down for you, but you took care of things. Fierce."

"Technically, Trunk took care of things," I point out, but my heart warms at his words.

"Only 'cause he was trying to prevent bloodshed."

11

BRICK

"CAN I WEAR my new snowsuit?"

Kiara is hopping from foot to foot in front of the TV.

Never thought I'd find myself hitting up a mall with a woman, two kids, and a baby, but that's exactly what we did this morning.

"When we leave in ten minutes, yes," I tell her.

This past week it's been snowing on and off, and all the kids were in dire need of winter clothes. Finn also needed more things. We got him a proper crib, a high chair—even though Lisa says he's too small yet—a bouncy seat, and a stroller.

Fuck, I didn't know babies were this damn expensive, or maybe I'd just conveniently forgotten. I dropped almost two grand this morning. Lisa didn't even argue when I put the older kids' new snow gear on my tab as well. She was too stunned.

Hope she stays like that a little longer, because I found a nice 2017 Ford Explorer for her that will comfortably transport all three kids with the third row of seats in the back. It'll be safe in the snow, and has only thirty-eight thousand miles on it. It'll set me back some, and I'm sure she'll balk at the price, but I've barely had any expenses since selling my shop in Grand Junction and moving here.

I'd like for her to take it for a test drive this afternoon after we drop the kids off at Lissie and Yuma's place up the road.

After finding the clubhouse and cottage broken into last weekend, we had Ezrah and Kiara stay with Lissie overnight, so they didn't have to come home to the mess those fuckers left behind. Lisa and I cleaned that night until we rolled into bed, exhausted, and did the rest in the morning before those two came home.

The sleepover apparently had been a success. Lissie called and invited them back for a winter cookout in their backyard tonight, complete with roasting marshmallows. Since it's been snowing on and off pretty much all week, Yuma is apparently taking them sledding tomorrow. I'd pay to see his ass on a sled coming down the mountain.

Tired of the news loop, I flick off the TV and take my coffee cup to the kitchen. Lisa is upstairs giving Finn a bath since he had an explosive diaper on our way home from the mall. Ezrah is hanging out up there as well, and Kiara is as restless as a squirrel, insisting on packing her own overnight bag on the coffee table. She has all her newly purchased clothes laid out and can't seem to make a decision on which ones to pack.

I do a quick rinse of the lunch dishes and load the dishwasher so it can run while we're out, when my phone buzzes in my pocket. Sophia's name comes up on the screen.

"Hey."

"Hi, Brick, how are things?"

I had her drop 'Mr. Paver' quickly, the moniker making me feel ancient.

"Going," I answer. "Meant to call to make sure you got home all right, but things were a little crazy here."

She chuckles. "Tell me about it. I came home to find my place was broken into. Can you believe that?"

Immediately my hair stands on end. I can still hear Luna saying she doesn't believe in coincidence. Well, neither do I.

"Gone for twenty-four hours and boom. I live in a townhouse for Pete's sake, not in the worst part of town either. Go figure."

"Anything taken?"

"That's the kicker," she says. "My five-year-old laptop and an external drive. That's it. Left a virtually new flat-screen TV, a few bits of jewelry on my nightstand, an expensive vase my mother gave me, all easily worth much more than that old laptop."

"You need to report that," I urge her.

"Oh, I did. Denver PD showed, took a report and I haven't heard a thing since."

"Sophia, do you remember Luna? Ouray's wife? I'm gonna have her call you right away."

"Why? Is something going on?"

"Yeah. Last Saturday, while we were all at Kelsey's funeral, the clubhouse as well as Lisa's place was broken into too."

For a moment it's dead silent on the other side. Then she says softly, "This is about Kelsey, isn't it?"

"Sure looks like it." For some reason I suddenly feel uncomfortable talking on the phone. "Sophia?"

"Yeah?"

"Are you home?"

"I am."

"Do me a favor, get into your car, drive to a coffee shop or something, and wait for Luna's call."

"You're making me nervous," she whispers.

"Good, then you'll be careful."

With that I hang up, walk to the front door, shove my feet in my boots, and head outside.

I don't even notice the snow coming down as I dial Luna's number.

"What's up?"

"Got a call from Kelsey's friend, Sophia, just now. Apparently she got home last Saturday and found her house tossed. Only thing missing was her old laptop and external hard drive."

"Shit, how come there's no report?"

"She reported it to the cop that showed up."

"Fuck. That should've been flagged for us."

"I told her I'd have you call."

"Good, I'll do that right now."

I take a deep breath in, wondering if I'm getting paranoid now. Fuck it, I'd rather be paranoid than stupid.

"Luna, I had this thought while I was on the phone with her. No one checked the house for bugs last Saturday, did they?"

"With bugs you mean listening devices? Not exactly standard procedure for burglary."

"I get that, but they weren't regular burglaries. We're all in agreement they're probably lookin' for something, what if they're listening in for the same reason?"

"Shit," she whispers.

"Yeah. And there's the clubhouse. Ouray's gonna shit bricks if I'm right and they bugged his office."

She lets another expletive fly.

"Where are you now?"

"I'm standing outside in the fuckin' snow talking to you. Also, I told the girl to wait for your call in a coffee shop. Just in case."

"Good. I'm gonna send Greene and Barnes over there."

"I won't be here. Dropping the kids at Yuma's and I'll be taking Lisa and the baby to a fuckin' hotel tonight."

"Good call. I'll be in touch."

I hear the door behind me open and turn to find Lisa standing in the doorway.

"What on earth are you doing standin' out there without a coat?"

Instead of answering her, I grab her hand and pull her outside with me. She doesn't object but scrutinizes my face.

"I need you to go inside and pack some clothes in an overnight bag for us. Finn too, and he'll need bottles. I'll explain later."

"You're scaring me."

I cup her face in my hands and press my half-frozen lips to her warm ones.

"I'm sorry. I'll tell you what's going on as soon as we drop off the kids."

She nods and I brush her lips again before letting her go.

Ten minutes later, we're all in my truck heading away from the compound.

LISA

I'VE BEEN ON eggshells since he told me to pack an overnight bag for us.

Lissie looks at me a little funny when I kiss the kids, say goodbye, and walk back to the truck where Brick is waiting with Finn. I clearly suck at acting. The moment I climb in the passenger seat and buckle up, he has the truck backing up.

"Tell me."

And he does. He tells me Sophia's place had been broken into the same day as ours. I agree that can't be a coincidence and am glad he notified Luna, but it doesn't really answer why our toothbrushes are in a bag in the back of the truck.

"Where are we going?"

He glances over and takes my hand, lacing our fingers.

"Ford dealership first. Found a car, secondhand," he adds when he catches my frown. "2017, not a lot of mileage, plenty of room for all three kids in the back so they're not squished together. That's only gonna get worse as they get older." He's playing to my common sense and he knows I know it, that's why the little smirk is under his beard. "Also, it's winter. Roads ain't gonna get any better, especially up the mountain. This car is safe."

"Mm-hmm." Man should've been a car salesman.

"We'll take it for a test drive."

"We?" I give him a look and he grins in response.

"Yeah, we."

He looks way too satisfied with himself and I have to admit, I like this talk of 'we,' but I'm not about to let him gaslight me. I give him a few minutes before I circle back where I started.

"Still doesn't explain the overnight bag."

His sigh is loud in the cab of the truck.

"We're staying at a hotel in town tonight. All three of us."

I twist my body toward him.

"Why?"

"Because it occurred to me today, whoever broke in may not have taken anything but could've left something behind."

It takes me a second to clue in and then I instantly feel cold.

"Listening in?"

"Luna is sending someone to check."

Then another thought hits me.

"Watching?"

The moment I suggest it, the truck swerves and Brick swears under his breath.

"They better fuckin' not have," he growls.

Each lost to our own thoughts—mine mostly trailing to anything I might've said or done this past week—we don't say another word until Brick pulls into the dealership across from Walmart.

We get out, Brick lifting the stroller from the back of the truck while I get Finn. Despite being creeped out, I smile to myself when the rather fierce-looking man confiscates the stroller and starts pushing it to the showroom. One of the things I'm learning to love about him is the fact he really doesn't give a crap. He doesn't apologize for who he is. Or who he's with for that matter.

A guy—dressed in preppy clothes and late thirties, I'd guess—exits the showroom and walks toward us.

"Hey, man," he greets Brick, giving me a nod. "Still have to get her detailed and topped up on fluids."

"That's fine. Need to take it for a run first anyway."

"Sure. Let me grab the keys."

The 'car' we're walking up to is actually an SUV. A large, black, shiny one.

"You call this a car?"

I catch a glimpse of a large sticker on the windshield with a nauseating price tag.

"Car, SUV, same difference," Brick says casually.

"Hop in."

I turn to the younger man. "Would you excuse us for a minute?"

"Sure."

He starts walking away and as soon as he's out of earshot, I turn to Brick.

"Twenty-two thousand dollars? No. Just no."

His gray eyes lock on mine.

"Take a look at him, Sugar." He points at Finn, who is just waking up. "What do you figure he's worth to me? Or Ezrah and Kiara? You? Lost enough in my life, Lisa. You have too. I'm just trying to keep the most important people I have left safe."

Oh no. Not fair. There isn't even an argument I can offer to that. To accept is to disregard a lifetime of hard lessons, but I can't refuse him. Not after those words.

"I see the struggle—"

"Okay," I interrupt. "But I still wanna drive it first. It's huge."

Of course, Finn picks that moment to exercise his lungs.

"You go," he says, waving the guy over. "I've got the baby."

I take the keys and climb behind the wheel, trying not to let the luxurious interior freak me out. Behind me are two additional rows of seats. I'll have to be careful parking this thing at the grocery store.

Starting the engine and hearing how smooth it is, my face breaks out in a smile.

It's still there when an hour later Brick pushes

open the door to the Homewood Suites across from the dealership. I can't believe we're picking up my beautiful new ride tomorrow. A Ford Explorer, Ezrah's going to lose his shit. My grin gets even bigger at the thought.

At the desk, Brick asks the hotel clerk for a travel bed, which she says they can provide, and is specific in his demands for a suite with a separate bedroom.

That's when the smile I was wearing becomes a little nervous.

I follow him down the hall, my anticipation building with every step. It's crazy; we've lived in the same house for two weeks. Heck, we've slept in the same bed for almost as long, but we've always had the baby in the room with us.

We've kissed, let our hands wander over our clothes, but that's as far as it's gone. Other than that one time when I tried to shove my hand down his shorts. Lordy, was that embarrassing. Still, I have a feeling if I did that now the outcome would be different, but this time I'll let him take the lead.

He unlocks the door and wheels the baby's stroller inside. I follow behind.

It's nice but nothing special: a couch, two chairs, and a dresser with a TV, a coffee maker and a mini-fridge. The bathroom has a separate walk-in shower and a nice-sized tub. I can't remember the last time I've had a bath, definitely before the kids were left with me.

I must've been staring at it because Brick taps me on the shoulder.

"Why don't you have a nice bath while I run to grab

us something to eat. The baby's sleeping again and I'll ask the desk to leave the crib in the hallway."

Oh, so tempting.

"It's been a while," I admit.

"Then go for it. I'll pick us something up to drink too. What would you like? Wine? Beer?"

I never really drink these days, but one won't hurt.

"I like moscato. They have those little bottles. If you don't mind?"

He turns me and wraps his arms around me. His face is inches from mine and his eyes are smiling.

"Not in the least."

He lowers his mouth to mine and doesn't hesitate slipping his tongue between my lips, kissing me deeply. This kiss isn't like the others, I can feel the hunger

12

BRICK

SOMEONE LEFT A folding crib just outside the door.

I already have my hands full with bags and walk in with those first. I set them on the coffee table, sneak a peek at Finn who's still sleeping, and try to ignore the sounds of water splashing in the bathroom. If I think of Lisa's body, water sluicing down her curves, I won't be able to hold myself back.

In the hallway I grab the travel crib, which I set up in between the two chairs. I leave one of the small bottles of wine and a beer on the coffee table and am tucking the rest in the mini-fridge when I hear the bathroom door open.

She walks out wearing a T-shirt, her lounge pants, and her hair up in a towel, showing off her graceful neck.

It's not like I haven't seen her this way before, unguarded and relaxed, it's the promise hanging heavy in the air.

"How was your bath?" I ask, my voice a tad gruff.

"Bliss." She moves into the room and goes straight to Finn's stroller, pulling down the blanket still covering him and unbuckling the harness. "We should put him in the crib."

"Let's eat first, before he wakes up."

I duck into the bathroom to grab one of the glasses I spotted on the vanity for Lisa's wine. She's already pulling the food out of the bag, as well as a paper bag I forgot I dropped in there.

She holds up the box of condoms, pressing her lips together.

Fuck. Smooth, Paver, you're losing your touch.

I force myself to walk to the table, unscrew her wine bottle, and pour a glass for her.

"Dinner?" she asks, setting the box smack in the middle of the table and challenging me with a look.

"Dessert," I return, holding her gaze until she looks away.

I stopped at Serious Texas BBQ across the street and picked us up stuffed taters with pulled pork and a couple of small garden salads. Sitting down at one end of the couch, I pull one of the containers my way before twisting the top off my beer, taking a deep swig.

Lisa moves to the other side of the table and for a moment I think she's going to settle in one of the chairs, but she grabs the remote lying under the TV and flicks it on. Then she rounds the table and sits beside me on the couch.

The tension is so thick in the room, I barely taste my meal, but I eat it anyway. I have a sneaky suspicion I'll need my energy later. I watch the news on the channel Lisa found with half an eye, suddenly eager for Finn to wake up so we can feed him and get him ready for the night. As if he read my mind, a small cry sounds from the stroller.

Lisa is on her feet first, lifting him from the stroller. She has an easy, confident way of handling Finn, like she's done nothing else her whole life. Occasionally, I'll catch her humming at him under her breath, something he seems to be fascinated with as his curious eyes focus on her face.

With the baby in a football hold under her arm and a bottle from the fridge in the other hand, she disappears into the bathroom and turns the faucet on, while I clear away the remnants of dinner.

My phone vibrates in my pocket and I pull it out. It's the lawyer. A little odd that she's calling on a Saturday night, but then again, Mel Morgan doesn't seem like a conventional lawyer anyway. It's that she came highly recommended, or I might've beelined it out of her office when the woman greeted me wearing bib-overalls that were half done up and on bare feet. Who goes around in bare feet when snow is piling up outside?

She didn't waste time either; while I was explaining the situation she had her assistant draw up a bunch of legal paperwork she had me sign on the spot.

"Mel," I answer.

"Had to chase the damn judge down, but I finally cornered him at a fundraiser this afternoon," she jumps right in. "Arm wrestled him into signing off on the order for allocation of parental responsibilities. That should get the caseworker off your back, but like I said before, CPS will still need to check out any complaints they get."

"Great," I grumble. "So some asshole can still mess with our life."

"Yeah, except the CPS doesn't take kindly getting sent out on false claims either. You should be fine. It helps your club has a good reputation for the work they do with those kids. Goes a long way."

I watch Lisa walk in, sit down in a chair, and settle Finn on her lap as she gives him his bottle. Her eyes are on mine the entire time, concerned.

"I appreciate your help," I tell Mel, keeping my gaze locked on Lisa. "You don't mess around."

Mel snorts. "Got nothing better to do anyway. I'll swing by on Monday, drop off a copy for ya."

I'm about to thank her again, but she's already hung up. Odd woman.

"Everything all right?" Lisa asks anxiously.

"Judge signed off on the order." I get up and lean over her chair, bracing my hands on the armrests. "We're all good. I'm gonna hop in the shower while you finish feeding him."

I bend down to kiss Finn's head, before turning my face to her and capturing her mouth with mine for an all too brief but potent taste.

"I won't be long," I promise.

The heat of her eyes follows me into the bathroom where I quickly strip out of my clothes and jump in the shower.

I'm primed. Years of waiting, weeks of building anticipation, have me close my fist around my almost painfully engorged cock and lazily stroke myself to relieve some of the pressure. It doesn't fucking help. Afraid I'll blow my load too soon—recovery time is a far cry from my twenties or even thirties—I focus instead on washing up quickly. I'm in a rush to feel her under me.

I dry myself in front of the mirror, looking at my reflection with a critical eye. I don't usually, only to trim my beard or check my nose for the odd stray hair. For fifty I'm in decent shape, at least I think so. A little softer than I used to be, hairier for sure, but nothing to scare her off. My ugly mug she's already used to.

Instead of putting today's clothes back on—I didn't grab clean ones—I wrap a towel around my hips, which does dick all to hide my hard-on. A little late for that anyway.

When I walk out of the bathroom, I'm greeted by Lisa's round ass in the air as she lays Finn down in the travel bed. My cock twitches at the fine view.

"He sleeping?"

She straightens up and turns around, her gaze hot as she scans my body. She focuses on the obvious bulge behind the towel, but when I growl deep in my throat her eyes shoot up to my face.

I snatch the box off the table, grab her hand and pull her behind me into the bedroom. Sinking down on the side of the bed, I tug her between my legs, and hold her there while I pull a string of condoms from the box and toss them behind me on the mattress.

Then I look up in her face.

"Let me see you."

LISA

FINALLY.

Hard to believe I've never seen the man naked before—that little towel leaves nothing to the imagination. There's a lot to look at, including the tight flex of his ass as he drags me into the bedroom.

"Let me see you." His hoarse voice tells me he's as turned on as I am, and I haven't even taken my clothes off.

I lift my hands to my head, unwrapping the towel from my hair, and shaking the last droplets out.

"Love your hair like that," he mutters, easing up the hem of my shirt.

I'm a little rusty when it comes to seduction, having spent too many years downplaying any attributes I may have had, but that doesn't appear to still the hunger in his eyes as I take over and whip my shirt over my head. They fixate on the deep cleavage my sturdy bra facilitates. Not once does he seem distracted by the belly pouch I've developed over the years.

I reach behind me and unclip my bra, letting it fall off my arms. He hisses sharply when my heavy breasts drop an inch or two, the deep brown areolas right at his eye level. There's no hesitation in the way his hands come up, cupping both and brushing the pad of his thumbs over my distended nipples.

"Fuck, Lisa," he mumbles, his lips already fitting over one, pulling it deep into the heat of his mouth. His beard brushes the skin of my stomach when he moves to the other side, giving it the same attention.

Arousal floods my core and my hands clumsily shove down the lounge pants I pulled on commando after my bath. Releasing my breasts, he slides his hands around to my ass, groaning as he digs his fingers into my bare cheeks.

"Like a fuckin' dream."

His lips move against my belly, his tongue licking leisurely at my skin until my knees buckle from need.

"Honey, please."

He lifts his head and those expressive gray eyes regard me carefully.

"You want me?"

"God, yes." I almost laugh at his question.

He stands up, his skin brushing mine, sending tingles down to my toes. Then he kisses me deeply, one of his hands tangling in my hair. The slight sting only turns me on more as I tug his towel free, and slide my hands over the tight globes of his ass. I can feel the hard heat of his erection press into my stomach.

He groans down my throat and I've never felt both this vulnerable and this powerful at the same time.

"Lie down on the bed, Sugar," he orders, turning to pull the covers down. "The first time I wanna look in your face when you come."

This man has seen me at my worst already, so there is not a trace of self-consciousness when I do as he asks and climb into bed, knowing he's watching my every move.

He waits until I scoot up the bed, tucking a pillow under my head. Then he reaches for my ankles, spreads my legs and wedges his shoulders between them.

Lordy, the man knows what he's doing.

The tight stream of air he blows from the inside of my thighs to their apex sends a hard shiver down my limbs. But when he uses his thumbs to spread me open, drags his tongue lazily through my slick heat, and then brushes it over my clit, I almost launch off the mattress.

I don't know how long he plays with me like that, long easy strokes, then hard little flicks. Driving me to the edge and then easing off again. My fists are clenched in the sheets, my hips undulating on the mattress, seeking more, until I finally plead.

"Brick, fuck me already."

His deep chuckle vibrates against my sensitive flesh. Then he lifts his face, his glistening lips smiling at me.

"At your service," he teases, grabbing the string of condoms and ripping one off, handing it to me.

He goes up on his knees, planting them in the mattress on either side of my hips. The blunt tip of his cock weeping as I tear the foil between my teeth. Then I reach for him, my hand not quite closing around the hot steel.

"You do too much of that and this'll be over before

we get started," he warns, and I grin up at him. "Two years, Sugar, that's a lot of load to blow."

My hands shake as I roll the rubber down his length, reeling at the fact he's withheld for that long.

Then he takes over, holding himself at the base as he slides down and drops his hips in the cradle of mine. I hold his eyes as he poises his cock at my entrance, and buries himself to the root.

"Okay?"

"Honey, I'm sure it didn't fail your notice I ain't made of glass." I cup his face with my hands and pull him close for a hard kiss. "Don't hold back on my account."

His eyes darken and his nostrils flare.

"Spread wide for me," he growls, hooking his hands behind my knees and opening my legs wide. "Yeah," he whispers, looking down between us where his cock gently rocks in and out of my body. "Brace, baby."

I raise my arms and place my hands against the headboard.

"Please."

That's all he needs to power inside me, balls slapping against my ass, and the pace punishing. It's hard, it's raw, it's filled with exposed need and hunger, and it's the single most mind-blowing sexual experience of my life.

When his heavy body, slick with sweat, collapses on mine, I welcome his weight. I can take it. I'll take anything this man loads on me.

"Jesus, Lisa, I think you've done killed me," he mumbles out of breath, his face buried in the crook of my shoulder.

"We're gonna need to work on your stamina," I tease, chuckling underneath him.

I feel his lips brushing the tender skin of my neck before they find their way to my ear.

"You're perfect," he whispers. "The reality beats every fantasy I've had of you."

13

BRICK

HOLY SHIT.

I can't move.

I'm boneless, watching from the bed as Lisa shrugs into her clothes to tend to Finn, who woke up crying. Not even the enticing jiggle of her ass can spur a reaction from any part of my body.

Waking up to her hand and mouth moving on my morning woody had been another fantasy realized. I didn't think I'd have anything left to give, especially after we had round two after Finn's middle of the night feeding, but Lisa surprised me. In a very good way.

I fold my arms behind my head and listen to her moving about the other room with the baby. I should probably get up and hop in the shower, and maybe give the clubhouse a call. See how things are there.

Groaning as I swing my legs over the edge of the bed, I note on the bedside alarm clock it's already almost nine. Been years since I've slept this late. Then again, it's been years since I had three explosive orgasms in a relatively short time span.

It's not until I'm standing under the hot spray I realize I'm not feeling an ounce of guilt.

Later, with Finn asleep on my shoulder and Lisa in the bathroom, I quickly dial Ouray.

"Morning. Quiet night?" he asks, and I almost laugh. Hardly, but I'm not about to share that with him.

"Yup. Gonna run an errand and then head up there. What's the verdict?"

"Motherfuckers. Greene pulled a high range transmitter from the light fixture over the kitchen island and another from behind the TV stand. One in my office in the clubhouse."

"Sonofabitch. He take them all down?"

"Leaving the one in the office up. Don't wanna alert them and Greene thinks they can use that to their advantage."

"And the house?" I'm not taking Lisa back there if someone is listening in.

"They're gone. Taken to the shed at the back of the clubhouse, along with an audio jammer. They'll still be able to pick up the signal but will hear mostly static."

"No cameras?"

"No. Still, doesn't mean there aren't eyes on the compound. On you. If that company is involved, they're not new to surveillance. Gonna put some security measures in place. Club meeting at three."

"In your office?"

"Smart-ass," he fires back. "No, your garage."

"Fine by me."

I'm about to hang up when Ouray starts talking again.

"You may wanna prepare Lisa she won't be going anywhere by herself in the near future."

"That'll go over like a lead balloon."

"Until the FBI can figure out what the fuck is going on, that's the way it's gonna be."

"No need to convince me, Chief."

"Convince you of what?" Lisa asks, coming out of the bathroom.

"That's my cue," Ouray says with a chuckle before hanging up.

Asshole.

As expected, Lisa isn't happy. Not about the bugs found in the house or the restriction on her movements, but she's not stupid or reckless, and would never do anything that might endanger the kids.

When we pull into the dealership, after grabbing a bite to eat, she's almost smiling again. Her SUV is cleaned, holds a full tank and complimentary floor mats, and by the time she gets behind the wheel, she's beaming. I check on Finn over my shoulder, who is awake and blowing bubbles in his seat, before I start the truck and ease off the lot, sticking close behind Lisa.

I lose sight of her for a minute when a light turns red for me on a left turn up the mountain, but the moment it turns green I speed across the intersection, releasing a relieved breath when I spot her SUV two cars ahead of me. The two cars turn off into the last subdivision and I'm able to catch up with her.

Lisa called her friend earlier to see how the kids were doing. They were having a late breakfast and Yuma would take them up on the slope behind their house to go sledding after.

Lissie said they were planning to stop by at the clubhouse later anyway—I assume because of the club meeting Ouray called—so would just bring the kids back at that time.

We have to stop at the gate to the compound, which hasn't been guarded in the past two years. Shilah is chatting with Lisa, admiring her new wheels, and waves both of us through before closing the gate behind us. I'm guessing one of Ouray's new safety measures.

"What do you want to do with your Toyota?" I ask when she gets out of the Explorer.

"Maybe I can sell it."

"Don't think you're gonna get much for it."

"Then what do you suggest?" she asks, looking at me with a raised eyebrow.

I shrug. "Have the boys work on it after school. We've got two boys almost old enough to get their learner's permit."

I run an apprentice program for some of the older kids after school at the garage. An opportunity for them to learn a trade while staying out of trouble. Every so often, I'll pick up an old car—or someone donates one—

and have the boys take it apart, fix what needs fixing, and put it back together.

"Yeah, I like that idea. A chance to give something back to the club."

I unlock the door and set Finn's seat down inside, toss the overnight bag toward the stairs, and turn to catch Lisa in my arms.

"You've got things backward," I tell her. "You don't owe the club a damn thing." Then I close my mouth over hers, swallowing her protest.

Nothing stops Finn from launching a complaint, however, he apparently does not appreciate being left on the floor.

"Come on, child," Lisa mutters, untangling herself from my hold before getting Finn from his car seat. "Let's get you some lunch, then a nap, and after that you can come keep me company at the clubhouse."

"You all set for groceries?" I call after her, kicking the door shut and grabbing the overnight bag. "I can run into town."

"Got all I need to make a vat of chili," she says when I walk into the kitchen.

She's by the stove heating water, Finn against her shoulder, trying to stuff her curls into his hungry mouth. I pull the strands from his fist and kiss his little head before walking into the laundry room with the bag.

"What are you doing?" I hear Lisa ask.

"Tossin' our stuff in the laundry."

Her head pokes around the door.

"You're doin' laundry?"

"You're feeding the baby, I'll get a load going."

"You're gonna wash my unmentionables?"

I chuckle at the old-fashioned term.

"Sugar, I've had my mouth between your legs," I point out.

"Hush!" She presses his head against her shoulder, covering his ears. "Not in front of the baby."

That only has me laughing harder.

"Babe, he chews on his toes, that should make it clear he doesn't have the mental capacity to know what we're talkin' about yet."

She harrumphs and disappears back into the kitchen, but calls out, "If you're gonna do laundry, you may as well grab the baskets from upstairs."

Right. Had my eyes open when I walked into that one.

LISA

"OH MY GOD, I'm so stuffed."

Lissie walks into the kitchen, carrying the last of the dirty dinner plates.

Good thing I planned chili for today, it stretches. Add a massive salad and about ten loaves of garlic bread and it feeds close to thirty people.

Ouray apparently called a club meeting, which meant all of the brothers were here, as were Lissie and the kids, Luna and Ahiga, and at the last minute Trunk's wife, Jaimie, showed up with their kids as well.

Ezrah adores Jaimie, who looked after him before

I moved to Durango. I noticed the two of them talking at one of the smaller tables, their heads bent close. As I anticipated, he'd been wildly excited about the new wheels, claiming the entire rear seat for himself. Yet other than that, he's still quiet like he has been for a while. He's chewing on something and part of me hopes whatever it is, he's sharing with Jaimie.

Yeah, I'd prefer he come to me, but since I have a feeling it's to do with Brick and me, it makes sense he'd unload with someone else.

"I can't believe the amount of food these guys put away," Lissie comments, rinsing plates in the sink and stacking them on the counter for me to slide in the industrial dishwasher.

It's Sunday night, so the boys have the night off from their chores. All the kids made a run for the large screen TV as soon as they were excused from the table.

"Big men, big appetites," I point out dryly.

"You can say that again." She giggles and winks at me. "I'm guessing things are good with Brick?"

"Mmhmm."

"By the way, I meant to ask you; Thanksgiving is Thursday, what are we doing?"

The holidays are big for the club, that's Momma's legacy, and so far I've done the same she did for years, put on a huge feast for the entire club family. Quite a few of the guys now have families, though, and may want to spend some quality time at home.

"I'll check with Ouray, but maybe we can do an early meal, maybe around two? After that everyone can do their own thing if they want."

"I like that. How about we make it a potluck? I don't think I'd trust anyone but you with the turkey or the sweet potato casserole, but we could split up the rest of the dishes. Why don't I check with the others?"

I smile at her and load another stack of plates in the dishwasher. Instead of slighted or dismissed, I feel included. Part of a whole.

"Lisa, do you have a minute?" Jaimie walks in, her eyes on me.

"Let me get out of your hair."

Lissie turns off the faucet and starts wiping her hands on a towel.

"No need," Jaimie says before turning back to me. "I just had a talk with Ezrah."

"I noticed."

"He was asking about Brick," she shares, taking a seat at the kitchen table. "Wanting to know if I thought he was a good man."

I press a hand to my chest and sit down myself before my knees give out on me. My boy, more damaged and confused than any of us. Guilt immediately follows. Should've talked to him more, spent less time teaching him and more time listening. Should've given more thought to him when I invited Brick and the baby into our home.

He's only ten, but a lot of his young years he was witness to—and ultimately victim of—the kind of racist evil the world still holds. The last two years here at Arrow's Edge, he's starting to learn what he experienced before was the exception, and not the rule, but for a ten-year-old boy, it must be confusing.

I'm at least in part to blame. It was me who made them say Mr. Brick, and Mr. Yuma, a sign of subservience instilled in us living in the Hinckle house but perpetuated by me.

I let Trunk always be just Trunk. Because he's a brother.

"Oh no," I groan. "What did you tell him?"

"That I like Brick, I trust him, but he shouldn't depend on anyone else to tell him how he should feel. I told him to trust his gut. I'm not sure how helpful that was, but I thought I'd let you know."

"Appreciate it. He's been quiet and I've wondered what was on his mind. Now I know."

Jaimie reaches over and puts her hand on mine.

"You know, when Ezrah stayed with us, he didn't trust Trunk and me as a couple. I guess in the beginning our differences were more obvious than our love for each other, but he doesn't question us now. He'll start seeing the love between you two as well."

Love…Lordy.

Just because I feel it doesn't mean I've allowed my thoughts to go there.

"And that man *looooves* her," Lissie butts in. "Have you taken a gander at that SUV he got her?"

"You got a new car?" Jaimie asks with a big grin. "That's awesome. Trunk'll be so happy you're not driving that rust bucket anymore."

I've got love on the brain and the two of them are

still yapping about my new ride when Brick walks in, Finn on his hip.

"You almost ready to roll? This one needs a bath and I think the afternoon sledding has worn out Kiara, she fell asleep on the couch."

"Go," Lissie urges me. "I'll finish this off. Get your family home."

I find myself doing something I hardly ever do; I pull her in a quick embrace. I'm not usually one to show much affection and it means something when I do. For good measure I hug Jaimie too.

Then I grab my purse and follow Brick out of the kitchen.

"What was that all about?" he asks when we walk home.

Ezrah runs ahead with the key, while Brick carries Kiara and I push Finn's stroller through the snow.

"What?"

"The hugging. That some sisterhood thing I need to know about?"

"Nah. We were just discussing our periods."

I burst out laughing when his face blanches.

"Right, I didn't need to know that."

"You asked," I tease, but then add on a more serious note. "Do you care about the kids calling you mister?"

"Sort of. Kinda bothers me, if you wanna know the truth. Makes me feel…I dunno, removed, I guess."

"Any preferences?"

He turns to me with a smile in his eyes.

"Don't care, as long as it's not mister or uncle

anything."

"Fair enough," I say, wheeling the stroller into the house.

Brick closes the door behind us.

"Why don't you ask the kids?" he suggests.

Kiara stirs when he lays her down on the couch, blinking her eyes open.

"Ask us what?"

14

BRICK

"PAPA, LOOK!"

I dry my hands on a towel and walk into the living room, where Kiara is lying on her stomach on a quilt with Finn.

Calling me 'Papa' had been her idea. One Ezrah is not quite on board with, opting to avoid calling me anything at all. Kiara's logic had been if they called Lisa 'Nana,' then I should be 'Papa.'

"He rolled over. All by himself."

She's right. I'd put down Finn on his stomach after Lisa explained it would build strength in his back and neck. She said nothing about rolling though.

"That's great, Princess."

At least I hope it is. I pull out my phone and dial

Lisa's number while walking back in the kitchen, so I can keep an eye on the pancakes Kiara demanded for breakfast. Lisa is already at the clubhouse, something about getting the turkeys in the oven.

She left at five this morning, even though we're not eating until two apparently. I guess when you're cooking for around thirty people; it takes a little prep work.

"Mornin'," she answers the phone after only two rings. "Everything okay there?"

"Is it normal for Finn to roll over?"

"He did? Good boy. He's about the right age."

Well, that's a relief.

"Should I do anything?"

"Roll him back on his stomach so he can do it again. How are the other two?"

"Ezrah's still in bed and Kiara demanded pancakes so don't yell if I make a mess."

Her warm chuckle puts a smile on my face. Christ, I've turned into a sap.

"Trust me, nothing you can do to my kitchen that isn't ten times worse than this kitchen here."

"Tse cooking again?"

"Not this time. This is all me. I took the turkeys out of the brine and tried to lift the tub to dump it in the sink, but I splashed some, slipped, and now the entire kitchen is covered in brine."

"You okay?"

I worry about her. She's been feeling a lot better on the beta-blockers and her doctor was pleased when she saw her earlier this week, but I still worry. Lisa is one of those people who'll put on a brave face and try to bulldoze her way through, instead of looking after herself. I'm going to have to do the looking after.

"Just a bruise."

"Are the boys up?"

"I've only seen Nosh, but I think Wapi may have come in."

"Check."

"Why?"

Her question is a challenge. She doesn't like me dictating things, but fuck it, someone's gotta look out for her.

"Because either he helps you clean up that kitchen or he comes here to mind the kids so I can come clean up the kitchen. Up to you."

"I'll check." The fact she so easily agrees has me more concerned. "He's here."

"Good. Ask him to help, or I can do it if you prefer." I ignore her grumbled protest. "Do it for me."

"Fine," she mutters before the line goes dead.

I slide the first batch of pancakes onto a plate and set the pan on a cold burner.

"Princess! Your breakfast is served."

She runs over and climbs on a stool at the island. Finn voices his displeasure at her abandonment loudly and I go to pick him up.

He's on his back again and hits me square in the chest when he greets me with a wide, gummy smile. I've had smiles before, but usually with some coaxing. This is the first 'hey, I'm happy to see you' smile. I tuck it away right along every other small treasure my days are filling with.

I lift him on my shoulder where his little fist quickly finds my beard.

"Ezrah! You want pancakes, your butt better be on a stool in the next few minutes or you're outta luck!"

Something incoherent comes from upstairs and I take it to mean he'll be down. A few minutes later I hear his feet clomping down the stairs. Finn, who I left sitting in his bouncy chair on the floor beside the island where I can keep an eye on him, starts babbling loudly when he catches sight of Ezrah.

The boy usually doesn't pay a whole lot of attention to Finn—it's his sister who tends to draw the focus—so I'm pleasantly surprised when he plops his butt down on the floor beside the chair. He picks up a rattle, which was tossed on the floor, the way most of Finn's toys are, and shakes it in front of the baby's face.

"How many pancakes, bud?"

"Four."

"Why can he have four and I only get two?" Kiara complains.

"Princess, you're having a hard time eating the two I gave you. Finish those up, you're still hungry, I'll make you another one."

"So why doesn't he have to finish two first?"

I lift my eyes to the ceiling and blow out a breath. Love these kids, but damn…

"Because I'm bigger," Ezrah answers before I can.

That doesn't help.

I can see the little girl's mouth form a pout and prepare myself for the waterworks, but we get a mini-explosion instead.

"You're stupid!" she yells, shoving her plate so hard, it flies off the other end of the counter, crashing to the floor.

Immediate silence follows, but just for a second before Finn opens his mouth and starts wailing. Then Kiara joins in.

I'm about to take her to task when I notice Ezrah sitting on the floor, staring at me, fucking fear in his eyes. I close my eyes and take a few deep breaths.

"Princess," I say in an even but stern voice. "Go up to your room. I'll come get you when I'm ready."

"I'm s-sorry," she wails.

"I'm sure you are, but I still want you to go upstairs. Right now."

While she scrambles down from her stool and stomps upstairs, I pick Finn up from his chair and bounce him on my shoulder.

"Hush, Little Man. It's all over. Shhh…"

With one hand I flip the pancakes before they burn, then grab an empty bottle from the cupboard, when I notice Ezrah inching his way toward the broken plate on the floor. Kid's gonna get cut with a shard if he's not careful.

"Bud, stop," I tell him. "Ezrah? I'll take care of that in a bit. Can you give me a hand with Finn?"

He's hesitant when he gets to his feet and takes a few steps closer. It's like he's approaching a land mine.

Ignoring his defensive body language, I bridge the gap and hand the baby to him.

"I'm just gonna get a bottle for him, why don't you take him into the living room? And be careful where you put your feet."

I turn and measure formula in the bottle, put the kettle on, and turn the burner off under the pancakes. While the water comes to a boil, I grab a broom and dustpan from the laundry room and clean the mess off the floor.

Then I pour myself another cup of coffee, fix Finn's bottle to temperature, and move the pancakes to a plate, setting it on the counter for Ezrah.

"Got your pancakes here, bud. I'll take the baby."

I'm sitting at the table, Finn on my lap, feeding. I'm watching Ezrah, who is eating but with little enthusiasm, and when the baby dozes off, the boy is still sitting there.

"You know you never have to be scared of me, right?" His shoulders pull up almost to his ears at the sound of my voice. "Sure, I'll probably get mad when you do somethin' wrong, but I'll never lay a hand on you. On any of you. That's a promise."

LISA

"NEED ANY HELP?"

Luna walks in just as I'm trying to pull the turkeys out of the oven.

"If you don't mind."

Relieved for the extra pair of hands, we make quick work basting them in their own juices.

"God, that smells so good," Luna mutters, shoving the racks back in the oven. "I always promise myself to snag some leftovers but there never are any."

"Nothing that'll last 'til morning anyway," I agree.

I straighten up and am immediately hit with a dizzy spell that has me grab for the counter.

"Sit," Luna snaps, wrapping an arm around me and guiding me to the kitchen table.

"I'm fine, I just got up too fast."

"Bullshit. You're doing too much. Wapi told me about this morning's mishap."

"That was just an accident."

She ignores me as she pulls her phone from her jeans.

"Are you coming over soon? Can you grab that casserole from the fridge? Yeah, I'm staying here. Thanks, see you soon."

Tucking her phone back in her pocket she sits down across from me, elbows on the table, waiting for me to say something.

"I did fine on my last checkup." She looks unimpressed and simply waits me out. "Fine, the stress may be gettin' to me." That's no lie. I hate not knowing what's going on and I have this dark cloud of impending doom following me around. "I don't like being in the dark."

"Fair enough. I was planning to brief Brick today anyway. When is he coming?"

"Should be here with the kids soon. Let me call him."

Ten minutes later the kids are busy with PlayStation, Nosh is looking after Finn, and Brick pulls up a chair beside me.

"Couple of things," Luna starts. "We urged Sophia to take a leave from work. She's visiting her sister in Oregon."

"Good," Brick comments. "I was worried 'bout her."

"Yeah, but our FBI office in Denver isn't getting anywhere with Safe Load. Lots of protective layers for these government contractors, which are not easy to get around. They're working on it, carefully approaching some employees Kelsey worked with while not alerting management, but it'll take time."

"No luck with Kelsey's car or her apartment?" Brick probes.

"The navy paint composition came back as a standard GM color on models 2016 and newer. We're talking many, many thousands of possible matches in the state of Colorado. If not for Kelsey's phone call to you, and the break-ins here and in Denver, this could've gone down as a simple hit-and-run. Not a lot of hot leads.

"Nothing remarkable in her apartment either. Dishes in the sink, unmade bed. Confirmed with the security guard in the building she walked out one morning and never returned. The baby's daycare confirmed she came in earlier than normal that day, seemed in a hurry.

"The last confirmed sighting was at an ATM machine in Glenwood Springs along the 70. She pulled out her daily maximum of a thousand dollars, but most of it was still left in her purse."

"She must've been on her way to Grand Junction," Brick observes. "Didn't know I'd moved."

"That's what we figure. That's why she called to find

out where you were."

I cover Brick's clenched fist with my hand, and he slowly relaxes and turns his palm up, his fingers slipping between mine.

"So what now?" I want to know.

Luna bites her lip and her gaze jumps between Brick and me.

"Well, it's clear they're looking for something, but we went over everything that was in her car with a fine-tooth comb and came up empty-handed. Unless we missed something."

The oven timer goes off and I automatically get up, but Luna stops me.

"You sit. Tell me what you need."

"Same thing we did earlier."

Brick ends up helping her baste while I look on. When the birds are back in the oven, he turns and looks at me sharply.

"What's wrong?"

Trust him to pick up on it.

"I just got up too soon earlier. I'm fine now."

He eyes me sharply.

"You feel off, you tell me. This ain't nothing to mess around with."

I mock salute him and Luna snickers.

"Tired?"

Brick walks in from the bathroom, catching me

trying to stifle a jawbreaking yawn.

I shouldn't be tired, not after having been forced to sit through most of the day. All I'd been allowed to do was give directions from the kitchen chair I was relegated to, while many hands got the meal ready.

I can't remember the last time I could sit back and enjoy dinner, being waited on hand and foot. If ever. So much food covering the large table the guys had extended with some of the smaller ones to fit everyone. Nosh rounded up the older boys for cleanup duty and there was nothing for me to do but sit Finn on my lap, watching all the activity.

The guys took the younger kids out on the sleds for a bit to burn off that turkey, and I sat with some of the girls, talking about our kids and men. That too was a new experience for me; being part of the group. Granted, I was the one always keeping my distance, but it sure felt good to be included.

"A good tired," I tell him.

The kids were all worn-out from the day's activities, and despite the fact it's only nine, they're already in bed asleep.

Brick checks on the baby before climbing into bed with me. I immediately snuggle up to him and he presses a kiss on my forehead.

"Happy Thanksgiving, Sugar. Best one ever." His voice rumbles in his chest.

"Me too, honey."

It's true, for the first time it felt like I was exactly where I belonged, and if not for that persistent worry, the day would've been perfect.

"We're gonna have to figure out something more permanent for Finn soon," he suddenly says and I hold my breath. "He can't stay in the same room with us forever."

I exhale deeply and hide my smile against his skin. Doesn't matter that circumstances forced our shared living arrangements, I don't want them to change.

"Mmhmm," I mumble.

"There's enough room on the back to bump the place out a bit. Family room, maybe a main floor master. Once Finn starts moving around on his own, I figure we'll get cramped pretty fast."

Typical Brick, not so much a man of words as one of action. We're not so different. I recognize his language and it makes my heart expand.

"Sounds like a good plan."

The way he pulls me tighter to his chest tells me he recognizes my language as well.

15

BRICK

"PHONE!"

I roll out from under the Kia I'm working on. We only have one hoist and Shilah is using it already to replace a set of brakes.

It fucking gets harder every time to get up from the creeper, it's basically a board on wheels to move around under a vehicle. Used to be I could hop to my feet easily, but I'm getting old and my knees aren't what they used to be.

"Fuck off," I toss out at the snickering prospect when I pass him.

The phone is off the hook in the small office.

"Arrow's Edge. This is Brick."

"Hi, I'm gonna need a tow. I'm up on the north end

of the Lemon Reservoir. Got my truck stuck off the road. We're gonna need a winch."

I glance at the clock. It's barely nine in the morning, wonder what the hell he's doing all the way out there on a Monday morning.

"Sure. I'm on my way."

I hang up, grab the keys to the tow truck, and walk back into the garage.

"Watch the shop," I tell Shilah when I pass him. "Got a tow up by the Lemon Reservoir."

His head pokes out from under the SUV.

"What the hell is someone doin' up there this time of year?"

He voices my thoughts exactly. It's a popular spot for serious fishermen but not in late November.

"Fuck if I know. No idea how long I'm gonna be, so when you're done with the SUV, can you check that Kia for me? If you run into trouble, get Tse, he's supposed to come in to look at that Beemer's transmission."

"Will do."

It's fucking cold out. No snow, but it sure looks like it could start coming down any minute. The wind is brutal though, biting through my padded flannel. I hoist myself up in the cab of the truck, starting the engine, and throwing the heat on max. It's only November; if this weather is anything to go by we're in for a hell of a winter.

I head down the driveway to the county road, but before I turn on I quickly dial Lisa's number. Better let her know I won't be around for a bit.

"Takes less time to walk over than to dial the damn number, you know? And yes, I'm fine. Just like I was when you left a little over an hour ago."

I grin as her sarcasm fills the cab. Clearly she doesn't fully appreciate my concern for her well-being, but that's too damn bad. The woman needs a keeper; she's too tough for her own good.

"I'm sure it does, but I'm on the road with the tow truck. Wanted to let you know in case you came looking for me."

"Be careful out there." She changes her tone to one of concern, and that feels damn good too. "Was just watching the news and there's a storm brewing."

"Doesn't surprise me. You guys bundle up when you go to the clubhouse later. How's the little guy?"

"Wide awake on his quilt on the floor, chewing on anything he can get his hands on. I think he's teething, he's making a drool puddle"

"Isn't he a little young for that?" I question.

"Almost four months. Kiara cut her first tooth at three and a half." In the background I hear Finn start crying. "Duty calls," she points out. "I better go."

"Okay. I'll pop into the clubhouse when I get back."

I traverse downtown and turn onto Florida Road, heading into the mountains on the east side. The Lemon Reservoir actually feeds into the Florida River, which runs parallel to the road once you get out of city limits.

My mind is on the conversation I had with Nosh and Ouray yesterday about the possibility of adding onto the cottage. I explained we'd need more room for the kids and both of those geezers had a long hard laugh at me at first, but then pulled out the original drawings for the compound. They'd been kept in the filing cabinet in the office.

I showed them the rough sketch and we were talking ballpark figures when Tse poked his nose in. He grabbed a few blank sheets of paper and in no time, had some layout ideas sketched out I wanted to show Lisa tonight after the kids go to bed.

It's not going to be cheap, but Ouray offered to have a talk with Jed Mason, a local contractor who rebuilt the clubhouse a couple of years ago. He seems to think the guy will give us a good deal. We'll see.

The snow starts to fall when I take the turn toward the dam. By the time I pass it and start curving around the reservoir the road is already covered. I have to lean over the steering wheel, crawling along to try and keep away from the shoulders, otherwise I'll end up stuck my damn self.

About halfway around, I spot someone waving their arms by the entrance into Miller Creek campground at the edge of the water. Strange, I could've sworn they mentioned the north side. I slow down further and carefully turn into the campground where I come to a stop.

The guy is jogging toward me, dressed in heavy winter gear. At least he was prepared for the weather. I roll down the window as he approaches. Younger guy, maybe thirties, with a look of relief on his face.

"Thank God. I thought I'd be stuck up here when

the snow hit. The truck's down that way." He points up ahead, but I can't see anything for the trees lining the dirt road.

"Sure, hop in."

I realize my mistake when he guides me through the campground toward the boat launch and there's still no sign of a truck.

"Look, I don't know—"

"Stop right here," he says, a gun pointing at my head.

LISA

LORDY, IT'S COMING down.

In that short walk from the cottage to the clubhouse, the quilt I threw over Finn for the trip is covered, as am I.

I stomp my feet to get the snow off my boots and shake it out of my hair.

"Here, let me take him," Ouray says, walking up and taking the stroller while I hang up my coat and scarf. "Pretty bad out there," he points out, uncovering the baby and lifting him out.

For a man who's never had babies of his own, he's pretty comfortable handling Finn. In fact, I've seen him handling Lettie, and Trunk and Jaimie's babies. He may be a little rough around the edges but he's a good man at the core. All of these guys are.

I really lucked out when I ended up here.

"How are you feeling?"

I bite off a grin. If there's one negative about this club, it's that very little stays secret. I'm sure Luna already gave him the update.

With Brick's help, she pushed me to put a call into Dr. Husse's office Friday. I did, and went to see her Saturday morning. According to her, there's no reason for alarm, as long as it doesn't become an ongoing problem. She did reiterate cutting down on stress, which I don't exactly have complete control over.

In fact, looking out at the storm outside reminds me how little control I have. I don't like Brick being out on the road in this. The sense of doom that's been hovering over me feels even heavier today.

"I'm all right. Just a little worried with Brick out on the road in this."

"He is?"

"Was called out on a tow," I explain, grabbing the diaper bag from the stroller and plucking Finn from Ouray's arms.

"Won't be the first time. Tow calls get more frequent during the winter months. Lots of idiots ending up in a ditch. He'll be fine."

"I'm sure," I mumble, not quite convinced as I make my way to the kitchen.

I notice one of the boys, Michael, lying on the couch watching TV and walk over.

"Why aren't you in school?"

It's clear when he turns his head to look at me the boy has a fever: eyes glassy, deep blush on his cheeks and forehead.

"Not feeling good."

"I can tell. Let me take care of Finn and I'll check

you for a fever."

Last thing I need is for the baby to catch something.

Ouray is in the kitchen pouring a coffee.

"If I get his bottle ready, would you mind feeding him?" I ask. "I think Michael's got a fever."

"Yeah, he puked after breakfast. Said his stomach was bothering him."

I put the kettle on the stove and pull one of the premade bottles out of the diaper bag.

"Could be a stomach flu, which is bound to spread. Might be a good idea to keep him away from the other kids."

"Fuck. Just what we need," he grumbles, holding out his arms for Finn.

"Not until you wash your hands, and you better warn everyone else too. Nosh especially. At his age a simple flu could knock him on his ass."

Once Finn is safely installed in Ouray's arms, his little hands folded around the bottle, I head to the bathroom down the hall to grab the medical kit.

"Sit up, boy, let me take your temperature real quick."

He barely lifts his head off the couch and he lunges over the edge, puking. Great. This is gonna be fun if more turn up sick. I grab a gauze pad and wipe his mouth.

"Stay like that. I'll be right back."

I rush to grab a few towels, a wet washcloth, and get a bucket from the laundry room in the back. Poor kid is crying when I return.

"Here, wash your face. You'll feel better." From the corner of my eye I see Wapi walking in. "Gimme a hand?"

He walks around the couch and instantly freezes at the sight of the puke, turning a little green himself.

"I'll take care of this, but I need you to get his stuff from the bunkhouse. We're gonna get him set up in one of the empty bedrooms here, otherwise it'll spread like wildfire."

Half an hour later, we have Michael installed in the bedroom closest to the main room so someone can hear him if he calls. He's got his bucket in case, and Wapi even borrowed a small TV from one of the other rooms so the boy wouldn't be bored out of his brain. I left him with some ginger ale and a bottle of water, hoping to at least keep him hydrated.

Five minutes after I get started in the kitchen, we get a call from the school. Ravi, our latest foster kid, showed up at the nurse's station feeling sick. Ouray goes to pick him up while Wapi gets a second bed set up with Michael. I keep my fingers crossed there won't be more.

Luckily Finn is clueless, Ouray put him in his stroller after his bottle and he's sleeping soundly, supervised by Nosh.

When Shilah walks in a little after noon looking for lunch, I tell him he's on his own. I have my hands full.

Ravi came in looking like death warmed over and spiking a fever as well, so he's been relegated to the bedroom with a bucket of his own. Not really surprising, since Michael sleeps in the bunk above him.

Ouray is calling Dr. Weinberg to see if he can make a house call, instead of trying to cart the boys over to the clinic. In the meantime, I'm deep cleaning the big room, starting with the TV area where the kids tend to congregate.

It isn't until I get back to the kitchen and see Shilah eating lunch at the table, I remember Brick saying he'd stop by.

"Is Brick back? Should I make him something?"

He looks up, the sandwich halfway to his mouth.

"I haven't seen him. I kinda thought maybe he'd gone home first or something. That's weird."

That heavy cloud over me just got significantly darker.

I grab my phone from my pocket and dial his number. It rings five times and hits voicemail. I try again with the same result.

"Where'd he go?" I can hear the edge of panic in my own voice. "Brick?" I prompt Shilah who isn't answering fast enough. "Where was he called to?"

"Up at the reservoir."

I dart out the kitchen and slam into Ouray.

"Hey, careful," he says, grabbing me by the shoulders. "The doc is on his way."

I shake my head, willing myself to calm down, but I know in my bones something's very wrong.

"You need to find Brick."

16

BRICK

FUCK.

I watch as three more men—two more armed with what looked like M16s hanging off their shoulders—step from the tree line. Dressed the same as guy number one, but with the distinct difference: these three have most of their faces covered with balaclavas.

That's not good. I can deal with one guy with a gun—maybe—but four is a different ballgame. My best course of action is to find out what they are after, because one thing I'm sure, they lured me out here for a reason.

"Mr. Paver…"

The only unarmed one of the three, a guy with a raspy voice, opens my door. He seems to expect me to get out so I comply.

"What's going on? I'm supposed to pick up a truck that ran off—"

The openhanded bitch-slap stings my cheek and my hand automatically comes up to cover it. I flex my jaw.

"We don't play games, Mr. Paver. I strongly suggest you refrain from doing so as well. You cooperate, this will be quick and you'll soon be on your way."

Somehow I doubt that when I feel the cold steel of a gun pressed to the base of my neck.

"Walk," the guy behind me orders, and I take a step.

The unarmed guy walks ahead and I do my best to go as slow as I can. Give myself time to think, because I'm not liking what I see when I look toward the end of the boat launch.

"Fucking move," the voice growls behind me.

"I've got arthritis," I lie. "My knees are bad."

"Maybe a bullet in the kneecap will help?"

"No bullets," the guy in front says.

Well, at least that's something, although, I have a feeling they wouldn't hesitate should I try to get away. There's an air of professionalism around these guys, like this is something they do on a regular basis.

The other two guys take the cinderblocks off the mechanic's creeper sitting at the end of the slope as we approach.

"What is it you want?" I try again.

"I have reason to believe you're well aware, Mr. Paver. I caution you not to waste my time." He gestures to the creeper, which I now see has ropes attached to it.

My heart sinks; unfortunately I can see where this is

going. The water in the reservoir would have cooled off significantly with the November we just had. It wouldn't take much for hypothermia to set in.

"Is this about my daughter?"

"Very good," he says in his raspy voice, and I have to clench my fists not to react to that patronizing tone. "Like I said, we can avoid a whole lot of unpleasantness if you simply tell us what we want to hear."

"If I knew whatever the fuck you're looking for, I could."

This time it's not a bitch-slap, it's a fist, and it hurts like a sonofabitch. I lean forward and blood drips from my nose.

I'd fucking fight to get away if there wasn't a possibility they'd just go after Lisa next. The longer I can drag this out, the better the chance the brothers will clue in something is wrong, and I trust them to make sure she and the kids are safe.

I'm pretty sure I still have the gun to my head when the two other goons walk up and take my arms. I keep my mouth shut and I'm not fighting, but I'll be damned if I make it easy for them; I let my knees buckle so they have to carry me. I'm not a lightweight, probably close to two hundred and thirty pounds, and I derive some satisfaction from their grunts of effort.

Of course the result is the same; they force me down on the creeper and boss guy pulls straps from his pocket. I panic when they pile the two cinder blocks on my chest and pull the straps through the holes before tying me down on the board, but with one of the guys sitting on my legs, strapping those down as well, there isn't much I can do.

"Last chance," he says, getting up.

"Fuck you."

One second I'm cursing him, the next I'm flying toward the water, and all I'm able to do is take in as much air as I can.

It is indescribably cold—painful. I have to resist the urge to suck in a breath as I come to an abrupt stop, reaching the end of the rope. I open my eyes and can see the snow hitting the surface of the water just a few inches away.

My lungs start burning and I let out the air a little at a time, watching as the last the bubbles break on the surface. An overwhelming sadness washes over me as I think of Finn, of Lisa and the kids.

Then suddenly I'm moving. The moment I feel air on my head I suck in a breath, inhaling water with it. I cough to clear lungs that feel raw like open wounds. Blinking to clear tears and water from my eyes, a blurry masked face comes into view.

"Where is it?"

"I…I d-don't know what you want!" I yell, the effort resulting in another coughing bout, even as the shakes take over my body.

"The. Fucking. Key. Where is it?"

He slaps my face again and again, but I'm already numb.

"I don't know what you're talking about," I mumble.

"Put him back in."

A second later I'm plunged into the water again. The cold this time not as painful. I try hard to empty my mind of everything while I'm under. Just as darkness starts pulling me down, I'm yanked to the surface again.

The questions, then the hits, and I'm back underwater.

I lose track of time, stopped feeling my body a while ago, and I have trouble thinking. The only thing I hear is the same question, over and over again, *"Where is the key?"*

At some point I must've passed out when I feel a weight behind lifted from my chest. It takes too much effort to open my eyes, but I hear them talk.

"...doesn't know."

"What about the feds?"

"Don't be a moron, would they be sniffing around if they had that kinda intel? We'd a been nailed already. We need to find it before they do."

"Well, if he doesn't have it, who does?"

"That snooty bitch from accounting; Sophia. It's fucking somewhere. We've got millions on the line, and time is running out."

I'm suddenly grabbed under my arms and pulled off the board. I hear my heels dragging over the dirt but I don't feel anything.

"You know it's easier just to shoot him."

"Won't look like a fucking accident with a bullet in his head, Einstein."

"What if he doesn't drown?"

"Hypothermia will do the trick. No one's up here this time of year. With a bit of luck they won't find him 'til spring."

LISA

"LEMON RESERVOIR."

Ouray swings on Shilah, covering his phone with his hand.

"What time did he leave?"

"He called me at nine fifteen," I answer for him. "He said he'd just left."

Ouray looks up at the clock, but I already know it shows twelve forty. I've been counting seconds in my head. It's all I know to do to keep from screaming. That darkness is no longer hovering over me; it's invading me.

He left almost three and a half hours ago.

"Shilah, get Tse, close down the garage. Call the brothers; tell them armed. You, gun safe." He tosses a set of keys at Wapi, who easily grabs them out of the air before heading to the office.

The prospect runs out the door while Ouray gets on his phone, snapping details to someone on the other side. Nosh covers my hand with his and I turn to him. His face is one of sympathy.

"He'll be fine," he says in his monotone rasp. "Ouray will find him."

I nod and grab on to the faith he offers. Brick will be okay. He has to be. Anything else is inconceivable.

The door swings open and Shilah is back, with Tse in tow. Both men focus on Ouray, who is still pacing and talking on the phone.

"Like fucking hell I'm gonna hang around, Sprite," he barks. "Heading out now."

He shoves his phone in his pocket and turns just as Wapi holds out a gun and what looks like an assault rifle. Ouray stuffs the one in his waistband and slings the other over his shoulder.

"Chief," Shilah pipes up. "Got a hold of Yuma, he's on his way here."

"Good. Get back on the phone and locate the others. Tse, with me. Wapi, you and Shilah have the clubhouse. I'll be in touch." Then he walks over to me, bends down, and kisses my forehead. "Gonna find him, Lisa. Gonna bring him back."

Then his long strides take him out the door, Tse close behind him.

OURAY

I LET TSE drive.

His fucking NASCAR skills come in handy as he flies through town, narrowly avoiding hitting anyone.

"Don't do anything stupid, Ouray," Luna snaps in my ear. Should've known she'd call me back after I hung up on her at the clubhouse. "We're getting on the road now. Ramirez was near the hospital, but he's making his way up there and he's putting Fire and Rescue on standby. Station Three is closest."

"Good."

"We could be overreacting. For all we know his truck broke down."

"He's not answering his phone."

"Could be bad reception up there," she counters.

"Or not. Got a bad feeling about this, Sprite."

It's quiet for a second before she answers.

"Me too. How's Lisa?"

Tse takes a sudden left and I brace myself when the back of my truck starts fishtailing precariously. The snow has mostly stopped falling but the roads are a mess. It gets hairy for a moment before he straightens it out. I glance over to catch him grinning at me.

Fucking lunatic.

"Stoic," I answer Luna. "I got the bad vibe from her."

"Shit. Let me call Lissie, see if she can head up to the clubhouse."

"She may already be there. Yuma was on his way." The phone buzzes against my ear with another call. "Gotta go. Got another call."

I take a quick look at the screen to see Kaga calling.

"Talk to me."

"I'm right behind you…" I glance over my shoulder and spot him. "…and tell Tse to keep his fucking hands on the wheel before he wipes us all out."

"Will do." I hang up and mutter at Tse, "If you could keep us alive I'd be much obliged."

"Doin' my best."

I guess that'll have to be good enough.

I'm trying to imagine what we'll encounter. Thankfully, I geared out the truck after the first snowfall. You don't drive winters in the mountains without a survival kit. Thermal blankets, an emergency warmer pack, shovel, ropes, gloves, extra clothes, and a first aid kit.

We're passing the dam on the left and I'm keeping my eyes peeled.

"Somebody drove out of here not too long ago. South."

Tse points at the faint imprint coming toward us in the opposite lane.

"There. They came from the campsite."

We follow the tracks on the narrow road between the pines until we break through the tree line.

About twenty yards into the reservoir only the top foot or so of the cab of Brick's black tow truck is sticking out of the water.

Tse hasn't quite come to a full stop when I jump out and start running and slipping down the boat launch.

"Brick! Brick!" I yell as loud as I can, scanning the waterline to my right and left to see if he's climbed ashore.

Then I look back at the roof of the truck and it doesn't even take a fraction of a second to make the decision.

I kick off my boots and jump into the freezing water.

17

LISA

"SIT DOWN."

I shake my head at Nosh. If I have to sit any longer I'll go nuts.

"I have to do something."

He nods his understanding.

Thank God Finn is still blissfully unaware, sleeping in the stroller. Wapi is sitting at the bar, my eyes briefly meeting his serious ones before I duck into the kitchen.

I'm just pulling vegetables out of the large fridge for a hearty soup when Lissie walks in. I barely have the chance to drop the produce on the counter before I'm wrapped up in a bone-crushing hug.

"He's fine," she says, looking me in the eye. "You'll see, it's gonna be one of those stupid things you'll be laughing about later."

"I know," I lie, just like I know she was. I can see the concern in her eyes.

"Okay, Nosh has the babies, Yuma is doing whatever Yuma does when he's in biker mode, so I'm here to help. What are we cooking?"

What an unexpected, amazing friend Lissie has become. Already she knows me well enough to guess I've got to keep my hands moving.

Unfortunately, that still doesn't keep my mind from churning out the worst scenarios. Top of the list is whoever killed Kelsey may have gotten their hands on Brick, and that puts the fear of God in me. People who don't think twice to kill a young woman and her child, surely won't blink an eye killing a silver-haired biker.

I'm not a fan of guns, but right now I wish I'd learned to shoot one.

For the past hour or so, Lissie and I have barely spoken while working side by side in the kitchen. The soup is simmering on the stove, and I have all the ingredients set out for a large pan of cornbread to put together closer to dinnertime.

I glance at the clock, it's coming up on two. We should've heard by now.

Inside Finn suddenly starts crying and I'm almost relieved for something to do. I pull a bottle from the fridge, but Lissie pulls it from my hand.

"I'll take care of this."

Her eyes dart over my shoulder and I turn to find Yuma in the doorway, his face grim.

"Need you to come with me, Lisa."

My knees almost buckle, but I force them straight.

"Finn needs—"

"I've got Finn, you go with Yuma."

"But the kids are gonna be—"

"I've got it," Lissie says softly behind me, giving me a little shove in my back.

My first steps feel like I'm wading through water.

OURAY

FUCK, THAT'S COLD.

I keep my eyes peeled on the roof of the truck as I swim closer, my strokes already slowing down. At first I don't see anything but when I get closer I notice him. He's in the driver's side; his head tilted back, face above the waterline.

Jesus, he has no color left.

I try the door, but it won't budge. I turn my head to yell at Tse, but he's already swimming toward me. Between the two of us we're able to wrangle the door open and Tse is already leaning in, feeling for a pulse.

"I can't f-feel anything, m-man."

"Get him out," I grind between my chattering teeth.

LISA

"TELL ME."

Yuma turns to me as he starts his truck.

"Kaga called. They found the truck in the reservoir, Brick behind the wheel." I suck in air through my teeth, my hands clenched in my lap. "They got him out, alive, but barely. He's in the ambulance on his way to Mercy."

Words won't come but I nod and lock the fear that threatens to overwhelm me down. No time for that. He's alive; that's what I'm holding on to.

The drive to the hospital is a blur. When we get there, Yuma helps me out of his truck, keeping his arm tightly around me as he walks me into the emergency entrance. The moment we come through the door I see Ouray walking toward us, pulling me from Yuma's hold into his arms.

"We just got here. He's alive, darlin'," his deep voice rumbles somewhere over my head. "He's in good hands. They're working on him now."

He guides me to a waiting area and urges me to sit. Then he takes the seat beside me, Yuma sitting down on my other side; the two large men like pillars holding me up.

In a low voice Ouray recounts how they found him and managed to pull him from the water.

"He's hypothermic. I have no idea how long he was in the water for, but according to Sumo long enough to lower his body temperature to a dangerous level."

"How did he get in the water?"

Yuma asked the question but I've been thinking it.

"He had help."

I swing my head around to look at Ouray.

"What does that mean?"

"Another vehicle had been there. We saw the tracks."

Someone did that to him. Like someone ran his

daughter and grandson off the side of the road.

Finn.

"The kids!"

I surge to my feet but Ouray pulls me back.

"Sit down, Lisa. They're looked after. My guys are there and Luna has a team heading to the compound."

I do as he says, and take my seat. I'm torn, wanting to be with my babies but needing to stay close to Brick as well. Ouray's hand lands on my knee just as Sumo walks into the waiting area, looking at me as he crouches down before me.

"The attending will come to talk to you in a bit, but I thought I'd come and let you know what's going on. They're working to get his core temperature up, which was dangerously low. Right now they're hooking him up to a heart bypass machine, which withdraws his blood, warms it, and then feeds it back into his body. It's one of the most effective ways to warm him up safely."

"Is he gonna to be okay?" I can't help ask, desperate for good news.

"The fact he's alive is a testament to his strength," he says gently.

I note he avoids answering my question.

BRICK

"Wake up, Mr. Paver."

The voice is unfamiliar as is the hand on my shoulder.

I struggle to open my eyes but it feels like they're glued shut. A steady beep can be heard but it sounds muffled, like I'm underwater. Sudden panic grabs me and I feel my body jerk.

"You're all right, Brick. You're gonna be okay."

That voice I recognize. Rich and soothing. I try opening my eyes again and this time I manage a crack, but bright light has me force them shut again.

"Turn off the damn light." *Ouray.*

A hand grabs mine and I try to wrap my fingers around it.

"Try again, honey."

It takes a minute for her face to come into focus, but when it does a surge of emotion blurs her again. My last thoughts had been of her; cursing myself for the two years I wasted waiting for the right time, before I gave in to the darkness.

"Lisa." I only manage a whisper.

"I'm right here," she says, her lips moving against the back of my hand.

I can feel that. I'm starting to feel a lot of other things too; pain, for one.

Blinking my eyes a few times, I scan the dim room, spot a nurse on the other side of my bed, and encounter Ouray's grim face at the foot end.

"Good to see you, brother."

"Likewise. You need to—"

I'm launched into a coughing fit.

"Let's have you sit up a little," the nurse says. "Looks like you may have inhaled some water."

She cranks the bed up and I immediately feel a little better. Then she lifts a cup with a straw to my mouth.

"Warm tea. Probably not your favorite, but it'll soothe."

Tastes like warm piss to me, but I sip it anyway.

The woman asks me a few standard questions to gauge my mental capacity, then tells me a doctor will come and talk to me about my condition. The moment she leaves the room I turn to Lisa.

"What condition?"

"You came in with severe hypothermia," Ouray answers instead. "Some of your toes and the fingertips of your left hand are frostbitten." That explains the pain. "The doctor's guess is you were in the water for quite some time before we got to you. You're on an IV with fluids and antibiotics."

Memories flood back of being submerged with concrete blocks on my chest time and time again.

"There were four of them. One waved me down, light hair, light eyes, clean-shaven, late twenties, early thirties." I pause and take another sip from the tea Lisa is now holding to my lips. "Wasn't until he pulled a gun on me I saw the three others. Those three wore balaclavas, two with assault rifles. The one interrogating me had brown eyes, almost black. Raspy voice."

"Interrogating you?"

"Yeah. About a key." I glance over at Lisa, who is listening intently, and I squeeze the hand I'm still holding in mine. For her sake I refrain from going into detail and limit it to, "Tried some creative waterboarding, but since I don't fucking know anything about a key, I had nothin' to say. Went on for quite a while."

"Fuck, man. I thought you hit your face on the steering wheel going into the water, but I'm guessing that was them too?"

I meet his eyes so he can read my answer.

"You may wanna call your wife. They mentioned Sophia, someone's gotta check on her."

I feel Lisa's hand spasm in mine as Ouray walks to the door.

Half an hour later, I'm recounting the snippets of conversation I recall, before passing out, to Luna and her boss, SAC Damian Gomez. They've already spoken to Sophia and alerted a team in Oregon to watch over her. Agents Greene and Barnes are at the Arrow's Edge compound keeping an eye out there.

"This key; did they ever mention to what?"

"No. I keep thinking maybe Kelsey put something in a locker somewhere? Maybe a post office box?"

"You didn't get any mail?"

I shake my head.

"Could be a USB-key," Luna volunteers.

"Don't have any of those either," I admit. "Don't even have a computer."

"Anything else?" her boss pushes for more.

"They're organized," I inform them. "Professional, almost military. The guy doing the talking was clearly in charge. Built, about my height. Cold and calculated."

"Any distinguishing features? Or clothes?" This from Luna, who's been taking notes.

"No. All similar gear. GORE-TEX jackets, heavy boots, but no markings I could see."

"Did you see what they were driving?"

I shake my head. I never did see a vehicle.

"If you think of anything, give Agent Roosberg or myself a call," Gomez instructs me, then he turns to Ouray. "Walk with us?"

He nods at Lisa while Luna gives her a quick hug, whispering something to her. Then they're gone and I'm alone with her.

"Them bastards tortured you," she whispers, her head lowered and her body almost vibrating with emotion, although I'm not sure if it's from fear or anger.

"Sugar, I'm fine."

Her head snaps up, eyes spitting fire.

"You are not—"

"Mr. Paver, how are you feeling?"

A doctor, followed by the same nurse from earlier, walks in.

"Better," I answer.

"Good. You weren't in the best condition when you came in and we weren't sure which way you were going to go. You've got a strong heart, Mr. Paver. Now, right now, your biggest problem is your toes and the fingers of your left hand." I look at the gauze-covered fingers. "We warmed those even as we were warming your blood. We'll have to wait to see the full extent of the damage done. I suspect your case to be mild, but it's possible you'll see blistering on the affected areas. We're going to keep you here and see what it looks like in a few days; then we'll make a decision on what to do.

"We also want to make sure you're able to clear

your lungs yourself, and have you finish the regimen of antibiotics before we send you home."

Not looking forward to spending any time in here, but I'm also not stupid; if I insist on leaving now, I only become a liability to my family who already has their hands full.

"Fair enough."

Lisa is still looking at me funny when we're once again alone.

"What?"

"Didn't think you'd be so agreeable."

"Not gonna fight them on this, Sugar. I'm guessing I've given you all enough worry. Not gonna add to it." Lisa's eyes go liquid and she immediately turns her head away. "Come here, baby." I tug on her hand with my good one, but she doesn't budge. "Come lie down with me."

"Bed's too small for my fat ass," she mumbles.

"Your ass is perfect and I'll move over. Need to feel you close for a minute."

She doesn't resist this time when I tug on her hand, and I scoot over as far as I can so she can lie down beside me. I curl my arm around her and pull her close, shoving my face in her hair and breathing deep.

"Didn't think I'd see you again," I croak, my throat closing with emotion.

"Don't say that."

Her hands curls into the hospital gown I'm wearing and her face presses into my chest.

"Last thought I had was how much time I wasted.

Was hanging on to the edge of tomorrow and almost lost it all."

"Don't…"

"Not gonna take that chance again, Lisa. You gotta know I love you."

The heat of her tears soaks through the thin fabric.

"I know."

18

LISA

I DIDN'T WANT to leave his side, but he gently reminded me of the kids.

According to the doctor, he'll be here at least another day or two, and I can hardly leave the kids without seeing us for that long.

Durango PD posted an officer outside his room, in case whoever tried to kill him found out they weren't successful and returned to finish the job. I shiver at the thought. Life without Brick is already unimaginable.

"You okay?" Ouray asks over his shoulder, navigating the truck Kaga and Tse dropped off earlier through Durango.

"No," I tell him honestly. "I'm at a loss what to do. Kids have school tomorrow; do I let 'em go? Will they be safe? Will Brick? I wanna be two places at once, but I can't."

He grabs one of my hands from my lap and gives it a squeeze.

"We'll keep the kids home for now, until we get this mess figured out. Lissie will help with them and so can Nosh. Most of the brothers will be staying at the compound as well. We'll have a guard at the gate around the clock."

"What about the FBI?"

"They're around, keeping an eye out." He gives my hand a reassuring pat and puts his back on the steering wheel. "You hungry?" he asks, and I feel his eyes on me.

I haven't eaten since…breakfast?

"Not really, but I can put something together when we get home."

"I'm gonna swing by Sonic, I'm hungry. What would you like?"

Just like Ouray, to find a way to make sure I eat.

"I'll have a cheeseburger."

I automatically grab for my purse, but it's not there and I remember running out of the clubhouse without taking it.

"I've got it, Lisa. Drink?"

"Sweet tea is fine."

He pulls into the drive-thru and places our order. He catches me glancing at the dashboard clock, which shows eight forty-five.

"Relax. Won't take more than ten minutes to eat and another ten to get home. Just breathe for a few minutes, otherwise you dive from stress into stress and we both know you can't afford that."

The reference to my health is unexpected. I caught him watching me a few times this afternoon but I didn't pay it much attention; I'd been too busy worrying about Brick than to worry about me. Maybe I should've.

Ouray is a good man, like Brick. They each have a rough way about them, but with big hearts. I trust both of them to do right by me.

While we wait for the food to be ready, I rest my head back and close my eyes, taking a moment to gauge how I feel. No dizziness and when I put my fingers to my pulse it feels steady and regular. Thank the Lord, last thing we need is me keeling over.

While we're eating, my mind is going over Brick's statement to the FBI. That key they're looking for, Luna mentioned they hadn't found anything in Kelsey's car, but what if she put it on the baby somehow? Maybe in the car seat? I'm not sure where it is, the one we're using Ouray brought when he first picked us up from the hospital with Finn.

"What are you thinking on so hard?" Ouray asks, licking mustard off his fingers.

"Wondering why those guys were so certain Brick had whatever they're looking for. When you came to fetch us from the hospital with the baby, you brought a car seat, right?"

He looks at me quizzically, the remnants of his burger halfway up to his mouth.

"Went and bought one. EMTs kept him in his original

seat when they brought him in to keep him secure, but it had been in an accident so potentially no longer safe. I'm guessing the hospital would've discarded it. Are you thinking…shit, never thought of that. Let me give Luna a call, because I'm not sure they have either."

I finish eating my burger and end up eating most of the extra fries he bought while he calls his wife. Guess I was hungrier than I thought.

"She's on it. She'll check with the hospital," Ouray volunteers when he hangs up. "Ready to go?"

"Yeah. I wanna see my babies."

When we turn onto the driveway to the compound, I notice the gate closed and lit by floodlights. I jump when a figure steps out of the shadows beside the truck. It's one of the brothers, Honon. Ouray rolls down the window on my side.

"All quiet?"

"Yeah."

"FBI still here?"

"The tech guy, Greene. Working on something with Paco."

"Where are my babies?" I ask him, eager to hug my kids.

Honon smiles at me. "At your house with Lissie and Yuma. They're fine." I let out a relieved breath and smile back, but Honon's face turns serious. "How's Brick?"

"He'll be okay. They're keepin' him for a day or two."

"Some fingers and toes were frostbitten," Ouray adds. "They want to see how deep the damage goes. Also inhaled some water, so he's on antibiotics."

Honon nods and knocks on the doorframe. "Lemme get the gate."

Ouray bypasses the clubhouse and drives me straight to the cottage. The lights from inside are welcoming and the relief is instant, but so is the guilt for feeling it. Brick just went through a horrible ordeal, and I left him alone at the hospital.

The moment Ouray turns off the engine, the front door opens revealing Ezrah, Yuma visible behind him. The boy comes running up to the truck as I'm getting out and slams me against the side, his spindly arms wrapping around me tightly.

It's on my lips to scold him—a knee-jerk response—but instead I hug him back equally hard.

"It's all good, boy."

"He comin' home?" he asks, tilting his head back to look at me and I notice how tall he's getting. Won't be long before he'll start outgrowing his nana.

"Couple'a days." I look beyond him where Yuma is waiting in the doorway. "Where's your sister?"

"Fell asleep on the couch. Mr. Yuma just carried her upstairs."

I cup his face in my hands and kiss his forehead.

"How about we call him Uncle Yuma instead? No more of the mister stuff. You got lots of uncles and aunties here. No misters or missus."

I glance up to find Ouray standing a few feet away, giving me a nod of approval. To my surprise, Yuma gives me a quick hug at the door before letting me pass. Lissie twists her head when I come in. She's on the couch, feeding Finn, Jesse asleep beside her and Lettie is in her car seat on the coffee table, also asleep.

"Hey."

She smiles sweetly and my heart swells. Who would've thought, two years ago, I'd have a good friend who doesn't ask questions and jumps in to help out, an extended family looking out for me like I was one of their own.

Ezrah kicks off his boots and I remind him to put them away properly. Then I pull him back for another hug.

"You okay, baby?"

"Yeah."

"Think maybe it's time to head to bed?"

He lifts his face. "Are you gonna be here when I wake up?"

"Promise. Maybe you guys can come and see Brick tomorrow, we'll see. Say goodnight to Lissie."

His arms tighten around me before letting go, lifting a hand at Lissie, and heading upstairs. My Ezrah; for all his attitude making him seem older, he's still my little boy.

I shrug out of my coat and toe off my boots before walking in, but I almost stumble when my foot catches on something.

"Sorry," Lissie says. "I should've put that away."

I bend over to untangle my foot from the strap of Finn's diaper bag. I'm about to put it at the base of the stairs to take up, when I suddenly remember the nurse handing us the bag in the hospital. *"The bag is his. EMTs brought it in with him."*

Instead of walking inside I turn to the front door and pull it open. Yuma and Ouray, talking on the front step, both look up.

"What is it?" Ouray asks, seeing my face.

I hold up the bag.

"This is Finn's diaper bag." When they still seem confused I add, "It came from Kelsey's car."

FBI AGENT JASPER Greene is unpacking the diaper bag on my dining table, examining every item he pulls out carefully. Yuma and Ouray flanking him. I have Finn on my shoulder, dozing off, and Wapi is driving Lissie home with the kids.

"Can I get some paper towels?" the agent asks Ouray, who grabs the roll off the counter and hands it over.

I watch as Greene opens the jar of diaper cream and digs his fingers in, feeling around.

"Nothing," he states, setting the jar aside and wiping his hands.

He's already gone through the spare clothing, examined every diaper, and now grabs for the wipes. Most of those things we put in the bag, but he said he needs to make sure.

The entire contents are spread out over the table and he turns his attention to the bag itself.

"Got it," he says, and we all bend closer to see.

He's feeling around the base of the strap, where it is sewn into the quilted fabric of the bag. From his jeans he pulls one of those pocketknives with numerous different utensils and pulls up what looks like a toothpick. He pulls at the threads to create an opening and reveals a small metal tab, not even an inch long. It looks nothing like a key. He snaps a few pictures and puts his phone away before pulling the item free.

"Thumb drive," Ouray mumbles.

"What is that?" I ask.

"It's a convertible flash drive," Jasper explains. "It's a storage system for computer files. You plug it in one of the ports of the computer or on your phone and you can save information to it." He turns the small thing around in his hands then he turns to me with a smile. "Good catch."

"So now what?" Ouray wants to know.

"Now I'm taking this back to the office, see what's on it." He tucks the thing in his pocket and looks at Ouray. "We're keeping this under the radar for now. I don't want it to get out we found something and the fewer people who know right now, the better it is."

Ouray walks him to the door where they spend another few minutes, their voices too low to overhear.

"Want me to put him down for you?" Yuma says, pointing at Finn, who appears to be fast asleep.

"I've got it. I want to check in on the kids anyway."

"Why don't you try to get some rest too?" he suggests. "I'm gonna stay here tonight, so you won't be alone."

"You don't have to do that, you got your own family

to get home to," I point out, but he shakes his head with a smirk.

"Have you met Lissie?" he jokes. "My wife would have my balls if I showed up tonight. In fact, the only way I could get her to take the kids home was if I promised not to leave your side. So there you go, take it up with the boss." I roll my eyes at him, but he just grins and leans in to kiss my cheek. "I've got you tonight. Get some sleep."

I walk through the living room just as Ouray shuts the door on the agent and turns around.

"Heading to bed?"

"Think so. I'm just worried about Brick alone at the hospital."

"He won't be alone. Jasper's gonna make sure he's well covered. I'm gonna head over to the clubhouse, see what's going on there. Yuma will stay here and we've got the entire compound covered. There's nothing to worry about."

I give him an awkward hug, trying not to wake Finn, and head upstairs. The baby barely registers me putting him down in his crib. Then I check in on Kiara, who is starfished in the middle of her bed. Her hair is starting to curl around her face and I remind myself to tighten her braids tomorrow morning. A quick kiss she doesn't react to, and I pull the door partially shut. Tonight I want to be able to hear all my kids.

Next is Ezrah, whose room is dark, but I can see his eyes are open when I approach the bed.

"Can't sleep?"

He shakes his head.

I sit down on the mattress beside him, running my hand over his dreads. Those could do with some work too.

"What's happening, Nana?" he asks, and I realize there's nothing wrong with that boy's sight or hearing. He's too young to burden with the truth, but Ezrah has seen and heard too much in his life already to be brushed off.

"I'm not quite sure myself, but I do know the FBI and the police are lookin' into it. With Brick in the hospital, we're gonna be careful for a bit so Yuma's spending the night here and tomorrow I'm gonna keep you guys home from school."

"'Cause if he was home he'd be lookin' after us, right?"

I bend down and put a hand to his cheek.

"You know he would. Now, try and get some sleep. Nana's goin' to bed too."

His arms come up around my neck.

"I'll look after us too, Nana," he promises.

When I walk into the bathroom to wash up for the night, tears burn the back of my eyes.

I hate for my grandson to feel that weight.

ARROW'S EDGE MC

19

BRICK

"Not looking too bad."

I check out my toes the doctor is studying. They're all still there with just a few small blisters. I've been warned some of the skin could turn black and would probably just slough off.

"I think your heavy socks and boots may have prevented further damage," he suggests, wrapping them back up. "You'll need to stay off your feet as much as possible for a few weeks, though. Now, let's have a look at your hand."

My little finger is the only one that blistered and it doesn't look too appealing.

"That's one to keep an eye on. See how the skin on the tip is still discolored? And that blister is blood-filled.

Both of those things indicate a more severe case." He starts rebandaging my hand while he talks. "We'll send you home with some medication to improve your blood flow and with care instructions. I suggest you follow those to a T if you want to preserve your digits. Especially that one." He points at my finger. "I'll want to see you again in a week to check up on you." He reaches out his hand and I shake it. "You're a lucky man, Mr. Paver. Your lungs sound like they've cleared, and hopefully the frostbite will heal. That was quite an ordeal you went through and many would not have come out the way you have, if at all."

With that he walks out the door, leaving me to consider the truth of his words.

I *am* a lucky man and walking in is more proof of that in the form of Lisa holding Kiara's hand and Ezrah following right behind them. Ouray is last to enter, carrying my grandson.

God knows I don't deserve this beautiful family looking at me. What if I put them in danger? It would fucking rip me apart, but maybe I should keep my distance. I spent a lot of the night thinking about how to keep them safe and the easiest way would be to…

"How come you're sitting up, Papa?"

Kiara's voice has me choke up to a point where I can't even answer. Was only yesterday I didn't think I'd hear that little chirp again.

"He's feeling better," Ouray jumps in for me, as he lifts Finn from his seat like he's done nothing else his whole life. "Here, say hello to your boy."

The big gummy smile directed at me when Ouray plants him on my lap is a fucking gift.

"Come here," I tell Lisa, catching her eye over Finn's head. She leans in and barely brushes her lips against mine. "You can try that again later," I whisper, and then add a little louder, "Sleep okay last night?"

"I did okay."

Right. I don't believe that for a second since I didn't sleep particularly well either.

"Can I get a kiss hello from you too, Princess?"

"Sure!"

Kiara tries climbing on the side of the bed but Lisa has to lift her up.

"Guess what?"

"What?" she echoes back.

"I get to come home today."

"Yay!"

From the corner of my eye I see Ouray slipping out the door and notice Ezrah keeping his distance.

"What's going on with you, kid?"

The boy shrugs.

"Missin' school today."

"I see that. How much longer 'til Christmas break?"

"Three weeks. Are you really comin' home today?" He changes topic.

"Doc said I could. They're gettin' the paperwork ready."

"Coulda brought you some clothes had I known," Lisa points out.

"Just found out myself, Sugar. I'm sure they can lend

me some scrubs to get home in."

"That ain't gonna keep you warm." Lisa blows a stray curl from her forehead. She's wearing her hair natural again, which puts a smile on my face.

"Taken care of," Ouray says, walking into the room. "Yuma is on his way with a change of clothes for ya."

He arrives with a bag just as the nurse comes in with my discharge papers. Ouray took the kids to the cafeteria to get them a snack five minutes ago, and Lisa just finished telling me they found a flash drive in Finn's diaper bag.

I fucking hope this is the beginning of the end and this mess will be over with soon, because I'm about ready for things to get back to normal. Although I'm not quite clear on what normal for us would look like, I sure as hell would like to find out.

"Need help?" Yuma asks, grinning as he pulls my stuff from the duffel.

"Respect, brother, but fuck off."

He chuckles, walking out into the hallway and Lisa's about to follow him when I call her back.

"Where are you going? He can fuck off but not you. Close the door and you can give me a hand."

She shuts the door but stays on that side of the room, leaning against it with her arms crossed and one eyebrow pulled up.

"That sounded an awful lot like an order."

I don't bother hiding the lecherous grin spreading on my face.

"You gonna stand there? You still owe me a kiss."

A smile plays over her generous mouth as she closes the distance.

It takes a little longer than necessary for me to get dressed, but eventually I'm pushed down the hall in a wheelchair—doctor's orders—with a much too gleeful Yuma behind me.

"Can I come with you, Uncle Yuma?"

"Sure thing, kid. If it's okay with your nana," he tells Ezrah.

I notice Lisa throwing Ezrah a worried look, but she concedes to letting him go with my brother. Something is up with that boy because he's been distant the entire time he's been here. I barely got him to interact.

The painkillers have done a good job and I barely feel a thing when I get out of the wheelchair and hoist myself up into Ouray's big SUV. Lisa insisted she'd sit behind me with the baby, and Kiara was thrilled to have the third row of seats to herself. Normally that's the spot Ezrah claims.

I twist around when Lisa is settled in and keep my voice down so Kiara can't listen in.

"Something wrong with Ezrah?"

"He worries. My boy don't believe good things last. It'll help you're comin' home."

"Not gonna let anything bad happen, Sugar," I reassure her.

"Your brothers fished you out of the freezing water yesterday, Brick. You were barely breathin'," she reminds me, a sad smile on her face.

Maybe Ezrah doesn't believe good things last, but

neither does his grandmother. Suddenly I feel guilty for my earlier thoughts.

I reach back, putting my hand on her knee.

"I'm here, I'm alive, and I'm *not* gonna let anything bad happen, Lisa. Swear to Christ."

Fuck. Hope I can keep my word.

Lisa

I JUST WANT things to go back to normal.

Don't get me wrong, I'm glad Brick is home, but with the kids both at home too, and the baby, there isn't a lot of room to get around.

On top of that it's just Tuesday and I'm scared to send the kids back to school, but I'm also worried about all they'd miss staying home until it's no longer dangerous. That could be a week, or weeks, God forbid.

I just snapped at Kiara, whose chatter has been constant since we got home a few hours ago. The child doesn't give me a chance to think and I'm trying to figure out what to do for dinner. The big crocodile tears in her eyes have guilt surge up like bile, tasting foul in the back of my throat.

"Kiara," Brick calls from the couch. "Why don't you come sit with me and we'll find something to watch on TV?"

I watch as she moves to him, hopping on the couch and cuddling under his arm. He throws me a wink over his shoulder. Great, the man who was just released from the hospital after almost losing his life has to come to my rescue.

Everything in the freezer is rock-hard, but I pull out a package of ground beef anyway. I'll zap it and then turn it into taco meat. It's not complicated and the kids love it so I won't get any complaints. I'm unwrapping the beef when Ezrah tentatively sidles up to me at the counter.

"Can I help, Nana?"

His sweet face is full of concern and I almost lose it right then. My kids count on me—everyone counts on me—I *have* to keep my shit together.

"Yeah, baby. Wash the lettuce for me? It's in the vegetable drawer."

Ezrah is helping quietly, washing and cutting the lettuce into narrow strips, Brick and Kiara are cuddled on the couch watching some Disney movie on TV, and I'm starting to relax while working on the beef.

Then the baby monitor crackles with Finn's cries and the doorbell rings.

I squeeze my eyes closed, take a deep breath, and turn off the burner.

"I can get the door," Ezrah offers.

"No, baby. I've got it, Finn can wait a few minutes."

I grab a towel and walk to the front door while wiping my hands. It's Luna. She winces when she sees me.

"I know this is a shitty time and I'm sorry, but I need to talk to Brick."

"No problem." I step aside and let her in, just as Ezrah walks to the stairs.

"I can get the baby," he offers, "I know how to change his diaper," and before I have a chance to answer he's heading upstairs.

"Kiara, baby," I call out to my granddaughter. "Wanna come learn how to make Finn his bottle?"

Bless the child's sunny disposition and short attention span, because those tears I caused earlier seem completely forgotten as she hops off the couch and joins me in the kitchen.

The voices from the living room are muted and I'd love to know what they're discussing, but I don't want Kiara to overhear.

"Always half from the can and half from the faucet," I explain to her how to mix the concentrate. "Make sure you shake it, and then you have to set it in hot water for a few minutes. It can't get too hot or the baby will burn his mouth, so you have to check."

When Ezrah comes down a few minutes later with a happy Finn in his arms, his bottle is ready.

"I'll take him," I hear Brick announce, and I take Kiara's hand and the bottle, and walk inside.

"Why don't you and Ezrah watch some TV in our bedroom?" I suggest. "I'll call you when dinner is ready."

The two don't argue and head upstairs as I take a seat beside Brick and hand him Finn's bottle. This is still my house and I don't feel like cowering in the kitchen, I have a right to hear what's going on. Luna is perched on the edge of one of the chairs, leaning with her elbows on her knees.

"I was just telling Brick we found some interesting information on the flash drive," Luna catches me up. "It has a bunch of files that look like military transport contracts, and a few audio files. One was a dictation by Kelsey in which she identifies the baby's father as someone she calls V. I was just asking Brick if he had any idea who 'V' might be."

"Like I said," Brick responds, "She never mentioned anything to me. She didn't even tell me I was a grandfather."

"Could it be someone she worked with?" I ask.

"Don't think so. We tried matching that with the employment records Jasper pulled, but nothing seems to fit. She explains being swept off her feet by someone she met at a company event last year, which resulted in a very brief fling. She since discovered a few things about the man that had her decide not to inform him when she found out she was pregnant. She doesn't elaborate what that was."

Luna leans back and runs a hand over her face, looking tired.

"She had reason to be scared," she continues. "The other voice recording was one of her boss, Devin Cranford, and another man. They seemed to be discussing hijacking one of the military transports. We're trying to determine which one, because Kelsey downloaded an entire folder that held information on several scheduled for December and January."

"What are they transporting?" Brick asks, and Luna's face turns grim.

"Have you heard of the Pueblo Chemical Depot?" Brick nods, but I shake my head. "It used to be—well, technically still is—a chemical weapons storage facility, but in part, repurposed to destroy any and all chemical munitions." She looks at each of us with a solemn expression on her face. "The contracts on the flash drive all appear to be weapons transports from various military facilities in the Four Corners area to Pueblo for destruction."

"They're transporting chemical weapons?" Brick's voice is almost a hiss.

"Yup."

"What would someone want with chemical weapons?"

Luna's eyes land on me.

"Good question. That's what we're trying to find out, and why it's so important to know who this 'V' character is. We've had to notify the CID, the Army Criminal Investigations Division."

"What does that mean?" Brick wants to know, shifting Finn to his shoulder.

"Well, things are no longer solely in the hands of the FBI. We have the CID on board, and also the National Security Agency."

"Terrorists?" I know that's what would involve the NSA.

"Jesus," Brick hisses. "You've got to be kidding me."

"Sadly, no. Which is why we have an undercover team from Denver currently making themselves comfortable in and around the compound."

It takes a minute for that to sink in. Undercover FBI agents in the club, I wonder how that is going over? That feeling dark clouds are gathering over my head is back and I don't like it much. This isn't over yet.

A thought occurs to me. "What about Sophia?"

"We already had a team on her. They know."

"Bring her here," Brick grumbles.

"She's looked after," Luna insists, but Brick won't be deterred, shaking his head so vehemently he wakes Finn.

I pluck the baby from his arms and get up, bouncing Finn back to sleep.

"She's with her sister's family and that might put them in danger too. Bring her here," he repeats. "Safer if we stick together. Easier to cover."

Luna seems to consider that and then nods.

"I'll get on that."

It's much later, after dinner and the kids are in bed, Brick and I have a chance to talk. He's been up from the couch a few times and says he's not in pain, but I can see from the deep grooves on his face he is feeling it.

"Do you want me to help you upstairs?"

"I'm good, Sugar, not ready for bed yet. Come here," he says, slinging his arm around my shoulders and tugging me close. "You're tense."

I snort. Of course I'm tense, shit has just gotten really serious and frankly, I'm terrified. Luna explained if it was up to her she would've made the discovery of the flash drive public, but those in charge had different ideas. The concern was that if that news came out, it would only result in whatever organization is behind this to go underground and find another way to get their hands on what they want. Instead the general consensus seemed to be to get more information before a move is made.

Which meant we're left as sitting ducks in the meantime.

So yeah, I'm tense.

"Tomorrow we're gonna have a look at the plans for this place," he says, his voice rumbling in his chest. "We'll figure out how much space we wanna add and where. We're gonna focus on the future, Sugar. You, me, the kids, we're gonna make this work. Fuck all we can do about the rest, but I'll be damned if we sit here waiting for that future to come. We're gonna build it ourselves."

"Not sure we'll be able—"

He shakes me lightly. "I am," he says with conviction. "We may not be able to start building right away, but we'll do what we can, and plan the rest. You and me, Lisa, we're not gonna let circumstances stop us."

I tilt my head back and find him staring down at me; his clear gray eyes warm with love I can feel even without him saying the words.

"Okay."

"Good. Now, there's a few ways I know to work out that tension. Wanna know which one I'd prefer?" he asks, a hungry glare in his eyes.

"The babies…"

"Are asleep in bed."

"You're hurt…"

"Not as much as I will be if you turn me down."

I can feel the dark flush of desire starting to climb up my neck.

"I don't want you hurt," I whisper, his lips already brushing mine.

"Good," he mumbles, "then take off those jeans and

climb on, baby."

The promise in his words has my nipples harden and heat pool low in my belly. I quickly check the blinds are closed before I stand, unzip, and slide jeans and panties off at once. Brick already has his dick in hand, stroking it lazily and instead of climbing on as he ordered, I sink down on my knees between his legs, sliding the tip between my lips.

"Jesus, *fuck*, Lisa…"

"Mmhmm," I hum around his cock, working him with my hand and mouth in tandem.

"Sugar…you're gonna make me come and I'm not near done with you."

The fingers of his good hand tighten in my hair, and I reluctantly let him slip from my lips. His cock, slick, broad, and darkly veined, is an invitation I can't resist. Climbing up to straddle his hips, I position him at my wet entrance and slowly impale myself.

So damn good.

20

LISA

"I'M DONE!"

I walk over to the kitchen table where Kiara and her brother are working on homework assignments.

Both kids got ill with whatever flu has been going around the school a couple of days ago. Brick luckily was well enough on his feet to take the lion's share of care for Finn, while I ran from one kid's room to the other for two days straight. Then last night finally their fever broke and this morning they seemed good enough to come with me to the clubhouse, but I'm worn out already.

We ended up contacting the school and got homework to last until Christmas break, just to be sure. The kids have been working to catch up with this week's assignments this morning and are eager to start their weekend.

This entire place has been like an infirmary; all four older boys got sick, as did Ahiga and Wapi. The rest of us seem to have lucked out. At least so far. Wapi is still a bit under the weather—so are a couple of the kids—and keeping to his room in the bunkhouse. Sophia seems to have taken on his care, checking up on him a few times a day.

She arrived Wednesday night, a little freaked out after Luna explained what was discovered about her employer, but she shook it off and seems to be adjusting. Aside from looking after Wapi, she's also taken on care for the boys, and has been helping Ezrah with his math.

This has left me able to pick up my responsibilities at the clubhouse, much to Ouray's chagrin. He greeted me with a scowl yesterday, but then proceeded to introduce me to the 'new members,' the undercover FBI agents. Five of them, masking as imposing bikers. Surprisingly they blend in well.

"Well done, child." I run my hand over Kiara's braids as she slips from her chair.

"Can I go play now?"

"Clean up your things first, and don't go bothering Papa, he's talking."

It's not a surprise Brick wouldn't stay put for longer than a day. He's supposed to stay off his feet as much as possible, but Tse found him an old golf cart. Brick now zips around the compound in that thing, and Kiara likes to take rides with him.

Last I saw him he was at the bar having lunch with

Shilah, who's been doing the lion's share of the work in the garage.

Kiara stuffs her work in her backpack and skips out of the kitchen.

"How about you?" I ask Ezrah, who has seemed moody. "Almost done?"

"Yeah."

"Are you okay, boy?"

He looks up at me with that stubborn set to his mouth. Something he inherited from Sunny, and maybe his nana.

"I'd rather go to school. This sucks."

It's on my lips to explain again why he's not at school, but think better of it. He knows it's to keep us all safe, but that doesn't make it suck less for him. I get it.

"I know. I'm not liking it much either. Afraid we're both gonna have to suck it up, though."

He grunts something, returning his attention to the homework.

"Hey, wanna start some Christmas baking later?"

I know damn well those cookies probably won't last much past dinner, but I sure like seeing that smile on my boy's face.

"Snowballs?" They're his favorite.

"Sure thing." I grin back at him, while doing a mental inventory of the pantry to make sure I have all the ingredients. "Better get that work done then."

He bends over the worksheet and starts scribbling furiously, while I give the pot of chili simmering on the stove a quick stir before getting together the necessary ingredients.

"Do you have a minute?"

I turn at the sound of Brick's voice and wipe my hands on a towel.

At some point while Ezrah and I were making cookies, Kiara wandered into the kitchen looking to help. So I leave the two of them to finish rolling the balls of dough while I follow the slightly limping man into the clubhouse.

Sophia is at the other end of the space, watching something on TV with Finn on her lap. A few guys are hanging at the bar, but Nosh and Tse are bent over blueprints spread out over the large dining table when we walk up.

"What are we looking at?"

I notice Tse is drawing something on a large sketch pad in front of him. Brick takes a seat and pulls me on his lap, not letting go when I struggle against his hold. Nosh is grinning from across the table and I send him an annoyed look.

"Have a look," Tse says, flipping the drawing around to face me.

I'm stunned. First of all, I had no clue he was that talented, and second, the sketch of the cottage plus extension is amazing. It's a side view with a bump out on the back and a fenced-in yard. The cottage doesn't have a yard currently, just a walk out to the mountain beyond.

"That looks amazing."

"Wait 'til you see the inside," Brick mumbles behind

me.

Tse flips over the page, revealing what looks like a main floor layout. I bend closer. The living room looks the same, as does the dining room, but instead of the kitchen in the short part of the L-shaped space, it now extends straight back from the dining room. Where the kitchen and laundry room used to be is now another sitting room and behind it what looks like a large bedroom with a massive closet, a bathroom, and a new laundry room.

"Two living rooms?"

"A living room and a family room, with three kids in the house you may want a quiet place to sit from time to time," Tse points out.

"It's so big. You figure we need that much space?"

"Sugar, three kids with little bodies now, but they won't be little for long."

"Footprint is already there," Nosh signs.

"He's right," Tse follows up. "Have a look at the original plans, the foundation is there." He points at some lines on the blueprints that extend beyond the house. "That's an underground bunker Nosh built. We can build on that."

"A bunker?" I glance at the old man with surprise. "Why?"

He looks a little sheepish. Tse saves him from answering.

"In those days the club was into some dangerous stuff." He taps on the print. "Good place to stash the family when trouble comes calling."

"How do you get in?"

"Laundry room," Nosh says in his rusty voice.

I mentally go over the laundry room but I'm sure there's no other entrance or exit than the door from the kitchen. Nosh points at the wall separating the laundry room from the stairs going up.

"He says there's a set of stairs going down behind the built-in shelves," Tse volunteers.

The shelves are to your right when you walk into the space. I use them to store cleaning materials and such.

"Awesome." Ezrah—who I didn't hear walking up—leans over the table to look where Nosh is pointing. "A secret doorway."

I can feel Brick's chuckle at my back. "Yes, one you're gonna steer clear of, you hear?" That's all I need, a child with broken bones when he goes tumbling down the rabbit hole.

"Can we go check it out?"

His eyes are on Brick instead of me. My boy knows he'd get nowhere with his nana. I twist around and glare a warning at Brick. He grins and turns to Ezrah.

"Sure thing, kid."

BRICK

I'M PROBABLY GONNA get an earful for this when we get back to the clubhouse, but I couldn't resist the look of excitement on the boy's face. He's still grinning big as he sits beside me in the golf cart.

Nosh wouldn't tell us how to open the door, which only adds to Ezrah's hunger for adventure. He's out of the cart before it even comes to a complete halt, but forgets I have the key. Before the door was never locked to my knowledge, but now it is.

"Hold your horses, kid," I grumble, as I catch up with the boy. "Don't do anything on your own, you hear?" I warn him as I unlock the front door. "Hey—boots," I remind him when he's poised to tear through the house in his winter gear.

He kicks off his boots, tosses his coat on the couch, and I don't bother correcting him again, I understand his eagerness.

He's already busy pushing on the frame of the shelving when I squeeze through the laundry room door. No method to it, though, just haphazardly pressing here and there.

"Hang on there, Ezrah. I've seen you try the same spot twice already. Be smart about it. Start up on one side first and then down the other. You're gonna miss spots otherwise."

I flip over a laundry basket for him to stand on and hoist myself up on the washer. Then I watch as his small fingers slide along the framing of the built-in. It takes him a good fifteen minutes, and some muttered, frustrated cursing, when he suddenly alerts.

"Found somethin'," he says softly.

I hop off and grab the laundry basket out of the way, setting it behind me.

"Show me."

I lean over his shoulder and slide my hand over his between the second and third shelves. He gives me some room and with my fingertips I feel the slightly raised ridge in the side corner, between the two shelves. I push on it and feel it give with a click.

"Sweet," the boy whispers, and we both take a step back.

"You push it open," I tell him and he twists his head, looking up at me. "Go on."

He puts two hands to the right side of the frame and gives it a good shove. The shelving creaks open like a door, revealing a dark stairway going down. As eager as he was earlier, he seems frozen now. I bite off a grin.

"Got a flashlight, kid?"

"In my room," he answers, sounding a little apprehensive.

"Why don't you go grab that? We'll need some light if we're gonna explore."

He squeezes by me, and moments later I hear his heavy steps running upstairs, returning almost right away.

"Here." He shoves the light in my hand, a clear indication he wants me to go first.

"Hang on to the back'a my shirt," I instruct him, and I wait until I feel him grab hold.

There's no railing and the stairs are typical wooden basement steps so I put one hand on the wall for stability. I go slow, so Ezrah can keep up.

I'm surprised the amount of light his small flashlight gives off. The space in front of us looks empty. Just a slightly dank basement under the house, much like any other. But when I swing around to the part that is hidden under the ground—the bunker—I'm surprised to see a fully furnished space.

Large racks of metal shelving house a stockpile of canned goods along one wall. In front of it a kitchen table with four chairs, and an old couch. In the corner I spot what looks like a small generator, probably to run the few light bulbs hanging down from the ceiling. The other corner is obscured by a shower curtain, which I suspect hides a chemical toilet or something. There are no faucets or pipes to be seen for running water.

Along the other wall are three sets of bunk beds end to end. Next are six large water bottles meant for a cooler stacked on their side, and a makeshift counter with a small two-pit burner on top.

Everything is covered in a layer of dust and grime. I doubt anyone's been down here in many years.

"This is so cool." Ezrah steps up beside me, and gapes slack-mouthed at the cavernous space. Then he lifts his face to me. "Can we have a sleepover here?"

I bust out laughing. Typical boy.

"Don't know about that, kid. It ain't too clean down here and there could be critters in them beds." He visibly shivers and I put a hand on his shoulder. "We'll see what we can do with the space, but first we've gotta make sure there's enough room in the house for all of us."

"You staying then? With Finn? You gonna live here?"

There's worry in his voice and I wonder what plays inside that head of his to make him doubt me. I turn to face him and put a hand in his neck.

"Bud, how many times I gotta tell you; I ain't goin'

anywhere."

"You almost got killed," he throws back, a stubborn set to his jaw. "What if they come back for you?"

I don't have the heart to tell him it might not just be me they're after.

"That's why we're all sticking together. You've seen the brothers, you think anyone can just walk in here and hurt one of us? They wouldn't dare try," I tell him.

I have no idea how far off the mark I'd turn out to be.

21

LISA

"CAN I HELP?"

I turn around as Sophia walks into the kitchen.

Two of the boys just finished setting the big table for the kids, and the adults will have to find their own spot. It's a pretty full house tonight with the new additions so I cooked a vat of chili—a favorite for the guys—and I'm about to pull the cornbreads from the oven.

"Sure, wanna dress the coleslaw and toss it?" I point at the massive bowl.

"The whole thing?" She holds up the Mason jar I used for mixing.

"Yep. Throw it all in."

She's a pretty girl. It's no wonder half the male eyes in the clubhouse follow her every move. All legs and ass, and she knows how to move all of it. Yet she seems oblivious to the attention. Her eyes are sad—I'm sure she misses her friend—and her friendly smile doesn't quite mask it.

"You settlin' in okay?"

"Sure. Everyone's been really nice." She doesn't look up and her answer is a little evasive.

"You know," I proceed cautiously. "You're fine to stay at my place if that's more comfortable." In my head I'm already bunking Kiara and Ezrah together, something the boy may not appreciate, but it'd only be temporary.

This time she does turn to me with a smile.

"Kind of you to offer, but I should be fine here. Besides, you already have a houseful."

I shrug. "Offer stands if you change your mind."

"Thanks, Lisa."

I focus on cutting the three pans of cornbread in pieces when Tse walks in. He's never far away when there's food to be found.

"Gonna be long?"

He leans a hip against the counter right next to Sophia, watching her toss the salad. I notice a faint blush on her cheeks as she tries to ignore his scrutiny.

"Not if you'll carry in the chili, the pan's heavy," I tell him.

He throws a rakish grin my way before straightening up and grabbing the heavy pot.

"We better get out there. Can't trust him alone with food."

Sophia snickers, grabbing the bowl of slaw. I carry

the cornbread as she follows me inside.

To my surprise, Wapi has surfaced, sitting beside Nosh. He's still looking a little green around the gills, but he has food in front of him. Somehow Tse manages to coax Sophia in the seat next to his, right across from Wapi, who doesn't look happy.

I can smell trouble. Tse is a relentless flirt and tease, and Wapi is a sensitive soul. It was clear last time the girl was here, he's sweet on her. Problem is, I'm not sure she sees him as anything more than a nice kid.

Ezrah and Brick walking in makes for a good distraction. Ezrah is more animated than I've seen him in a while, especially talking to Brick who smiles indulgently. The two pull up chairs and, with everyone scooting over a little, find room at the table.

"You've gotta see this," Ezrah tells the other boys in between bites. "It's like a cave down there. Creepy as shit."

"Mind your mouth, boy," I warn, pinning him with a glare. "And while you're at it, mind your manners too."

"Sorry, Nana. Can we have a sleepover in the bunker?"

All that is said in one breath and seems to strike the men as funny. I don't find it funny.

"Me too!" Kiara pipes up.

No way on this earth I'm gonna let my babies sleep down there. Lord knows, there could be mold, bugs, rodents. Nu-huh. No way.

"When you're twenty-one," I declare firmly. "And not a day before."

Loud complaints go up from the kids at the table, and I catch Brick watching me, amusement making his gray eyes dance, while I shush the young ones.

"Feeling better, kid?"

I look down the table to where Tse is leaning back from the table, his arm resting on the back of Sophia's chair, directing the question at Wapi.

Oh boy, here we go.

"Don't call me kid. I'm your fuckin' brother," he spits his response, clearly agitated and going from zero to sixty in a hot minute.

"Not at the dinner table," I announce, but neither listens.

Tse is wearing his relaxed shit-disturber smile, while Wapi stares back shooting daggers.

"Just askin' if you're feeling better, *brother*," he says, sarcasm dripping from his words. I notice his fingers lightly stroking Sophia's upper arm. Poor girl sits ramrod straight beside him. Wapi notices too.

"Enough." Ouray's voice is low but firm, inviting no argument. "We've got kids at the table. You wanna piss all over each other, do it outside."

"I've lost my appetite," Wapi announces, shoving his chair back and getting to his feet. Then with a last angry look at Tse he marches out, slamming the door behind him.

I notice Sophia leaning into Tse, her head jerking slightly as she says something softly before moving her chair back as well. She turns to me.

"Dinner was delicious, Lisa. Thank you."

Then without another glance at Tse, she grabs her coat from the rack at the door and hurries outside.

"Kids, you done with dinner?" I ask, attempting to distract from the tension at the table. A choir of yeses goes up. "Good, Kiara? Wanna grab that big tin from the kitchen table? You guys can have dessert in front of the TV."

For the next two minutes all you hear is chairs scraping over the wood floor as the young ones make their way over to the large sectional on the other side of the clubhouse. The adults now have the table, and it's suddenly quiet.

"Care to share what that was about?" Brick is the first one to break the heavy silence.

"Was simply asking a question," Tse dismisses with a shrug.

"Goading is more like it," Ouray corrects. "Which I'm sure has nothing to do with the pretty girl who just ripped you a new one in her soft, sugar-sweet voice, now would it?"

"Hardly a girl," Tse immediately reacts, and with that confirming Ouray's suggestion. "She's thirty-four years old, for fuck's sake."

"And you're forty-one, yet here you are, throwing down with a baby brother like a couple of teenagers with a hard-on for the same girl."

Tse forces a grin on his face and shrugs. "Nah, just ribbin' the kid."

He's lying through his teeth. Ouray knows it, I know it and so does the rest of the table, but more importantly;

Tse knows it.

"Keep telling yourself that," Nosh signs, a smirk on his scraggly face.

"I need a drink," Tse announces.

"Right behind you." Ouray gets up from the table as well, following his brother to the bar.

"Going to my room." Nosh's hands indicate as he shoves back his chair. *"Watch the news."*

Watch the news, my foot. He'll be asleep in front of the tube in minutes.

I get up as well and start gathering the plates.

"I can help," Brick offers.

"You sit. You've already been on your feet enough today. Thought the doc told you to keep off 'em?"

"I'm fine," he pouts and I hold back a grin.

"Yes, you are." I bend down to him and kiss his mouth. "You most definitely are."

His hand in my neck holds me in place, when suddenly a sharp yelp sounds from outside followed by a window shattering.

Above the screams of the children and the barking voices of men, a staccato volley of cracks can be heard outside.

BRICK

I LET GO of Lisa and reach for my gun with my good hand.

"Under the table," I bark at her, already on my feet.

Should've guessed she wouldn't listen, not when

kids' loud fearful screams can be heard from the other side of the clubhouse.

I notice only three of the undercover agents taking up positions by the shattered front window, weapons in hand, while Ouray runs to the back. I've lost sight of Tse when Finn starts to cry in his stroller, where he was asleep next to the kitchen door. I duck and aim for the baby, snatching him up, and clutching him one-armed against my chest. Crouching low, I make my way over to where Lisa is pulling the kids away from the large side window, pushing them down behind the sectional couch.

"To the back," I yell at her over the shouting and the gunfire. "Nosh's room."

"Follow me," I hear her tell the kids, scooping a hysterical Kiara in one arm and grabbing Ezrah firmly by the hand. "Stay low."

I coax the other boys to follow them, backing up behind them as I keep my body turned to the front of the clubhouse until I enter the hallway.

Ouray is already barking into his phone inside Nosh's room, who is herding Lisa and the kids into the small adjoining bathroom. I follow in behind them. The boys are huddled in the bathtub as Nosh pushes Lisa down between the toilet and the small vanity, Kiara clutching to her like velcro.

When Nosh moves past me out of the small space, I meet Ezrah's eyes, wide and afraid, but still he holds his arms out.

"I'll take him," he says, his voice tight.

I'm reluctant to let go of my grandson, but I hand

him off anyway. I'm needed out there and he's safer in the tub.

Ezrah must see the struggle on my face as he curls his ten-year-old body around Finn and says, "I'll look after him, Papa."

Words stick in my throat so I nod instead, turning next to Lisa who is as wide-eyed as her boy.

"Go," she urges. "But by God you come back to me."

"Take this." I shove my gun in her hand. "I'll grab a weapon from the office." Then I step out and shut the bathroom door behind me.

Nosh is peeking between the closed blinds covering his window, a weapon by his side. He waves me into the hallway where I can still hear some gunshots from the front of the clubhouse but more sporadic than earlier.

Ouray is in the hallway, his weapon trained toward the back, where someone is banging on the door.

"Fucking let me in!"

"Tse."

I recognize his voice. So does Ouray, and both of us rush to the back door. Ouray takes up position in the corner while I unlock it. I slowly pull it open, Ouray training his gun on the widening gap.

Tse shoulders his way inside, Sophia in his arms.

"Fuck, what happened?" I follow behind him into his room, leaving Ouray to relock the door.

"Fucking saw her come out of the bunkhouse, heading this way, and suddenly she went down," he mumbles, as he lays her on his bed, tugging at her long, thick, winter coat. She's white as a sheet, her dark hair plastered against her skin. "Blood in the snow underneath her but I can't find where it's coming from."

I help him roll her and as soon as she's on her side, we both see the dark stain blooming on the back of her left leg.

"Scissors," I bark, and start pulling off her boots while Tse rummages in the bathroom.

"She okay?" Ouray asks from behind me.

"Leg shot."

"Got this?"

"Yeah. Go," I assure Ouray.

Tse hands me a pair of scissors and I quickly cut open the leg of her jeans. "That's an entry wound," I conclude, looking at a relatively tidy hole in the back of her leg, but when we roll her on her back, the front of her thigh is a mess. "Towels, brother," I nudge Tse who seems frozen on the spot, his eyes locked on the gaping wound. "And a belt. She's bleeding a lot."

That seems to jar him and he rushes back into the bathroom, returning with an armful of towels. I leave them folded, pressing one to the front and one to the back of her leg.

"Wrap the belt around," I instruct him, pulling my hands out of the way.

I suddenly notice it's gotten quiet. No gunshots, no yelling. I can't even hear the baby crying.

"How tight?" Tse demands my attention.

"As tight as you can."

When he cinches in the belt Sophia moans and I round Tse to get to her head. I stroke the hair off her face.

"Hey, sweetheart. You're gonna be okay."

"What…"

"You got shot, babe." Tse pushes me out of the way and leans over her. "We wrapped you up until EMTs can get here."

As I try to squeeze by Tse to go check on Lisa and the kids, I notice blood on the back of his shirt.

"Brother…"

"I've got it," he says, dismissing me before he turns his attention back to the pale-faced woman in his bed.

"Tse, man, take off your shirt. I think you got hit."

ARROW'S EDGE MC

22

LISA

THE GUN IS shaking in my hand.

I've never held one before, although there've been times I wished for it.

I'll never wish that again, it terrifies me.

What if I have to shoot and the bullet bounces off something and hits one of the kids? I couldn't live with that.

I don't know how long we've been hunkered down here, but Kiara stopped screaming, although her little body still shakes against me. Finn is quiet after I noticed Ezrah pop a knuckle in the baby's mouth, something he's seen me do from time to time to soothe him.

Outside the sound of gunshots seems to have died down, but instead of bringing relief, in here it only raises anxiety. The boys are all staring intently at the door and I find myself doing the same, waiting for someone to burst through, and my hand starts shaking harder.

My heart is hammering hard in my chest when I hear someone moving around on the other side. Then the doorknob turns and my breath sticks in my throat.

"It's me," I hear whispered on the other side before the door slowly opens, revealing Brick's face.

The clatter of the gun falling to the tiles is loud in the small room as it slips from my hand.

"Papa," Kiara wails, releasing her death grip from my neck as she flings herself at him.

"It's okay, Princess. It's gonna be all right," he coos, pressing her head in his neck. Then he turns to the kids in the tub. "You doing okay, guys? Ezrah?"

"We're fine." His words may be decisive but his voice wobbles.

I try to get up to take the baby from his arms, but I barely have my ass off the floor when I drop back down. I'll try again in a few minutes, when I'm not so shaky.

"Is it over?" Ravi asks, his eyes large in his face.

"Not sure, kid," Brick tells him honestly. "I wanted to check on you guys first before I go out there. Can you hang tough for a little longer?" The boys nod, but Kiara clamps on to his neck tighter. "Lisa?"

"Go check." I nod at him and hold my arms out for my baby. "Kiara, let Brick go, honey."

Just that one sentence leaves me out of breath and I force myself to inhale deeply. Luckily Kiara doesn't put up too much of a fight and climbs back on my lap, as

Brick leans down and kisses our heads.

"Right back," he mumbles before he disappears out the door again.

I don't even bother with the gun anymore, it's on the floor by my knee, but the effort to pick it up seems too much. Instead I fold my arms around my granddaughter, and lean my head back to the wall. Then I turn my eyes to Ezrah, who has the baby's downy blond head tucked under his chin.

BRICK

NOSH IS STILL standing guard by the window when I carefully tap him on the shoulder.

"You good here?" I mouth at him when he turns around.

He nods and waves me out the door.

It's quiet in the clubhouse when I walk in. The only person I see is Shilah standing by the front door, looking out at something.

"What's going on?"

He turns at the sound of my voice. "I'm not sure. One minute we're getting peppered with bullets and the next it's over."

I look over his shoulder and see a crowd stand around something on the ground. Then Ouray breaks away from the group and starts this way.

"We've got ambulances en route," he informs me when he gets close. "She hanging in?"

"Tse's with her. He got winged himself while rescuing

her. Left upper arm, minimal damage."

"The kids?"

"Freaked but unharmed. I kept them in the bathroom for now. Anyone else hurt?"

"None of ours," he says. "Wapi is still holed up in the bunkhouse with the other two boys. They're all in one piece."

Elan and Ishtu are the last victims of that stomach bug that's been doing the rounds. After Wapi got it too, we moved the sickbay from the clubhouse to the boys' dorm, trying to minimize the spread.

"They had a fucking armed drone, those cowards," Ouray continues. "One of the agents shot it out of the sky."

I don't have time to wrap my head around the implications of that when the sound of a rapidly approaching vehicle has us turn to watch an SUV barreling through the gate, spitting gravel as it grinds to a halt just feet from us. Luna jumps from the driver's side and marches up to Ouray, who's already waiting with his arms open.

"Situation under control," she says, her voice muffled by her husband's chest. "We caught a navy blue Silverado coming out of the closed-down campground just north of here. As suspected they were close. Gomez is on the scene there."

That's all I need to hear and I turn and hustle back to Nosh's room. I give him the thumbs-up and am about to reach for the bathroom door when it opens and Michael sticks his head out.

"Something's wrong with Lisa."

I squeeze by him and have to lift Kiara out of the way to get to her.

"Everyone into the bedroom," I order, my eyes locked on Lisa. "Michael, take Kiara. Ravi, go get Ouray. Now!" I vaguely hear my princess start crying again, but tune it out to focus on Lisa.

She's breathing, but her color is almost gray, her lips dark. Lack of oxygen? She's still awkwardly wedged between the vanity and the toilet and I try to lift her out. She's dead weight when I pull her free, and I prop her up with her shoulders and head resting against the bathtub. Somewhere in the far recesses of my mind I seem to recall that's what you're supposed to do with a suspected cardiac event.

"Lisa?" Ouray's voice fills the small space and I turn around. He's looking over my shoulder. "Fucking hell," he hisses, catching sight of her.

The sound of sirens from outside are welcome.

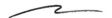

IT'S A BLUR; two EMTs I don't know pushing me out of the way to get to Lisa, running after the stretcher to the waiting ambulance, and Ouray's assurances they'll be right behind us with the kids.

I'm instructed to sit up front so they have room in the back to work on her, and the entire drive to the hospital I have my nose pressed to the small window giving me a view of only her bottom half. Still, I can't peel my eyes away.

When we pull into the ambulance bay at the hospital, I just catch sight of Tse rushing in behind a stretcher. They beat us by a hair.

Lisa's eyes are open when they pull her out of the back of the ambulance. The smile she directs at me is faint, but definitely there, and a little of the pressure on my chest lets go.

"Love you," I manage to tell her right before a nurse holds me back at the doors to the ER.

I give the nurse Dr. Husse's name and the name of the medication Lisa's on, and she gets on the phone immediately, directing me to a waiting area with a wave of her hand.

I don't see Tse anywhere and assume he's being looked after as well. Time seems to crawl while I wait until I hear a familiar chirp.

"Papa!"

Kiara pulls from Ezrah's hold as they come through the door and starts running toward me. I stand up and easily catch her in my arms.

"Where's Nana?"

"The doctor's looking at her, Princess."

"Can we see her?"

"In a little bit." I hope, anyway. "We'll have to wait."

Ezrah and Ouray—who is carrying Finn in his car seat—join us and I ruffle the boy's hair.

"Nana okay?"

"She was awake when we got here, Son. She's gonna be okay."

I have no choice but to believe that. His body presses close to mine and stays that way even after we sit down.

"Most of the brothers are at the clubhouse dealing with the mess, so their women are stuck at home with their own kids," Ouray informs me, "but Trunk and Jaimie will be on their way as soon as Jaimie's mom gets to their place to look after the babies."

"Thanks."

"Any word on the others?"

"They got here moments before we did. I'm assuming they're both being looked at."

"I'll go check," Ouray announces, setting the car seat at my feet before walking over to the nurses' desk.

I lean back in the seat and put my free arm around Ezrah, tucking him closer. Kiara is dozing off against my chest and Finn sleeps obliviously between my feet.

Fifty fucking years old—a shit father for most of those—and here I sit, the responsibility for three young lives weighing heavily, but I'm grateful for a chance to do better. I just don't know if I can do it alone.

"Papa?"

I look down at Ezrah. "Yeah?"

"I'm scared."

Fuck but that boy breaks my heart. I lean down and kiss the top of his head, gathering him a little closer. It would be easy to brush off his fear, but he's proven again tonight he's more mature than he should be at ten years old.

"Nothing wrong with that, kid. I am too, but I do believe she'll be all right."

"Okay." He slumps back against me.

"By the way, thank you for looking after Finn tonight. I knew you were the best person for the job."

"Okay," he mumbles again, but this time I feel him sit up a little straighter.

Not long after, Ouray comes sauntering back and takes a seat.

"She's gonna let us know as soon as she hears anything."

The words have barely left his mouth when his phone rings and he gets up again, walking away as he answers.

Finn starts fussing in his seat at the exact moment Trunk and his wife rush through the door. Perfect timing, since I don't have formula or a change for him, but Jaimie comes prepared with a diaper bag over her shoulder.

"I'll take her," Trunk says by way of greeting, plucking a now sleeping Kiara off my lap before sitting on Ezrah's other side.

"You're a lifesaver," I tell Jaimie, who roots around in the bag and comes up with a bottle, handing it to me.

"I'll change him quick and give him back to you," she offers, lifting a now crying Finn from his seat and carrying him to the nearest restrooms.

"News, brother?" Trunk asks.

"Nothin' yet. Still waiting."

He nods. "She'll be all right. Strongest woman I know."

Damn right she is.

It takes another half hour before someone comes out to give us an update.

Ouray's already gone to deal with the FBI, all three kids are asleep—Finn with a full belly—and Tse has joined us with nothing more than a handful of stitches.

"You're here for Lisa Rawlings?"

"And Sophia Vieira," Tse corrects the young doctor.

"Ah, yes. Okay, Ms. Vieira first. All damage was to soft tissue, no bone involvement, which is good news, but injury wasn't insignificant. They're working on cleaning and closing the wounds."

His eyes drift to Ezrah, who's fallen asleep with his head on my thigh, before lifting them to me.

"As for Ms. Rawlings," he says, guessing correctly Lisa is mine. "She's stable. She had what we call a syncope, which is an episode where not enough blood reaches the brain."

"So not a heart attack?" I ask hopefully.

"No. A syncope occurs sometimes when the heart beats too slowly, but it can also happen when it beats too fast and therefore not effectively. Dr. Husse just arrived and is with her discussing the placement of a device to regulate her heartbeat."

"A pacemaker." I remember Dr. Husse mentioned that as an option should things not improve on medication alone.

"Yes," he confirms. "Although these days they're a little more refined than what you might think, but Dr. Husse will discuss that with you."

"Will I be able to see her before?"

"Let me check for you."

Five minutes later, I'm leaning over Lisa's bed,

brushing a kiss to her lips.

"It ain't gonna take long," she says. "But maybe you wanna take the babies home. They're gonna keep me at least overnight."

"The kids are sleeping now and won't wanna be far from you. It's been a traumatic enough night already, they'll feel safer close by. We're staying until you can come home with us," I state firmly.

She smiles a little and lifts one eyebrow. "The kids?"

"Fine," I admit. "I don't wanna be far from any of you right now. So we're all sticking together."

"Brick?"

I lean closer.

"You know I love you," she whispers.

"Yeah, I know."

LISA

"COME HERE, MY babies."

The early morning sun is leaking through the blinds, as Brick gives the kids a little nudge into my room.

I'm a little sore after the procedure. I was awake the entire time, but it didn't feel like the four hours it apparently took for them to place the device. I keep wanting to touch the spot under my left collarbone where they inserted it under the skin to see if I can feel it, but I had clear instructions to leave it alone.

Brick looks exhausted and the kids are rumpled from sleeping in the waiting room.

"Careful," Brick tells Kiara when she threatens to

climb onto the bed. He scoops her up and holds her over the bed so I can kiss her.

I reach out and brush a hand over her cheek.

"Hey, baby. You doing okay?"

"Papa is taking us for breakfast after," Kiara chirps, her sunny disposition thankfully unchanged after the events of the past twelve or so hours.

"Exciting." I smile at her.

Ezrah, however, looks grave. Too grave. He stands a few paces behind Brick, who lowers my granddaughter to her feet and steps out of the way. Ezrah doesn't move.

"They made a tiny cut," I decide to explain. The boy's always done better with the truth. "Right here." I pull down the gown with my right hand so he can see the dressing. "It only hurts a little. Do you recall last year when Nana's car would sputter sometimes when the weather got cold?" I wait for him to nod. "We had to put a new battery in to help the engine run better, remember?" Again he nods. "Nana's heart was sputtering a bit, that was the problem. Now they put a tiny battery in here," I point at the incision, "so my heart will run better, just like the car."

"Sweet," he mumbles, looking a little more animated.

"Now, I need you to come over on this side so Nana can give you a hug."

I hold out my right arm and he approaches my bed. As soon as he's within reach, I curve a hand around his neck and pull his head down on my good shoulder.

"Love you, boy," I softly mutter in his dreadlocks.

"Love you too, Nana," he whispers, before

straightening up.

"Where's Finn?"

My eyes find Brick's tired ones.

"Jaimie's feeding him in the waiting room."

"You gonna say hello, or just stand there?" I tease him.

In two steps he's beside my bed, leaning down, and I slide my hand along his jaw.

"Hello," he croaks, as he leans his head into my touch.

"You need some rest."

He nods. "As soon as we have you home," he declares. "Lissie is taking the kids and we're gonna sleep all damn day."

I tug on his beard and he lowers his mouth to mine for a sweet kiss full of promise.

"Sounds like a plan," I mumble against his lips.

Kiara clearly has run out of patience and pipes up.

"*Now* can we go for breakfast?"

ARROW'S EDGE MC

23

BRICK

I LEAN AGAINST the doorpost watching Lisa putz around the clubhouse kitchen.

"What are you doing here?"

She swings around at the sound of my voice.

"Workin'," she snaps, before turning back to what she was doing.

Things have been tense since the kids went back to school on Monday. Turns out, Lisa doesn't do well with nothing for her hands to do. Without the kids around to keep her busy, she became restless, unable to sit still. Apparently me pointing that out wasn't helpful.

Then yesterday I had an appointment with my doctor at Mercy, and since Tse was already heading there to pick up Sophia, who was being released—and neither

Lisa or I were cleared to drive—I caught a ride with him, which didn't sit well with her either.

To my surprise I was cleared. The feeling back in all my fingers and toes which are all pink again, and the blisters mostly healed, the doc didn't see a reason why I couldn't slowly start back to work.

Things came to a head with Lisa last night when I tried to be nice and was cooking my very basic spaghetti and meat sauce for her and the kids. She asked me where the vegetables were and I pointed to the jar of tomato sauce. I found out that was not the right answer and she dove into the fridge, pulling out the entire vegetable drawer and slamming it on the counter. I made my second big mistake when I asked her what the big deal was going one meal without a side of vegetables. She looked at me like I'd just pledged allegiance to the devil, turned on her heel, and marched straight upstairs.

I made my third mistake when I decided to let her cool off a little. I served the kids dinner at the island, fed Finn and put him on his blanket on the living room floor, and left Ezrah and Kiara in front of the TV with orders to keep an eye on the baby. Then I went upstairs.

She was in bed, the cover over her head and her back turned to the door. I stood there for a moment, watching the steady rise and fall of her breath before going back down to join the kids.

I didn't have a chance to talk to her until this morning when I found her already up and in the kitchen, packing lunches for the kids. I leaned over and kissed her cheek, asking if she slept well. She took one look at my work clothes, pressed her lips together, and returned her focus to the sandwiches. Then the kids came thundering down the stairs, Finn started wailing upstairs, and the opportunity was lost.

She went with Wapi to drop the kids off at school, and I was already at the garage when I saw his truck driving past toward the cottage.

Now I find she's at work, when she should be home resting.

I step into the kitchen and close the door, shutting us inside.

"Lisa, we gotta talk."

"What do we need to talk about?"

I can tell her defenses are up and decide to break those down before I say another word. I grab a kitchen chair, turn it around, grab her hand, and sit down, pulling her on my lap. Then I lock her in my arms when she struggles to get up.

"Sugar, settle. What's going on in your head?"

"Nothing. I'm just going nuts at home when there are people who need looking after. Sophia needs someone around and the club has enough on their plate."

"You got out of the hospital just a few days ago yourself."

"Don't remind me," she mumbles.

"That may explain why you're working when you shouldn't be, but it still doesn't tell me what's going on in your head? You haven't been yourself."

I try to look at her face but she turns away. Then I feel her body stop resisting and she slumps against me. I have to strain to hear her when she starts talking.

"Those kids, Brick. I couldn't even hold up that gun. What if it hadn't been you comin' in? And to make things worse, I passed out. I had five babies in there, countin' on me, and I fuckin' pass out," she sobs. "Anyone could'a walked in. Grabbed them. Hurt—"

"That's enough, Sugar," I stop her.

Guilt. It fucks with people's heads, mine included.

"They count on me, Brick, and I wouldn't have been able to do a thing. I failed."

I set her on her feet and get up, before I move and lift her to sit on the counter. Then I wedge myself between her legs. I need to be face-to-face with her. I leave my hands on her hips and lean close.

"Ahh, Lisa. Wanna talk about guilt? About failure? Remember, it was me who promised to keep you and the kids safe." Her body goes tight and surprise registers on her face. "And then insisted Sophia comes here, only putting a bigger bull's-eye on the club. Think I haven't struggled with that these past days? Jesus, Lisa, for a while there I thought I might lose you."

"That wasn't your fault," she protests, as I guessed she might.

"No. Just like you being unwell wasn't yours. I wanna bet we aren't the only ones feeling guilty for one reason or another. I can think of a handful who are right now wishing they'd done something different. Truth is, no one can go back and change anything, so all we can do is learn, move forward, and do it smart." She cups my face in her hands and I'm glad she's softening, but I still have a point to make. "And what ain't smart is starting work too soon. You're taking a risk, Sugar."

"I called Dr. Husse." Now it's my turn to be surprised. "After I dropped off the kids," she clarifies. "I'm climbing the walls if I can't do somethin' with my hands."

"Can't you take up knitting?" I tease unwisely, which earns me a dirty look and a growl. I bite off a grin. "All right, what did she say?"

"That if I feel I'm ready, I can get back to work," she says, but from the way she's avoiding my eyes I can tell she's holding something back.

"But?" I prompt, to which she pinches her lips closed and I give her hips a squeeze.

"Fine. She said to take it easy," she reluctantly admits. "I can't lift and am supposed to mind my left arm so I don't open the incision."

I'd still prefer her resting, but realize the inactivity may cause more stress than it relieves, so instead of pushing her to go home, I look for a compromise.

"You need some help," I suggest.

"Everyone's already stretched thin," she counters.

"Then why don't we see if Lissie is able to give you a hand? Jesse is at school and maybe she can bring Lettie. Finn will like the company and Nosh can keep an eye on them."

She opens her mouth to protest but quickly closes it again. Then she nods.

"I'll call her."

"Good. Now, gimme a kiss."

Her lips are soft, pliant, and open willingly when I

slick my tongue along the crease. I haven't had a proper taste of her in days and my body responds immediately. Pulling her butt a bit closer to the edge, I press my hardening cock against the apex of her thighs and swallow her resulting moan. Fuck, yes, I can't wait to get inside her soft, welcoming body again.

Her fingers tighten behind my neck when I end the kiss and rest my forehead against hers.

"Does that mean you have the all-clear in the bedroom?" I mumble, rubbing my nose along hers.

"Do not fucking answer that question," Ouray's voice booms from behind me. I hadn't even heard the door open. "I don't wanna know."

I help an embarrassed Lisa down from the counter before I turn to him.

"You barge through a closed door, you're asking for it," I inform him with a grin.

"And here I thought the kitchen would be safe," he fires back, but he shoots Lisa a wink. "You're both wanted out there. FBI is here."

LISA

NEVER BEEN CAUGHT in the act by a boss before.

It's embarrassing.

"How are you feeling?"

Luna leans close while the men greet each other. Her boss, Damian Gomez, and Jasper Greene are here as well.

"I'm good." I inadvertently touch the spot on my left

side. "A little weirded out I got somethin' stuck under my skin, but no pain."

"Can we use your office?" Gomez asks Ouray. "Now that it's clean?"

"Jasper cleared all the bugs on Sunday," Luna informs me softly.

"Sure." Ouray leads the way to the back of the clubhouse.

Finn is on Nosh's lap when I walk past, but he stretches his little arms to me. I can't resist and carefully pick him up, perching him on my right hip as I follow.

Special Agent Gomez pulls out a chair at the large table by the window and gestures for me to take a seat. Lordy, I may be ass over teakettle for Brick, but that doesn't make me blind. That man is *fine*. All class. Tall and dark, with just the right amount of gray peppered through his hair and goatee, and dark brown eyes as smooth as melted chocolate. When I first met him in the hospital, right after Brick's ordeal, I was too focused on my man to notice.

"I got her," I hear Brick behind me as I sit down, and I smile inwardly at the possessive tone in his voice.

He pushes in my chair and takes the one beside me, scooting it close enough so our thighs touch. Marking his territory. It shouldn't make me feel good but it does anyway. Finn busies himself with the buttons on my shirt.

I hear muffled arguing from the hall moments before Sophia walks into the office on crutches, Tse hovering behind her.

"I can handle it from here," she snaps at him and

shoves the door shut in his face.

Oh boy. Those are some fireworks. My heart bleeds a little for Wapi; I don't think he stands a chance against that kind of chemistry.

Ouray helps Sophia in a seat, trying hard to hide his grin. Seems Kelsey's friend is making an impression in this club. Her attitude fits right in and I smile at her across the table.

"Apologies you had to wait for an update," Gomez starts. "But as I understand you already know there are multiple agencies involved in this case." He throws a raised eyebrow at Luna, who told us that, but she seems unfazed and grins defiantly at her boss. "As you also already know, we we're able to intercept four men leaving the campground up the mountain from here in a dark-colored pickup truck.

"I have some pictures I'd like you to take a look at," he addresses Brick before turning to Sophia. "It's important he identifies them first. If you recognize them, please wait to confirm."

She nods her understanding.

He opens a folder he'd carried with him and pulls out four mug shots, spreading them out on the table in front of Brick, who immediately points at one.

"He's the guy who waved me down at the reservoir." Then he bends over the other three for a closer look and taps his finger on a second one. "This one was in charge."

"Are you sure? You mentioned his face was covered," Gomez probes.

"Positive. I'll never forget those eyes."

I put a soothing hand on his knee under the table. The anger in his voice a testament his ordeal at the hands of these men is far from forgotten. Finn stills at the biting tone of his grandfather and his bottom lip starts to tremble. Brick notices and immediately his face softens as he plucks the baby from my lap, cuddling him against his shoulder.

"The other two?" the agent presses.

"Never got a decent look, but it wouldn't surprise me if it was them."

"Good enough," Gomez declares "The men you identified are Kenneth Greer, second in command to Devin Cranford of Safe Loads, and Cody Hannah, one of its operatives. Did you know them?" he asks Sophia, pushing the mug shots her way.

"Kenny was in the office quite often," she confirms. "Not so much Cody, but I've seen him around, as well as Matt Jenkins and Barney Pasternak." She points out the other two men.

Gomez confirms with a nod, stacks the pictures, and slips them back in the folder.

"As of Monday, Devin Cranford is in custody and the Safe Loads offices are being dismantled as we speak. All military transports under their contracts have been delayed or rerouted."

"Does that mean what I think it does?" I ask, not wanting to get excited too soon.

Gomez grins at me—oh boy, that makes the man positively lethal—but it's Luna who answers.

"Yes, I think we all can breathe a little easier," she

indicates. "Cranford is out of play and his employees are all held for questioning to gauge the level—if any—of their involvement."

Then Gomez takes over again. "Friday night's events appear to have been targeted toward Ms. Vieira. It was our mistake."

I glance over at Brick, who raises an eyebrow at me as if to say, *"See?"*

"Given the direct approach they took with you," the agent directs at the man beside me, "we weren't expecting the calculated attack with a fully armed, military drone, and we were lucky one of our agents was outside at the time and was able to bring it down."

"So it's done," Ouray observes.

"For you it is," Greene speaks for the first time. "For us…" he glances over at his boss who appears to give him a nod, "…there are a few loose ends to wrap up."

"The other guy on the tape," Brick offers.

I'd all but forgotten about the other man. The one Kelsey said was Finn's father. Judging from the approving nods sent Brick's way, no one else had.

"Exactly," Greene confirms. "The NSA is eager to know, but no one is giving us a name."

I watch as he pulls what looks like a small dictation device from his pocket and places it in front of Sophia on the table.

"If you could have a listen. You'll hear your boss's voice, but see if you recognize the second one."

He plays the tape.

"…guys are prepared. When the transport crosses

the New Mexico border, around five in the morning, right as they hit Savage Canyon, the SUV in the rear will blow out a tire. That will bring the convoy to a stop and your men move in. The lead crew of two and vehicle are expendable."

Chills raise goosebumps on my arms as I listen to the businesslike voice. It's hard to believe he's talking about lives. Then a second voice takes over.

"We'll use an RPG, take care of both of them at once. It'll stun the guys in the truck long enough to give us…"

I suck in a harsh breath and lunge to my feet. I barely notice Jasper stopping the tape.

"Jesus, Lisa," I hear Brick beside me, but my eyes are on Gomez.

"You recognize him," he says, more as a confirmation than a question.

V for Victor. Not in my wildest dreams would I have come up with that on my own. The towering, arrogant, frequent guest at my former employer. The man with the cruelest blue eyes I've ever seen.

"Victor," I manage to share as a shiver runs down my spine. "I don't know his last name, but he was a good friend of Hinckle."

24

BRICK

HINCKLE, I RECOGNIZE that name.

James Hinckle, a former member of the Utah Senate, and Lisa's old boss.

I notice the three FBI agents exchanging glances. Gomez doesn't show much more than a muscle twitching under his eye, but the others—including Ouray—are obviously shocked.

Apparently, it's just Sophia and I who have no fucking clue what's going on.

"You have *got* to be fucking kidding me," Ouray barks, startling Finn who immediately shoves his hand in his mouth.

"Someone enlighten me?" I shoot a sharp look Ouray's way.

"Lisa," Gomez starts gently, completely ignoring my question as he focuses on her. "Does the last name Nowak ring a bell?"

"No."

She's still shaking and I grab her hand and tug her back down in her seat.

"Sophia?" Gomez turns his attention to her.

"Afraid not. Why? Should it?"

"Here," Jasper holds up his phone and Sophia peers at the screen. "Have you ever seen him at the office?"

She shakes her head. "I can't be sure. It's possible, but a lot of people are in and out of that office, and the accounting offices are at the other end of the building, so unless I'm coming in or heading out, I don't usually see visitors," she explains with a shrug.

"Can I see?" Lisa asks, holding her hand out for the phone. She takes one look and nods. "That's him."

I glance over her shoulder at the screen. He looks early or mid-forties, with short-cropped hair and piercing blue eyes. Despite the mellow smile on his face, his eyes are stone-cold.

"Now can someone tell me who this Victor Nowak is?" I rephrase my earlier question.

Luna does the honors.

"Remember that case early last year? Those murder victims found in that new development outside town?" Shit, yes I remember that, how could I forget? "Victor Nowak is that big media honcho. He's bought up almost three-quarters of the media outlets in over twelve states in the past fifteen or so years."

"I remember he got away," I point out.

"Technically, we let him go," Gomez fills in. "Had no choice, there was nothing concrete we could pin on him. He slipped through the cracks when we brought down Hinckle as well."

"Can't believe we missed this," Jasper grumbles. "We've been up the guy's ass for years."

"Apparently not far enough," Ouray observes dryly.

"Will this help?"

I glance over at Lisa's profile and note tension around her mouth. With the pad of my thumb I rub the back of her hand I'm still holding, until she turns to me and sends a tentative smile.

"Yes," Gomez states firmly. "It definitely will."

He suddenly seems fascinated with Finn, who is starting to fuss on my lap and I notice Luna is staring at the baby as well. Then it hits me.

Victor Nowak is not just the voice on the tape; he's also the man my daughter had a fling with a little over a year ago.

I look down on Finn's downy blond hair.

"Fuck." Ouray voices my exact feelings.

It appears everyone around the table has clued in, including Lisa, who grabs my arm before she aims a furious glare at Special Agent Gomez.

"Do not even think about it," she spits. "Do not acknowledge it, do not discuss it." Her gaze travels around the table. "This child will never know."

When there's no response, she slams her hands on the table and pushes herself to her feet.

"Promise me," she hisses, turning to me and lifting Finn off my lap. She presses him against her and repeats, "He will never know."

With the baby clutched to her chest, she steps away from the table and marches to the door, yanking it open. I rush up and plan to go after her when Luna's voice stops me.

"Nowak doesn't know." She looks at me steadily. "Kelsey never told him. He doesn't know."

"It's true," Sophia confirms. "When she first started showing and people asked questions, she claimed the father was an old high school friend and would not be involved in the baby's life. No one questioned her too hard after that. I'm the only who knows it was a lie." She turns to me and adds almost apologetically, "I was half-convinced she'd gotten involved with a married man and that's why she called the situation complicated."

"Right," Gomez takes over. "We have one big problem."

"Which is?" I snap.

"We're not the only ones who heard that tape and will come to the same conclusion. The CID and NSA both have copies. Proving Nowak as the father would lend credibility to Kelsey's recordings."

"No."

"Brother…" Ouray tries. I turn angry eyes on him, but that doesn't appear to stop him. "Think of it this way; it could mean the difference between putting him away for the rest of his life, or walking, and then you'll be looking over your shoulder the rest of *your* life. The man has money, he has power, and he wouldn't hesitate one second to mow down whoever gets in his way to get what he wants."

I lean with my hands on the table and hang my head. Goddammit, he's right. This will not please Lisa.

"No guarantees, but for now we'll keep this information to ourselves," Gomez offers. "We'll build the best case we can against Nowak with what we can find. Hopefully it's enough, but you'll be the first to know if, for whatever reason, that changes."

I look up at him and nod.

"Appreciated," I mumble.

A few minutes later, it's just Ouray and me left in the office.

"Don't want that boy to grow up knowing he has an evil bastard as a father," I share.

Ouray walks up behind me and claps a hand on my shoulder.

"In the end, I don't think it'll matter much who the sperm donor was. Finn will be raised by two of the best people he could have as parents."

LISA

"THERE YOU GO, Little Man."

Finn's little hands clasp the bottle as if he's afraid I'll take it away again.

Now that I've calmed down a mite, I'm embarrassed for the way I flew off the handle. In front of Ouray, of Luna. Lordy, even in front of her team. But I'll stand behind what I said. Over my cold dead body is this beautiful little boy going to be burdened with the sins of his father.

I glance at the clock, it's almost two already. The kids will need to be picked up at four and I haven't even started dinner yet. Maybe I'll give Lissie a call after all. See if she's able to fetch the kids from school, it would give me more time to get something going.

The kitchen door opens and Sophia comes in balancing on her crutches.

"I hope you don't mind me barging in, but I need something to occupy my hands or I'll wrap them around a certain person's neck."

I chuckle at her dramatic entrance.

"Which one of the two?"

She lowers herself on a kitchen chair and blows a strand of hair out of her face.

"Tse of course. He's hovering and I'm fed up. I need to figure out what I'm gonna do with my life, now I don't have a job to go back to, and I'd like to do that by myself."

"How about you start by feeding this boy?"

She smiles big. "Yes, gimme him." She stretches out her arms and wiggles her fingers. "By the way, I almost jumped up to applaud you in there."

"For real?"

"Oh yeah. I think you scared them a little."

She grins at me and I grin back as I hand Finn over. She immediately kisses his head. "Lucky boy, you are," she coos, snuggling him close.

When I turn to pull the makings of dinner out of the large fridge, I bump into Brick who immediately closes me in his arms.

"I was a little scared," he says, grinning down on me.

"I meant every word," I stand firm and his face turns serious.

"Don't think anyone doubts that, Sugar. Gomez is gonna do his damndest to keep the baby out of this, but it ain't just up to him."

Letting my forehead drop to his chest, I mumble, "I know."

"Hey…" He tilts up my chin with a finger. "No matter what happens, he has us to look out for him." His eyes drift over my shoulder to Sophia. "All of us."

"You bet," I hear her confirm behind me.

"Now, kiss me, woman. I gotta get back to my transmission service."

His arms tighten around me and I lift my face, pressing my lips to his. Not the kiss I'd like to give him, but as far as I'm willing to go with an audience. I can feel his soft groan all the way to my toes when I break away.

"This job shouldn't take me much longer, I'll be able to pick up the kids from school," he announces on his way out the door after kissing the top of Finn's head.

That means I don't have to bother Lissie. I turn to Sophia.

"Got plans this afternoon?"

"Other than hiding out in here? Nope."

"Good. I could use a hand."

Sophia keeps me company—and Finn occupied—

while I make a start on a hearty stew. It's the kind of day for it. We've had flurries off and on, but when I glance out the kitchen window I notice snow's coming down steady now.

"How much are we supposed to get?" Sophia asks.

"Hard to tell from the forecast. They could predict a couple of inches in town and we get fifteen up here. Or nothin' at all, that's been known to happen as well. Best way to predict the weather up in the mountains is to look out the window."

The next couple of hours we spend chatting about odds and ends, getting to know each other, and the more we talk, the more I like the independent younger woman. At some point, Tse poked his head in, but was quickly dismissed by her when he grumpily reminded her she should have her leg elevated, as per doctor's instructions. I almost felt sorry for him. The moment he disappeared though, she pulled up another chair to rest her leg.

By the time I hear the kids come into the clubhouse, Finn is asleep in his stroller in one of the bedrooms in the back, and we're at the kitchen table peeling potatoes.

"Nana! It's snowing! Can we go build a snowman?"

Kiara, as usual, starts chatting at high volume before she even gets to the kitchen.

"Inside voice, child," I scold her as she comes storming in. "And hello."

"Hi. But can we?"

"Hey, Nana." Ezrah pokes his head in behind his sister. "Can we have a snack?"

I wipe my hands on the towel I have tucked in my

waistband and get to my feet.

"Got homework, you two?" From the pout forming on Kiara's face it's clear she does. Ezrah has homework every day so that's a given. "Right. I'll get you a snack, you two do your homework, and if there's time after that before we sit down for dinner, you can go out for a bit."

Ezrah disappears at once, but his sister is slower, dragging her feet out the door while mumbling, *"not fair,"* under her breath.

"I could always change my mind," I call after her.

Sophia snickers. "She reminds me of me growing up. All princess, all the time."

"You got that right. Only girl with all these boys, she gets away with a lot."

"I bet."

A few minutes later, I walk out with a large plate of sliced apples, cheese, and crackers and set it down in the middle of the large table where all six kids are bent over their books.

"Share," I warn them. "Four of each, apiece." Five heads nod except for my granddaughter's. "You hear me, Kiara?"

She glances up with a mutinous look on her face, but knows me well enough to nod. Lordy, that child's gonna turn me gray before my time.

When I turn back to the kitchen I notice Wapi sitting at the bar, his eyes peeled on the doorway.

"What's with Wapi?" I ask when I sit back down at the table and grab the next potato.

"Why?"

"He's out there starin' at the kitchen, and I'm pretty sure it ain't because of me."

She shakes her head, her eyes on the potato she's peeling.

"I don't know. He's nice, and up until last week I thought he was a buddy. He reminds me of my younger brother."

I wince. From that pining look I caught, I'm pretty sure Wapi sees her as anything but an older sister.

"Not thinkin' he looks at it the same way."

"Yeah, I'm starting to get that," she snorts, her eyes meeting mine, a hint of humor in their depths. "If I'd known getting hurt would draw this much attention, I could've ended my relationship drought six years ago."

I don't bother pointing out she'd caught their eye long before she was shot.

"Six years?"

"Hmmmm," she hums.

What a waste. My mind goes to the many years I stayed willfully single, and then the last two years keeping my distance from the man I knew could break my resolve.

I may not be particularly smart or educated, but experience has given me some wisdom to share.

Putting down my knife I put my hand on her arm.

"Life's too short, honey."

ARROW'S EDGE MC

25

BRICK

KIARA'S GIGGLE JOINS her nana's.

"He's messy," the little princess points out and I look at Finn.

He *is* messy. Lisa decided it was time to try him on solid food and sent me out in the snow last night to get him the high chair from the shed. He's still listing a little to one side, but she says he'll get the hang of sitting unassisted soon. Until then, the harness seems to keep him in the chair.

This morning I have the honor of trying to fit a tiny spoon, with some orange guck Lisa says is good for him, between those constantly moving lips. Needless to say he's wearing it—everywhere—to my frustration and apparently to everyone else's hilarity.

"You're not helping," I grumble when Finn breaks out a smile, showing off the beginnings of his very first tooth.

While he has his mouth open, I try to shove in another spoonful. Of course the moment I do, his little jaws slam shut and most, if not all of it, ends up under his nose. Before I have a chance to scrape it off, one of his waving hands lands on his mouth and rubs the gunk around. Then he shoves his fist in his mouth and tries to suck it off.

"At least he's not spitting it out," Lisa observes, a smile in her voice.

"I suppose one could call that a win."

"Don't be so glum, you'll see, in a couple of days he'll get the hang of it."

She approaches the high chair with a wet towel and with a sure hand easily wipes a squirming Finn clean.

"I'll quickly change him before I go," I offer.

"Let me, you haven't even had breakfast yet. What time is Ouray picking you up?"

We're heading to Albuquerque to pick up a new tow truck. The one we had was pretty old, and even though Ouray hasn't heard from insurance yet, he didn't think we'd get a whole lot back for it anyway. He calls it a capital investment, which is fine by me, I'm just glad I don't have to pay the tab.

We've been bleeding money these past few weeks, having to pass on tow calls, and believe me, with the weather we've been having there were plenty. Every year it's the same thing, the first couple of weeks winter hits in earnest, it's like the road is full of idiots who forget how to drive in slick conditions.

It's generally a busy time of year for us and not just with tows, with snow removal as well. A few of the club trucks are outfitted with blades and every snowfall we're busy plowing the growing number of businesses the club owns in town. We're missing out on tows, though, and with another storm on the way this weekend, we really need that new truck. If this is any indication, it's gonna be a brutal winter.

"Eight," I tell her.

She plucks Finn off his chair and smartly turns him with his back to her clean front.

"That's in ten minutes. Pour yourself another coffee and grab some toast at least."

I manage to pull her close when she tries to walk past and lean in for a kiss.

"Yes, Mother," I tease her with a wink.

Then I watch her walk to the stairs, her rounded hips swaying with every step. My dick hardens in response. I turn to the counter, pouring myself that coffee to give the tent in my jeans a chance to deflate.

Lisa never answered my question about sex when Ouray interrupted us in the clubhouse kitchen a few days ago, and I haven't brought it up again. Doesn't help we're still sharing a room with my grandson, and I'd like to get started on that extension sooner than later, but it'll have to wait until spring.

Fuck, it's gonna be a long winter.

"Uncle Ouray is here!"

Kiara is already running for the front door, pulling it open.

"Mornin' Sunshine," he grins at Kiara.

"Papa tried to feed Finn sweet potatoes, but he got it all over hisself!" she announces.

"That a fact?" Ouray raises an eyebrow at me over her head and chuckles. "Sounds like your papa needs to practice a little more."

"Nana says he'll get the hang of it in a few days."

I don't bother explaining her grandmother was talking about Finn, not me. Ouray clearly finds it all very amusing.

"I'm sure he will."

"Go finish your breakfast, Princess," I tell the little girl, pressing a kiss on her head. "You have to leave for school soon."

Lisa is driving Finn over to Lissie's this morning before taking the kids to school, because she has an appointment with Dr. Husse. I told her I'd come with her—Ouray and I could've gone on Monday—but she insisted since it was just a checkup, she'd be fine.

"I'm just gonna tell Lisa I'm gone. Be right out."

With that I close the door in the asshole's still grinning face, and hustle up the stairs.

"Is that Ouray?" she asks when I walk into our bedroom.

"Yeah, we're headin' out."

She picks up Finn and props him on her hip before lifting her face for a kiss. Instead of taking her offering, I place my hands on either side of her face and lean close.

"We're gonna need to find a solution for the baby, and soon," I whisper, watching as her eyes flare. "Fuckin' blue balls are painful at my age."

"Mind your mouth," she whispers, mostly by rote.

"He's been sleepin' through the night for a couple of weeks now, Sugar. He don't need to be in the same room."

"I'll think about it."

She follows her words with a brush of her lips, which I immediately capitalize on to show her how serious I am. Finn has little patience though, and almost immediately yanks on my beard.

"All right, buddy," I tell him, kissing his forehead. "You be good for Nana."

His face breaks into a smile and he lets out a lusty cry of agreement. At least that's what I hope it is.

Ouray is waiting in his vehicle with the engine running.

"Shut it," I warn him, when I see from the smirk on his face he's about to give me a hard time.

"Finally a good woman in your bed and she comes with a house full of babies. It's too fucking funny." He laughs at my expense as we drive away from the cottage.

I almost tell him to fuck off, but I know it wouldn't do a lick of good.

"You laugh, but I gotta house full 'a love so you won't hear me complainin'."

Much.

He pats my knee as we head down the drive to the road.

"Pleased as fuck for you, brother."

I grin out the window.

So am I.

LISA

"Everything looks great. I'm going to be away for Christmas and won't be back until the first full week of January, so why don't we book you in for the Tuesday. Same time?"

I nod. "Sounds good."

She stands so I do too. It's been on my lips to ask, but it's not a subject I'm necessarily comfortable discussing. She rounds her desk, if I don't do it now, I'll have lost my chance. She reaches for the doorknob and stops, looking at me with narrowed eyes.

"Was there something else?"

"Sex," I blurt out panicked, and immediately feel the heat of a blush creeping up my cheeks.

Dr. Husse chuckles. "Hell, yes. The more the better," she jokes, putting me immediately at ease. "I'm sorry, I should've mentioned it when I had you on the phone the other day. You should be able to go back to your regular activities."

"Technically that falls under new activities, but okay, good to know."

I grin when she barks out a laugh.

"I'm sure it is," she says with a twinkle in her eyes. "Don't forget, I met the man."

I'm still smiling at the doctor's words when I pull up

to Lissie's place. She has the door open before I can get out of the SUV.

"What's that grin for?" she asks when I walk up to the door.

"Today's a good day," I share, as she waves me inside.

I hand her the bag of fresh muffins I picked up on my way from the hospital. She glances at the name on the bag before opening it up to take a sniff.

"Perfect. They'll go nicely with the fresh pot of coffee I just put on."

In the living room, Lettie—who is a month and a half older—and Finn are playing on a blanket on the living room floor, babbling at each other. The moment Finn spots me, his little legs start kicking and his arms come up.

"A-da…"

I pick him up for a kiss.

"Havin' fun, Little Man?"

His hands slap my face and I bend down to blow a raspberry in his neck, making him giggle. I smile at the contagious sound.

"I've got your coffee here, come doctor it up yourself," Lissie calls from the kitchen.

I give Finn another kiss, put him back on the blanket with his little friend, and go fetch my coffee.

"So what makes today a good day?" she asks when we sit down in the living room.

I swallow down the bite of muffin before I answer.

"It just is. I have my independence back. Don't need

a guard to drive the kids to school, or to go see my doctor. It feels good."

"How was the doctor? What did she say?"

I can't stop my smile and quickly take a sip of my coffee to hide it. Not soon enough apparently, because Lissie narrows her eyes on me.

"It's all good," I answer obscurely. "Stitches came out, wound looks good. I can return to *all* regular activities."

"Mmhmm," she teases, grinning at me. "All of them? So how come you're here and not stopping off at home to celebrate the good news with your man?" She wiggles her eyebrows and I snicker.

I'm lucky to have found a friend in Lissie. Something else I've done without for too damn long. My life's been all about the kids for so long, I'd almost forgotten how good it feels to share everyday things with someone who gets it.

"He's on his way to Albuquerque with Ouray. Pickin' up a new tow truck."

"Well, that's poor timing."

"Storm coming in for this weekend," I explain. "They're gonna need the truck. Besides, we still have three kids in the house, and this one," I point at Finn, who is chewing on a corner of the blanket, "is still sleeping in our bedroom."

"So move him. Put him in with Kiara. From what I remember her bedroom is big enough to add his crib. He sleeps through the night, yeah?" I nod. "Then it shouldn't be an issue. It's only until you guys have a chance to build the extension. She's six, she's gonna love her bunking with her little brother."

She's probably right. Kiara is a happy kid, loves the baby, and doesn't like hearing she's not big enough to carry Finn around like her big brother does. She'd be thrilled to be given a little responsibility.

The only thing that's held me back was Finn still feeding during the night—but now he sleeps right through—and not wanting to take away the first bedroom Kiara has had to herself. The first is no longer an issue, and the second may well have been about me wanting to give that to her instead of what she might want for herself.

"Good point."

"I know." Lissie grins at me. "You've gotta get creative when you have kids running around and you want a little fun time with your man." She holds up two fingers. "One; set your alarm at four thirty, it gives you enough time for some early morning nookie before the rugrats need attention. And two; lunch hours are underrated. Older kids are in school, baby's down for a nap, and you've got the whole house to play. Why do you think Yuma comes home for *lunch* almost every day?"

"Every day?" My eyes about fall from my head.

"Mmhmm," she hums again, her eyes twinkling.

Wow. Shows you how limited my experience is. I don't think I'd mind more of Brick every day. Since we got together, we really haven't had a chance to find our groove. Too much shit kept happening. But with the latest report that Nowak is in Mexico somewhere and the FBI is poised to nab him the moment he steps over the border, there's no longer anything stopping us from living a regular life.

Maybe it's time to find a new normal.

"Do you have time?" I ask Lissie who looks at me questioningly.

"For?"

"Helping me move Finn in with his big sister."

She immediately gets to her feet.

"Damn right I do."

Standing up as well, a few butterflies start swirling in my stomach from excitement.

I'm standing on the edge of a new tomorrow.

26

BRICK

IT'S CLOSE TO eleven at night when I pull the new tow truck up to the garage.

Much later than I had anticipated.

We got to Albuquerque a little after noon, had a quick lunch, and Ouray helped me run an errand before we finally got to the dealership. That took a few hours and on the way back we ended up stopping at the diner in Bloomfield. The snow started falling when we passed Aztec and got worse the closer we got to Durango.

The big storm arrived early.

Lisa left on the hall light I notice when I walk to the cottage. I talked to her when the snow started falling and told her not to wait up, but I'm still a little disappointed. Goes to show you how deep I've fallen for the woman.

Trying to keep the noise down, I kick off my boots and head for the kitchen for a glass of water. Then, making sure we're all locked up, I tiptoe up the stairs, peeking my head around Ezrah's door first. He's lying on his back in bed, one arm folded up under his head, in a typical guy-pose. Next I look in on Kiara, and I immediately notice her room has been rearranged. Her bed, which was first jutting into the room with the headboard butted up to the middle of the wall on the far side, is now lengthwise along that wall. To my surprise, Finn's crib is along the other wall, foot end to foot end.

My woman's been busy.

I bend over Finn's bed and notice he's also on his back, both his little pudgy arms flailed up beside his head, his little lips pursed in sleep. Leaning over, I press a kiss to his forehead before turning to Kiara—starfished across her bed as usual—and do the same with her. Then I walk to Lisa's bedroom, *our* bedroom, and notice a faint light coming from under the door.

The light on the nightstand on my side of the bed casts a soft glow and I can see a few of the tight curls of her hair sticking out of the blanket she is buried under. I'd love nothing more than to dive under the covers and pull her in my arms, but first I want to wash the day off me. A two-minute shower takes care of that.

With Finn in the other room, I forfeit putting on clean boxers and slide into bed in the buff. There I discover I wasn't the only one with those thoughts and fling back the covers to find luscious stretches of silky soft, dark skin.

"Hey, honey," she murmurs, rolling over to face me. "Sugar…"

Suddenly grateful for that quick rinse in the shower, I reach out, tuck a curl behind her ear, and let my hand slide down her neck, over her shoulder, and down her arm.

"I have the all-clear."

Her accompanying smile has me lean in and kiss those plump lips, while my hand continues exploring her curves. I taste her deeply, her mouth still flavored with a touch of mint. Lisa's lean fingers on a path of discovery of her own. She scrapes a nail lightly over my nipple, and I hiss in her mouth as goosebumps break out over my skin.

"Wanna take my time with you," I mumble against her lips before pushing against her shoulder, pressing her back into the mattress, and partially covering her with my body.

I wedge a leg between hers, sliding my hand over her breast and brushing her nipple with the pad of my thumb. I can feel the heat of her core pressing against my thigh, already so wet, and my cock gets impossibly harder.

"Brick," she pleads against my lips when I let my fingers trail down between her legs, testing her slick folds. "Don't make me wait."

She may have different ideas than I do, because she groans in complaint when I start sliding down her body, my lips and tongue marking every delicious inch of her skin. I spread her legs, wedge my shoulders under her thighs, and grabbing her hips firmly, lift her to my mouth.

Her fingers tunnel in my hair, and I see her back arch off the mattress when I lift my eyes. I flick and roll her clit with my tongue, every so often running it flat along her crease. I love hearing the sounds she makes as I drive her to the brink and then back off.

"Don't. Stop," she grinds out between clenched teeth when I do it again.

"Tell me what you want," I hum against her sensitive flesh.

"Brick…"

"Gotta tell me what you want, Sugar. Give you the world, all you gotta do is ask."

"Fuck me."

Jesus. I almost lose my shit hearing those words from her.

"How do you want me?"

Her fingers slide from my hair as I push up on my arms and her eyes blaze in mine. Instead of answering she rolls over, pulls up her knees—so her fucking gorgeous rear sticks up in the air right in front of me—and looks at me over her shoulder.

"Like this."

There's nothing fucking sexier in the world.

I nudge her knees wider so mine fit between, and run my hands over the round globes of her ass. Taking my cock in hand, I slide the bulbous head through the wetness gathered between her legs. Then I take a firm hold of her hips and surge balls-deep inside her.

The tight, vice-like grip her body has on my dick has my eyes almost roll to the back of my head.

"Nothing like it, Sugar. Bein' inside your beautiful body is the closest I've been to heaven. Ever."

"Less talking, more moving," she complains over her shoulder.

I don't need to be told twice.

Doesn't take long to have me hanging on by my nails, waiting for her to let go first. Sliding a hand around her hip and between her legs, I work her clit until I feel the walls of her pussy spasm. She throws her head back, crying out as I pump inside her, grunting my own release.

"Fuck, I missed that," I whisper in her hair, when we're spooned under the covers a little while later. My arm is tucked around her and she grabs on to the hand I have pillowed between her breasts.

"Me too. Now get some rest. Your alarm's gonna go off in a few hours."

If it weren't for the snow piling up outside, I'd be tempted to play hooky in the morning.

Seconds later I drift off, my body tired and well-sated.

LISA

"WHY DIDN'T YOU stay in bed?"

Brick is standing at the counter, pouring a coffee in a travel mug.

It's four in the morning; he may have gotten three-and-a-half hours of sleep in.

"Because I can go back to bed and sleep another few hours before the kids wake, but I need to make sure you have some food in your stomach before you go out there."

"Been takin' care of myself for a few years now," he observes, only half-joking.

"I'm sure you have, just like I've been looking out for myself for plenty 'a years, but that hasn't stopped you yet either, has it?"

"Stubborn," he grumbles, reaching for me.

"You sure are," I fire back, leaning into his embrace, just in time to feel the rumble of his laugh.

I receive his thorough kiss and disentangle myself, pulling a bag of bagels out of the breadbox. I pop one in the toaster.

"Butter or cream cheese?"

When his answer is not forthcoming I glance over my shoulder to find him grinning at me.

"Cream cheese," he finally says. "But I'm gonna have to take it with me. Tse is coming with me. We're doing the Riverside apartments first. He's helping shovel the sidewalks."

"Should I make him one too?"

I'm already starting to pull another bagel out when his arms wrap around me from behind, and a hand squeezes the bag shut.

"He's a big boy, Sugar. He can make his own damn bagel."

"If he's anything like you, he won't."

"Then let him get his own woman so she can worry about him."

I snort just as the toaster pops the bagel up. "He's

already got his eye on one." I quickly slather it with cream cheese and wrap it in a paper towel, handing it to Brick. "Although I get the sense he's mucking that up."

Brick barks out a laugh, grabs his travel mug, and still snickering, presses a hard kiss on my mouth.

"She'll need to be made of stern stuff to straighten him out. Tough, like you," he says with a wink.

I give his arm a shove and follow him to the door where he gives me another firm kiss.

"You be careful out there," I caution him. "I'm gonna need you back."

"I will. Should be done around noon or one. What are your plans today?" He shrugs on a coat and shoves his feet in his boots.

"Sleep a little more and I promised Kiara pancakes."

"Save some for me?" he asks, pulling the door open and a burst of cold winter air blows straight through my nightgown. When I nod, he stops for another brush of his lips before stepping outside. "Love you, Sugar."

"Love you too."

I stand in the doorway for two seconds, watching him walk toward the clubhouse, before it gets too cold and I shut the door.

Upstairs I climb back under the covers, still smelling of Brick.

***

"Now CAN I have another?"

Kiara shows me her empty plate.

She wanted three pancakes like her brother and I gave her two with the promise she could have another if she cleaned her plate.

"Yes. Boy? You want another as well?" I ask Ezrah, who is keeping Finn busy in the high chair.

I just fed the baby some sweet potatoes—which is fast becoming his favorite thing—and his clothes are still miraculously clean. He's currently chewing on his spoon.

"I could eat another."

I load the kids up with more pancakes and head for the laundry room to switch the loads around when the doorbell rings.

"I'll get it!" Kiara yells.

"Sit your butt down and eat your pancake, child. I'll get the door."

The woman on the doorstep is a surprise and I keep hold of the door and block her line of sight into the house. I'm grateful the kitchen can't be seen from the small entryway.

"Ms. Lunsden. I'm afraid Mr. Paver isn't home."

She tries to peek over my shoulder into the house, but I close the door a little farther so only my head is sticking out.

"I'm here to see the baby," she announces arrogantly.

"I'm afraid that won't be possible, but if you give me a minute, I'll give Mr. Paver a call. Maybe you can schedule a time with him."

I start closing the door but the woman pushes from the other side and suddenly I'm staring down the barrel of a gun.

"Where's the child?"

Her face has gone hard and I fight the urge to look over my shoulder to make sure the kids are still hidden from sight. I look beyond her outside, hoping I can see someone—anyone—so I can yell out. I don't care what happens to me, but I can't risk her getting anywhere near my babies. I need to buy time.

"They're not here," I lie, praying none of them decide to come checking. I squeeze myself through the door opening, walking straight into the gun, causing her to take a step back. I pull the door almost shut behind me.

"What the fuck is taking so long?"

The hair on my neck stands on end when I recognize that voice, and to my shock, from the rear of her car—which is parked right in front of my door—steps a tall, and all too familiar figure.

"She says the kids aren't here."

He pins me with those cold blue eyes and steps up behind the woman.

"She's lying," he bites off. "They're inside. Aren't they, you black cunt? Remember me? Always wondered what happened to you. Did you miss me?" Bile surges up my throat as he grabs his crotch. "Bet you remember this, though, don't you?"

I'll do anything—absolutely anything—to keep this man from my children, but the thought of having this man force me to do something, I never wish to experience again, sends cold fear up my spine. I can't hide the shiver.

He laughs, apparently satisfied with just my reaction to his threat, as he takes the gun from the woman's hand. With the hard touch I recognize, he grabs me around the neck and presses the barrel to my head.

"Move," he growls, as I claw my fingers into the forearm he holds pressed against my throat. He doesn't even seem to notice.

The social worker pushes open the door, walking in, and I'm pushed inside behind her. My eyes fill with tears as I'm led straight through to the kitchen.

To my surprise it's empty.

"Where are they?"

"I told you; not here." My voice is hoarse, the sparse air burning my throat.

The woman looks at me disbelieving. Their half-eaten pancakes are still on their plates.

He presses the barrel into the side of my skull and his arm around my neck squeezes tighter.

"Where?" he barks in my ear, the foul smell of his breath wafting up my nose.

"Not…here…" I repeat, forcing the words out.

I feel him let go of my neck, but before I can register what he's doing, a sharp blow hits the side of my head and I start falling.

"Look for them!"

Right before I hit the floor, a gunshot rings out.

Then everything goes black.

ARROW'S EDGE MC

21

BRICK

"FUCKING FLOOR IT, brother."

Tse, who refused to let me behind the wheel, is driving through the snow like a fucking maniac, but it's still not fast enough for me.

We'd just been finishing up the parking lot of the club's bar/restaurant, The Brewer's Pub, when my phone rang. I about had a fucking heart attack hearing Sophia's voice on the other end. She told me Michael had come running into the kitchen at the clubhouse, where she'd been alone; warning her there was trouble at the cottage. That's when she'd heard a shot. I instructed her to call 911 and then dial Ouray's house right away.

I've been trying to call Lisa's number but there's been no answer. I don't want to think what might've happened to her or the kids. I try Ouray again; he's not been picking up either. Just as I get kicked to voicemail again, Tse's phone starts ringing. Maneuvering the heavy truck with one hand, he pulls his phone from his pocket with the other and tosses it to me.

"It's Ouray," I tell him and hit speakerphone before barking, "Talk to me."

"Lisa's here. We've got a situation, brother. CPS chick was in cahoots with Nowak. Nosh walked in on them, armed, and hit Nowak but the bitch took off running. Fucking old coot must've gone after her. Her car's still here so I'm guessing she ran into the woods."

"Lisa okay?"

"She'll have a goose egg, but she's got a hard head she says."

"And the kids?"

The silence that follows lasts too long, and dread creeps up my spine.

"Brother…"

Tse turns right onto County Road 205 and makes an immediate left up the Arrow's Edge driveway.

"Can't find the kids," he finally answers, but by then we're already blowing past the clubhouse and are pulling in beside Ouray's SUV.

I'm out of the truck before the wheels stop turning and storm into the house, finding Luna on her phone, barking orders at someone, and Lisa sitting on the couch with Ouray pressing a towel against her head.

"Shit, baby…"

I drop down on my knees in front of her and only

then do I notice the body of a man lying in a pool of blood on the kitchen floor.

"Who the fuck is that?"

"Victor Nowak," Lisa says in a flat voice.

Pissed off I turn to Ouray.

"You make her sit here and look at that?"

He gets to his feet and shrugs. "She won't leave. Besides we have some more pressing issues."

"My babies," Lisa reminds me.

Shit.

"We figure they could've gone out the back, maybe the CPS woman took off after them," Ouray suggests. "Luna is getting her team up here to track them. Cops are on the way. All our guys are heading in as well. Yuma is already out there going after his old man. Paco is a good tracker; if they're out there he'll find them."

I don't think they've gone outside at all, but I don't say anything. I don't want to get Lisa's hopes up to then disappoint her. As I get up off the floor I hear sirens in the distance.

"Stay with her," I tell Ouray, as I head into the kitchen.

"Don't fuckin' mess with that scene," Luna barks at me, all business.

I step over the body, vaguely recognizing blond hair in the bloody mess left of his head. The laundry room door is closed, but when I open it and look around the corner to the built-in shelving, I see the right side of the framing protrude a little and am able to pull it open. The only thing I can see is the first stairs going down, but beyond that is nothing but inky darkness.

Taking a few steps down, I can hear muffled crying and a sharply hissed shush. My chest expands with relief, as I pull my phone from my pocket and flick on the flashlight.

"It's okay, guys. It's me," I call out.

"Papa!"

I make my way over to where all three kids are huddled on one of the bunks, Ezrah shielding them with his ten-year old body, in complete protector-mode. Kiara is trying to struggle free, but her brother will not let her move.

"It's okay, Son. I've got you," I mumble, carefully touching his shoulder. "You did good, Ezrah, keeping them safe. I'm so proud of you."

Slowly I feel the tension draining from his tight muscles, and it's not until he finally releases his arms and turns around I see Finn, wedged between the boy and his sister. Kiara flings herself at me and I can barely catch her, but my eyes never leave Ezrah's, filling with tears.

"You did good, Son. You kept them safe." I prop Kiara on one arm and hook a hand behind the boy's neck, pulling him close. He presses his face in my shoulder and I feel his body shaking.

"Ba!" Finn announces loudly, as I hear footsteps coming down the stairs.

"Here you are." Luna walks up to our huddle, relief clear on her face. "Thank God."

"You wanna take Finn? I've got these two."

I wait until she's picked up the baby, who is blissfully

unaware of the ordeal they just went through. Then I hoist Ezrah on my other hip without a word of protest from the boy.

"I need you both to push your face in my shoulder, okay? I will explain later, but I need you to do as I say."

With their faces averted, I rush up the stairs, walk into the kitchen where several officers are standing around the dead man. I ignore them, carefully step around the lifeless body, and move into the living room.

"Thank you, Jesus," Lisa whispers, when she sees us.

Blue, one of the EMTs, just enters the front door as Lisa jumps to her feet, holding out her arms. Kiara throws herself at her nana, but Ezrah's hold on my neck doesn't let up.

"Let's get them out of here first, Sugar."

Blue nods her understanding and grabs coats from the coatrack in the hallway, tossing them over the children as we pass her.

LISA

"ARE YOU SURE?"

Blue puts the last of the butterfly bandages on the small cut the butt of the gun made on my head.

She would've liked me to go with them to the hospital to get checked out, since I did pass out briefly. Other than a bit of a headache, though, I don't feel any ill effects, and I think the kids have been through enough of an ordeal today.

"Positive. If I feel anything weird at all, I promise

I'll go in, but for now I think we need a break from upheaval."

She nods her understanding, smiling at the kids plastered to my side. Brick is across the kitchen table from me, feeding the baby his bottle. I don't think any of us will let any of the others out of their sight for the foreseeable future. Except the next minute Detective Ramirez—Blue's husband—and Special Agent Gomez walk into the kitchen.

"Sorry to interrupt, but we'd like to ask you a few questions."

Right, I should've known. Hopefully this'll be the last time I need to give a report to the cops. The absolute last time. I've given enough statements to last me a lifetime but this round I'm telling it all. It's not going to be pretty.

"Can you give me a minute to get the kids settled?"

"Of course. Why don't you join us in Ouray's office?"

"I'm coming with you," Brick announces.

"What about the kids?"

"Sophia's here and Lissie is on her way to wait here for word on Nosh and Yuma. Trunk is coming too," he clarifies. "They can wait until we've got the kids sorted." He reaches over and brushes a curl from my forehead. "You okay?"

"I'll be fine," I assure him with a tight little smile. I'll be fine when that woman is caught and the men after her are back safe and sound.

Five minutes later—my kids installed on the couch with Trunk and Jesse, Lissie's oldest, and his mother and

Sophia not far away with both babies on a blanket on the floor—Brick grabs my hand, gives it a squeeze, and walks me to Ouray's office.

Both Gomez and Ramirez are sitting at the big conference table, Gomez on his phone while the detective indicates for us to sit. Even when we do, Brick doesn't let go of my hand.

"Sorry about that," the FBI agent apologizes when he ends the call. "That was Luna; the coroner and crime scene team just arrived. I'm sure they'll be a while. You may want to consider staying somewhere else, at least for tonight. Remind me to give you a number for a cleaning company who handles things like this after we're done here."

"I'll clean it."

Three pairs of eyes look at me disbelieving.

"Sugar…"

"Brick, I'm cleaning it." I turn to him, slipping my fingers between his. "I want to." Holding on tightly to his hand, I face the officers. "I know that man as Victor, a friend of the Hinckles and he was a regular visitor at the big house in Moab."

"You saw him there," Gomez confirms.

I don't bother stopping the derisive snort forming. "More than I cared to."

Brick's hand spasms in mine. "What do you mean?"

"He was a special kind of racist. A bigot," I take a deep breath in and blow it out before I add, "the kind who enjoys bullyin' and violatin' those he hates. I imagine mopping up his blood'll give me some satisfaction."

The sudden silence feels thick in the room when Brick suddenly lets go of my hand and surges to his feet, slamming his fist on the table.

"He raped you?" he says on a whisper that holds more venom than a rattlesnake, and I duck my head. When there's no answer he bellows, "That piece of shit fucker raped you?"

"Easy, brother…" Ramirez cautions, pushing himself out of his seat, but Brick is already on the move, hauling out with his fist and planting it through the wall next to the door. Then he yanks it open and stalks into the hallway, the detective rushing out behind him.

I know I should've told him before sharing a bed with him. I avoided it because that existence, where I had no choices and no power, was behind me and what would be the purpose in bringing it back to life? I'd given those people all they were going to get. In the two years since I've been here, I was treated with more kindness and respect than I'd received my entire life. Why would I risk letting old harm sully the beautiful life I was building?

Still, I should've told Brick. Shouldn't have held back with him, that was a mistake.

"I'm sorry that happened to you," Gomez breaks through my thoughts. "Why didn't you ever report that?"

I shrug. "And then what? Wouldn't have made a difference. I'm pretty sure the cops have a stack a mile tall of sexual abuse accusations just like it. The word of a black woman against a powerful white man? How far do you figure that would've gone?"

The agent looks uncomfortable and I know I got my

point across.

"Got my amends, though. Man's in my house, no longer breathin' so don't feel bad for me. Like I said, cleaning his blood off my floor will feel like a sweet justice."

Ramirez walks in right at that moment and takes his seat.

"He's cooling off," he says by way of explanation. "Ouray's got him."

"Good. Now if you don't mind, I'd like to get this over with," I suggest, and for the next twenty minutes give them every detail I remember of the events from earlier today.

They share what they were able to piece together from the boys' accounts. Apparently, Nosh had just come back with the boys from a hike, and some target practice up the mountain, when he spotted a guy getting out of the car parked in front of the cottage. He sent Michael to the clubhouse and told the others to stay put. They watched him sneak into my house and heard a gunshot seconds later. Then they saw a woman bail out the back door with Nosh on her heels.

If not for Nosh, I realize things might've ended a lot differently today. Once again I owe the old man a huge debt of gratitude.

Just as I come out of the hallway, the front door to the clubhouse opens and Yuma walks in, a supporting arm around his father. I rush over and help him get Nosh out of his coat. The old man is frozen.

"I'll get him something warm," Lissie announces,

having rushed over as well.

Nosh is trying to sign something but I have trouble making out the words, his hands are shaking too hard.

"He says you're a sight for sore eyes," Yuma translates. "He didn't know what state you were in when he took off after the woman, but he was afraid she snatched the baby. He noticed the empty high chair and ran after her."

I cup Nosh's grizzly face in my hands.

"You're a fool, old man, but I love you anyway," I tell him, making sure he can read my lips. The grin on his confirms he did.

"He had her pinned in the snow," Yuma explains. "Sitting on her back with his gun to the base of her skull and didn't want to let up. Feds were two steps behind me when I found them and took her into custody. They were both near frozen."

The front door slams open again, this time revealing Brick and Ouray. Brick's eyes find me right away and he stalks over, pulling me into his arms roughly as he buries his face in my hair.

"Fuck, Sugar," he mumbles.

I wrap my arms around his waist, holding on tight, offering my silent apology and understanding his. That's what love should be, acceptance and forgiveness.

When I finally let go my head is throbbing but my heart is full.

28

BRICK

IT STILL LOOKS dark outside when I open my eyes. The only indication it's later than it looks is the fact Lisa's no longer in bed with me and the baby is gone from the crib.

We stayed in the clubhouse last night. Ouray let us use his old bedroom behind the office, the only one big enough to house Finn's crib as well. Lisa had been adamant having the baby sleep with us, and I didn't object, sharing her need to keep him close.

Law enforcement roamed around the compound until about eight last night. I almost had to sit on Lisa to keep her from preparing food for all of them. Ouray ignored her protests and simply ordered a stack of pizzas for dinner, to the kids' delight.

She put the kids to bed, and didn't last much longer herself, the events of the day catching up with her.

I spent some time drinking with my brothers after that, but when I rolled into bed and pulled her in my arms, I was suddenly not tired anymore. We never mentioned what she'd revealed in Ouray's office, unable to change the past or claim revenge for her, I'd pushed it to the back of my mind.

Until I felt her soft skin under my fingers. Skin that piece of scum had defiled, the body I loved so much violated by his touch, and the rage I felt earlier came back in full swing with nowhere to direct it.

Spent half the night lying awake, reminding myself how grateful I should be to be listening to the steady breaths of my grandchild and of the woman who claimed my heart. Could've lost them like I lost my daughter, and I don't think I'd have been able to come back from that.

A quick glance on my phone shows it's high time to get my ass out of bed. A cool shower in the en suite wakes me up the rest of the way, and by the time I walk into the great room I feel half-human. To my surprise most of the brothers are here, as are all the kids.

"Papa!"

Kiara comes running toward me and I scoop her up in my arms.

"Morning, Princess." I kiss her forehead.

"Nana said we shouldn't wake you, but you took soooo long." She sighs dramatically.

I walk over to the large sectional where Ezrah's eyes are locked on the screen of the TV. Some kind of

PlayStation game involving a lot of shooting, by the looks of it. I set Kiara back on the couch and ruffle her brother's dreadlocks.

"Sleep okay, Son?"

He tilts his head back and looks up at me.

"Yeah. Took me a while," he admits.

"Me too, kid. Your nana in the kitchen?"

"Probly," he mumbles, his attention drifting back to the game.

On my way to the kitchen, I'm greeted with some chin lifts and 'mornin's,' which I return. I find Sophia and Finn, who welcomes me with his wide smile from the high chair Ouray fetched from the cottage before dinner yesterday.

Last night had been filled with regrets and guilt on the part of just about everyone over the empty comfort of a few beers. Hindsight being twenty-twenty we should've never left the old man to guard the compound by himself, but we all assumed the threat was dealt with. The FBI thought they had Nowak covered in Mexico. We were all wrong.

I'd voiced my gratitude to Nosh for his quick actions, which may well have saved Lisa from a fate worse than the cut on the side of her head. The old man brushed it off and luckily hadn't seemed any the worse for wear following his chase after the Lunsden bitch.

Hopefully we'll get an update today, because I'm curious to know how she got involved in this scheme.

I lift my boy from his chair and onto my arm. His little fingers instantly tangle in my beard. Sophia turns from where she's washing dishes at the sink, her crutches leaning against the counter.

"Morning." She smiles as she wipes her hands on a towel. "Lisa said you were restless all night and to let you sleep."

Damn woman looking after me again, when I should be looking after her.

"Where is she?"

I know the answer before hearing the words. I can see it in the way her eyes suddenly avoid mine.

"She said she had something to do at the house."

Goddammit. She's over there by herself. I'm sure it's not by accident she took off while I was still asleep. I bet she knew there'd be no way I'd let her go over there alone.

I quickly kiss Finn and plop him back in his seat.

"Mind keeping an eye on him a little longer?"

"Not at all," Sophia says with a twitch of her lips.

The smell of bleach greets me when I open the door. I find Lisa on her knees in the kitchen scrubbing at the stain on the floor, her ass up in the air. She doesn't even bother turning, she already guesses it's me.

"Was hopin' to get this done before you got up." There's a note of irritation in her voice.

"Figured as much," I return immediately.

"You don't need to be here, Brick."

Hell no, we're not going to go there.

I step up to her from behind, reach down, and grab her under her arms to pull her to her feet, ignoring her grumbled protests as I turn her in my arms.

"Yes, I fuckin' do," I growl at her, ignoring the heat of her glare. "I get you need to scrub your life clear of that sumbitch, but, Sugar, so do I. Can't save you from the pain he caused, can't make him pay for it either, since the asshole is already dead, but I sure as shit can help you eradicate him from your life. From *our* life." Her eyes soften as she pulls off a rubber glove and reaches for my face.

"Brick…"

"Tell me you can give me at least that."

She nods, her fingers stroking my cheek. "I can give you that, honey." She lifts up and brushes my lips with hers.

"Terrific. Now where's another damn bucket?"

LISA

I WAS RIGHT.

Washing him off my floors gave me some closure.

I was wrong as well.

Doing so with Brick helping didn't take away from that; it was an added fuck you to the man who thought I was something to be used and discarded. Brick showed I was something to be respected and treasured.

Two men, who may have appeared similar on the surface; yet one was pure evil, while the other is good and decent.

"Are you sure?" Brick asks again, as he empties the last bucket in the sink in the laundry room.

"Positive. The kids have school tomorrow and we

need to get back to normal." I watch him walk into the kitchen and over to the sink to wash his hands. The house smells of a combination of bleach and cleaning detergent. Brick had insisted on mopping with cleaner after we got rid of all the blood. "The kids will be none the wiser. They didn't see anything."

"Ezrah knows," he answers. "He may not have seen but not much passes him by."

He may have a point. I noticed the way my grandson looked at me.

"I'll have a word with him." I get up from the stool I'd been perched on and walk up to him, placing my hands on his chest. "Thank you."

He locks his hands in the small of my back and leans down for a kiss.

"My pleasure. But how about we both have a word with Ezrah?"

He may have a point. The boy is very protective of me, but seems to know he has that in common with Brick. I get the sense he may believe Brick before he believes me when it comes to my welfare. I should be offended, given I raised those kids by myself for years, but oddly, I'm not. I *am* thankful Ezrah has someone worthy to look up to.

"I'm good with that."

I take one last discerning look at the kitchen before we put our coats and boots on. It's just my kitchen, nothing more, nothing less, and when Brick takes my hand in his; I follow him out the door feeling lighter than I have in years.

Sophia is still hiding out in the kitchen where I found her earlier this morning. I say hiding out, because she seems keen on avoiding certain club members. She's kept busy, judging by the number of containers with chopped vegetables on the counter and the spotless kitchen.

"Hope you don't mind," she says when I walk in, looking a little sheepish. "I may have gone overboard, but you mentioned making a big pot of soup for dinner. I wasn't even sure what vegetables you wanted in there so I cut them all."

I grin at her. "Perfect. I try to hide as many vegetables as I can get away with in soups and stews. Don't know if you noticed, but some of these guys are as bad as the kids. If it ain't meat, potato, or deep fried, they won't touch it." I notice Finn's high chair is empty. "Is the baby with Nosh?"

She shakes her head, chuckling. "Wapi. I'm sorry in advance, but he said he'd change his diaper. I'm not even sure he knows how."

I'm about to go chase down Wapi when Brick walks in, Finn on his arm. The baby grins wide and reaches for me.

"Hey, Little Man." I blow a raspberry in his neck, making him giggle this belly laugh I love so much. His hands grab in my hair and I do it again.

"I just came to grab his bottle, but if you want him…" Brick grumbles.

Untangling little sticky fingers from my hair, I grin up at him. "You take him, I've got soup to put on."

"Kids were looking for you," he says with a serious

face.

I nod my understanding. "I'll get things started in here and I'll come find you guys."

It takes a few minutes to get his bottle ready while I listen to Brick asking Sophia about some job she was apparently looking at. The moment he leaves the kitchen to feed Finn, I turn to her.

"You've got a lead on a job?"

She nods and smiles, but it's not convincing. "Yeah. A job in payroll for a parts manufacturer in Denver."

"Denver." I raise an eyebrow at her, as I put the largest pot I have on the stove and light the burner. "So you plan to go back?"

She shrugs, looking conflicted. "For now, yes. I mean, I have my apartment there, friends, a life. I can't just drop everything."

"I guess." I drop a pat of butter in the pan along with a drizzle of olive oil, and toss in onions and garlic. "Be sad to see you go, and I'm thinking I'm not the only one."

It takes a while for her to answer, and I occupy myself stirring the onions around until they're glazed.

"I think it's better. At least for now," she finally says softly. "I think we can all use a little breather. It's been an intense couple of weeks."

I turn to face her. "I was hoping you'd be here for Christmas."

"Well, I still may be. I have another checkup at the hospital in eight days. I'm hoping I can ditch the crutches, but it'll just be a short week to Christmas then. I don't really have any plans so I could stay. Unless of course a job comes up that won't wait until after."

"I'll keep my fingers crossed."

With the soup simmering on the stove, I head into the clubhouse to find my family. Brick is sitting at a table, Finn dozing off on his shoulder. The kids are still planted in front of the TV. That's one thing about winter here; it's easy for them to get addicted to the tube. Now that things have settled down, I'll have to come up with some other ways to keep them occupied, especially with their Christmas break looming.

I notice Ezrah watching me and I crook my finger at him. Kiara doesn't even notice when he slips out of his seat and heads this way.

"Want me to put him down?" I ask Brick, indicating the baby.

"Nah, leave him here for now. I'll put him down in a bit."

I take a seat across from him and pull out the chair beside me for Ezrah to sit down.

"Am I in trouble?" are the first words out of the boy's mouth, and Brick barks out a laugh.

"Not this time, Son. Your nana and I just wanted to talk about what happened yesterday."

Ezrah flinches and immediately glances over at me.

"It's over, boy. It's over for good."

"I heard a gunshot," he says in a soft voice. "I thought it was you who got hit."

I know he's getting too old for hugs, especially in view of his friends, but I don't care. I need one and I'm grateful to note he wraps his spindly arms around me as best he can.

"I'm fine, honey, but someone got shot. He was not a good man and he meant to hurt Nana, but Nosh stopped him."

"Dead," my boy concludes correctly. "What about that woman?"

"She was caught. The police arrested her," Brick answers. "Everyone is safe now and we'd like to go back home after dinner, but we wanted to see how you felt about that."

"It's okay here, but I like my own room better. Can I go play now?"

I catch Brick's eye and he winks at me.

"Sure. Go ahead."

We watch him join his sister and his friends on the couch.

"You think he'll be okay?" I ask, turning to Brick who is already looking at me.

"Kids are resilient."

Yeah, they are, and thank God for that.

BRICK

LISA IS ALREADY in bed when I come upstairs.

Her head turns to the door when I walk in.

"Who was that?"

She's referring to the phone call coming in just as we were starting up the stairs.

"Luna," I tell her, stripping out of my clothes and slipping between the sheets. Lisa instantly fits herself against me. "Jane Lunsden talked."

"What did she have to say?"

I don't want to share—hearing it myself gave me chills—but she deserves to know.

"Nowak was at the hospital. He was watching us. He'd somehow pieced together Kelsey's baby might well be his."

"Why didn't he step up?"

"Luna figures the information on the USB key was more important to him. Finn's case was Jane Lunsden's very first assignment with Durango Child Protective Services. That was not by accident. She transferred from Albuquerque two days before."

Lisa lifts her head and looks at me sharply. "How is that even possible?"

"Nowak. The man apparently has connections everywhere. American National League connections. Lunsden was one of them. She's all about the cause. She was supposed to find a legal excuse to remove Finn from our care, but when the FBI started sniffing around was told to hold off until after the planned military transport heist."

"But why risk coming here?" she asks, the same question I posed to Luna.

I stroke the pads of my fingers down her spine, delaying my answer because it turns my stomach and would mean insult to injury for Lisa.

"Apparently he could not abide the thought any of his offspring being raised by a black woman."

Her eyes grow big. "Un-believable…" she mutters.

Then suddenly she chuckles, surprising me.

"Sugar, I'm not sure what's funny."

She rolls partially on top of me and props her chin on my chest, grinning wide.

"Seems like sweet justice this particular black woman gets to help raise that precious boy into a fine young man, in the very same house where that evil man released his final breath. I'm not normally a vengeful person, but yeah, I think that's funny."

Her eyes shine when she smiles into mine.

Fuck, but I love this woman.

29

LISA

"THAT ONE?"

I desperately point at another tree, hoping this one will pass scrutiny.

We've been up and down the side of this damn mountain for what feels like hours. Don't get me wrong, I love snow, especially this time of year, but for looking at not trudging through.

I thought it would be a fun excursion with the kids when Brick suggested going to pick out a tree. It became clear, when he told everyone to bundle up and packed Finn in the new backpack carrier he'd come home with last week, we weren't heading to town to one of the Christmas tree lots to pick one out.

"Too skinny," Ezrah declares, my grandson's grin

big in his flushed face as he continues plodding through the deep snow, his sister on his heels.

My toes are starting to numb in my fur-lined boots and I stopped feeling the tip of my nose about twenty minutes ago. For the sake of the kids I keep my grumbles to myself, but that doesn't hold me back throwing a heated glare at the rear of Brick's head. He seems to be enjoying himself altogether too much.

"Found it!" I hear Kiara yell up ahead, just as I step out of the trees into a small clearing.

"Nice one, Princess," Brick rumbles in front of me, his breath a white cloud in the cold air.

"Bah-pa!" Finn gurgles from his perch high on his grandfather's back.

The tree is pretty. A full base, tapering into a perfect peak that looks too tall to me, but I'm not about to argue that point. If this is the tree they want, then by God it's the tree we'll get. The sooner we get back inside where I can defrost, the better it is.

"Can I cut it down, Papa?" Ezrah wants to know.

"Hard work, Son. You sure you're up for it?"

His enthusiasm turns out to be no match for the thick trunk, and after giving it his all for a few minutes; the boy finally gives up. He's barely a quarter through.

Brick unclips Finn's carrier and turns to me.

"Can you hang on to him for a minute?"

I nod because I don't trust my frozen lips to form words, and slip my arms into the straps. Still warm from Brick's body heat and Finn—who is like a little stove—I actually welcome the weight.

Five minutes later, the tree is down and Brick is tightening a rope around the trunk. Then he hands the rope to the kids, relieves me of Finn, strapping him to his back, and grabs my gloved hand.

"I think it's time for hot chocolate," he announces.

"Yay! With marshmallows?"

He grins at Kiara. "Is there any other way? Gotta get that tree down first, though."

It's all the encouragement the kids need as they start pulling the tree through the snow. It's a slow process, and it's not long before Brick hands me the saw so he can give them a hand.

My relief is great when I finally see the cottage through the trees.

"I think ours is prettier than the one in the clubhouse," Kiara declares when I help her out of her snowsuit.

Some of the brothers had gone to cut down a massive tree for the clubhouse a few days ago, which I'm sure gave Brick his brilliant idea to make this a new family tradition.

"Can we decorate it? Are we still going to bake cookies?"

"Child, give your nana a chance to defrost her toes first, okay? Let's get that hot chocolate going in the meantime."

"With marshmallows," she reminds me.

"Why don't you check the pantry and make sure we have some."

She runs ahead into the kitchen, while I take Finn from Brick and start peeling him out of his snowsuit.

"Put those boots on the mat, boy," I call out to Ezrah, who is about to take off after his sister, leaving his boots dripping in the middle of the floor.

Brick's arm slips around my waist from behind as he sticks his cold face in my neck.

"You done glarin' at me?" he asks, amusement in his voice, and I growl in response, making him chuckle. "That was fun, admit it."

"Ask me when blood flow has returned to my body," I return.

"I can help with that," he mumbles, and I curse my body for responding to his suggestive comment instantly. Especially since the kids are in the kitchen waiting for their hot chocolate and Finn is squirming in my arms, probably ready for a diaper change.

"Stop teasing, the kids are waiting." My tone is terse, but the smile I throw him over my shoulder has him grin back. His eyes focus on my lips and in the next moment he covers them with his, kissing me with a heat that warms me right up.

"Bah!" Finn rudely interrupts, his little fingers tugging on my wild, hat hair.

Brick releases me with clear reluctance before his eyes drift to his grandson.

"You're already a menace, you know that?"

The baby's response is a wide smile.

Later that afternoon, I'm in the kitchen pulling a tray of snowball cookies from the oven when the front door slams open. Dropping the cookie sheet on the cooling rack, I wipe my hands and follow the kids' excited squeals into the living room where Brick is wrestling with the tree. We cleared a spot in the far corner by the window where we can see it from every vantage point, even from the kitchen island.

"Still too damn tall," Brick grumbles, when the tip of the tree scratches against the ceiling.

I bite my lip to refrain from telling him 'I told you so,' which I did, more than once. He glares at me anyway and I mimic zipping my lips, trying hard not to laugh while doing it.

"I'm sure it'll be fine if we cut a little off the tip," Ezrah suggests diplomatically.

"Shears are in my back pocket, Son. Have at it."

Ezrah must have a carpenter's eye because after he snips about five inches off the top, the tree easily slides into place.

That night after a simple meal of soup and grilled cheese sandwiches, we set to decorating. It's Christmas Eve and Ouray insisted I take the day off because tomorrow night we'll have a clubhouse full for dinner.

The tree is packed with decorations, with only a few clusters on the lower branches. Brick quietly stops Ezrah from correcting his sister's work who, because of the long, activity-filled day, is already tired and cranky.

"We forgot Mommy's star," she mopes.

We didn't exactly forget, but with the tree so tight to the ceiling, there isn't any room for the topper so I snuck it out of the box and hid it under a pillow. Trust Kiara to notice.

"There's no room, silly," her brother informs her,

which results in the tears I could've guessed were next.

"I want Mommy's star," she wails inconsolably and Brick raises a questioning eyebrow in my direction.

I fish out the star and hold it up behind Kiara's back.

"Let me see what I can do," he says, reaching for it.

Ten minutes later, after a few failed attempts, a goodly amount of muttered cursing, some kitchen twine, and a collection of twist ties, the star is haphazardly fixed to the top of the tree.

"It's perfect," Kiara sighs.

"It's crooked," Ezrah states.

"It's exactly right," I intervene before a new drama starts.

BRICK

HER HAIR IS bouncing wild around her face, her skin shimmering, her lips slack, but those fierce eyes are holding mine captured.

"Get there," I groan, waiting for her as she rides me with abandon.

"Almost…"

"Can't wait, baby," I warn her when I feel my balls draw tight, ready to explode.

Desperate, I slip the pad of my thumb over the tight bundle of nerves right above where we are connected. Almost instantly, I feel her pussy convulse around my cock and I let go in long, hot streams, bucking underneath her until we're both spent. She collapses on top of me and I hold on tight.

"Merry Christmas, honey," she whispers, her pants stirring the hair on my chest.

"Damn fucking right it is, Sugar."

I feel her chuckle against me and smile.

We lie like that for a few minutes, enjoying each other in the early morning quiet, when the doorknob rattles and we both dive for the covers.

"You can't go in there," I hear Ezrah whisper outside the door.

"Oh God, we woke 'em up," Lisa groans.

"But I wanna go see if Santa was here and Nana said not without her say so."

"Get your nightie on in case she barges in, baby," I suggest, digging around for my boxers. I pull them on under the covers as Lisa slips her nightshirt over her head. "We'll be right out, guys!" I call to the kids before they get into an argument and wake up Finn as well.

Ten minutes later, the coffee machine is gurgling and Lisa is sliding a tray of cinnamon buns she prepped yesterday into the oven. It's barely six thirty in the morning.

The kids were told to look but not touch, so both are on the floor in front of the tree, trying to figure out which gifts are meant for who. A squeal over the baby monitor signals our youngest is ready to join us.

"You go grab him while I make his bottle," Lisa suggests.

"Do we gotta wait?" Kiara asks, when she sees me heading back upstairs.

"Bet your booty you've gotta wait," I tell her,

ignoring the responding whine.

I try not to take too long getting a very wet Finn cleaned up and into dry pajamas. I'm at the top of the stairs, ready to head down when I hear Lisa's rich melodious voice from below.

"We're not touching anything until the whole family is here, child."

The whole family.

I'd meant to save it for tonight, after the kids are in bed, but now I'm changing my mind. What I have for Lisa involves the whole family.

With the gift I picked out in Albuquerque when I was down there with Ouray a few weeks ago tucked in my pocket, I head downstairs.

We tried not to go overboard for the kids, so we got all of them a gift from both Lisa and I jointly, and one from each of us separately. The kids got each of us something as well. I suspect we have Lissie to thank for that. She offered to take all the kids into town a few days ago to see a movie.

As for Lisa and me, we decided Christmas was for kids, so didn't buy each other anything. We'd save that for birthdays. I'm already breaking that rule, but I hope Lisa won't be too upset when she opens it.

The kids seem happy with their gifts, even though Finn appears to be more fascinated with the crinkling paper than any of the toys we got him.

Lisa's about to get up to get us another cup of coffee when I grab her hand to stop her, and with my other, pull the box from my pocket. Then I slide off the couch onto one knee and am rudely reminded why this romantic gesture might be better left to younger men. But Lisa was never asked this question and she deserves everything that comes with it, even if she may need to help me get back up after.

"What are you doing?" Kiara pipes up, curious as always.

"Shh, he's asking her," Ezrah tries to explain.

Lisa's beautiful brown eyes shimmer as she looks down at me, a sweet smile on her lips.

"What's he asking her?"

"To marry him."

I groan, so much for giving her a proper proposal. Beaten to the punch by the kids.

"Really?" Kiara jumps up and squeals, which Finn finds highly amusing and happily joins in. "Nana, does that mean I can wear my pretty dress?"

The first tear rolls down Lisa's cheek as she chuckles at my exasperated sigh.

"Let me ask the question first, yeah, Princess?"

"Okay," she says happily and I shake my head, grinning myself.

"Gave me back a family I didn't know I was missing, Sugar. Gave me a home I didn't know I needed. Gave me love I'm still not sure I deserve. Gave me a new tomorrow to look forward to and all I have is this ring…"

I flip open the box to show her the simple white gold ring made up of two parallel bands, holding a single solitaire diamond wedged between two turquoise bars.

"And with it the promise I'll spend the rest of my life

making sure you never regret any of it. Will you marry me?"

"So can I?" Kiara jumps up. "Wear my pretty dress?"

Lisa starts laughing through her tears.

"We'll get you a brand new pretty dress," she tells her granddaughter, but she's looking at me.

"Is that a yes?" I want to know.

"That's a yes."

"Thank God," I grumble grinning up at her. "Now help an old man to his feet."

I try not to groan too loudly when she pulls me up. I quickly slip the ring on her finger before pulling her body flush to mine, and kiss her smiling lips.

"Love you, Brick," she tells me when I finally lift my head.

"Thank fuck for that."

"Mind your mouth," she snaps, and both kids giggle at my expense.

"Don't mind if I do," I fire back, taking her lips again.

ARROW'S EDGE MC

30

LISA

Five months later.

I NEVER KNEW I'd enjoy the wind blowing in my face as much as I do.

Tightening my arms around my husband's waist, I look over his shoulder as he turns up the mountain.

It had taken a lot longer to convince me to get on the back of his bike than it took for me to enjoy it. We'd barely made it out of town before I was grinning wide.

This had been Brick's idea, to take off for a few days after the small wedding Ouray officiated last week. A honeymoon, biker style. Just the two of us for three days in Mesa Verde at the Far View Lodge.

If possible, I fell in love with the man even more

when he explained we'd only be forty or so minutes away from home in case of an emergency with the kids, who were staying with Lissie and Yuma.

Since we've lived in a house under construction since early April, those three days away have been bliss. Views from our room at the lodge were stunning, the food phenomenal, and the hikes we took invigorating, but I'm ready to see my babies again.

Brick called ahead to let Lissie know we were on our way back, so when he rolls the bike up to the clubhouse, I'm not surprised to see the door open and both older kids come running out to greet us. I barely have a chance to get off the bike before I'm almost tackled by Ezrah and Kiara.

"Missed you," I mumble, as I bend down to them.

"Got some of that left for me?" Brick sounds behind me, and I let both kids go so they can give him the same welcome.

"Nana!" There's no mistaking Finn's high-pitched voice as Lissie carries him out on her hip.

"Hey, munchkin." I take him from her and am immediately rewarded with some of his sloppy kisses. "Hope he wasn't too much trouble?"

Lissie shakes her head. "He wasn't. Lettie, on the other hand, decided to start walking and has been hell to keep up with. But enough of that. So how was your trip, Mrs. Paver?"

"Perfect." I grin at her as Brick plucks Finn from my arms. "It was the perfect little break. You guys ever want to get away without going too far; I highly recommend it. We'll look after Lettie and Jesse, right, Brick?"

"You bet."

"God, I might take you up on that," Lissie says, hooking her arm through mine. "But don't say I didn't warn you. My daughter is a handful and then some."

As we walk inside, I ask if Sophia got off okay. She'd been there for the wedding but had to get back to Denver the day after. There may have been a little tension around her brief visit, but I'd been too busy enjoying my day to pay it much notice.

"Ouray ended up driving her to the airport," Lissie says on a whisper.

"Oh?"

"Yeah, he stepped in when Wapi got all up into Tse's face about driving her. The chief wasn't having it."

"Poor girl. She comes here for our wedding and has to deal with those two fightin' over her."

I respond to a few greetings shouted out from around the clubhouse and give Nosh a kiss on the cheek, before walking into the kitchen—my domain—and sit down at the kitchen table with my friend.

"Good to be home," I tell her and she laughs at me.

"You've only been gone three days."

"I know." I shrug. "But this is the only true home I've ever known. I miss it when I'm not here."

She grins at me. "On that note; are you ready for some more juicy gossip?"

"Oh Lordy…what did I miss now?"

"Nothing yet, I don't think, but Paco got into it with that lawyer of Brick's after you guys took off."

"Mel?"

Both Brick and I really like her so we'd invited her. Especially after she managed to finalize all the paperwork securing Finn's place with us before the wedding.

"Oh yeah. Paco was already a few sheets to the wind when he commented she'd be even prettier if she'd dye her hair and put on some makeup. Boy, did she shut him up fast."

I chuckle. Mel is definitely not one to mess with, and I have no doubt she ripped him a new one. Paco is a good guy underneath all that cocky bluster, but I can see how those two would rub each other the wrong way.

I'm about to comment on that when Ouray ducks his head around the corner.

"Got a minute?"

BRICK

THE CREW BUSTED their asses while we were gone.

As much as our mini getaway was intended as a honeymoon of sorts, I planned for it to give the guys time to finish up the add-on.

Three days ago the bathroom was bare; no tiles, no hardware, no vanity. Same thing with the bedroom, the drywall was up, but nothing had been painted and the flooring wasn't down yet. I'd offered to pay Jed Mason's crew double if they could finish up before we got back.

I just went for a quick look and clearly my club had used some elbow grease as well, because all our stuff was already moved into the new master suite. Our old bedroom upstairs is now Kiara's, as per her brother's instructions. We offered it to him, given he is the oldest, but he insisted it made more sense for a girl to have a bathroom to herself.

The kid kills me. For all his occasional attitude, he is wise beyond his years and I'm gonna love seeing him grow into the fine man I know he's destined to be.

I promised the kids they could come have a look as soon as I showed their nana around.

"Are you serious?" she says when she walks up with Ouray. "They're done?"

Should've known she'd clue in the moment she noticed the dumpster and the equipment gone from the side of the house.

"Come have a look."

I step aside to let her through but she stops in front of me.

"You did this?"

"Well, technically it was Jed's guys and our club family who did this."

"But you set it in motion," she insists.

"I might have put in a good word."

She lifts up on her toes and brushes my lips with a kiss.

"Thank you."

"Why don't you have a look first?"

I nudge her farther in the house and she makes a sound in the back of her throat when she notices the family room we added on behind the dining room is fully furnished. Something I had Lissie's help with.

She walks through, running her hands along the sturdy woven fabric of the new sectional sofa.

"I love it," she mumbles, before turning around to the new French doors opening off the family room onto the new patio.

"Check out the master suite," I prompt her.

"It's beautiful."

She hasn't even seen it all when she turns to me and throws her arms around my neck.

"You can stop now," she says, her face lifted up.

"Stop what?"

I'm not quite clear what she means.

"Stop makin' sure I won't regret saying yes to you." She remembers my promise when I proposed. "I never will. You already gave me a life I never would've dared dream of."

THE END

ABOUT THE AUTHOR

Award-winning author Freya Barker loves writing about ordinary people with extraordinary stories.

Driven to make her books about 'real' people; she creates characters who are perhaps less than perfect, each struggling to find their own slice of happy, but just as deserving of romance, thrills and chills in their lives.

Recipient of the ReadFREE.ly 2019 Best Book We've Read All Year Award for "Covering Ollie, the 2015 RomCon "Reader's Choice" Award for Best First Book, "Slim To None", and Finalist for the 2017 Kindle Book Award with "From Dust", Freya continues to add to her rapidly growing collection of published novels as she spins story after story with an endless supply of bruised and dented characters, vying for attention!

www.freyabarker.com

Lightning Source UK Ltd.
Milton Keynes UK
UKHW021122040522
402471UK00007B/1223